BEHIND *the* Larch

T.J. DEAL

Word Candy
PUBLISHING

Reader Advisory

This novel contains scenes depicting domestic violence that may be distressing to readers. If you or someone you know is affected by domestic violence, please prioritize your well-being and seek support. Resources and helplines are available to help those in need.

To the audacious and badass women who have not only escaped the shadows of their past but have also opened their hearts to the love they deserve, proving that resilience can lead to joy.

Prologue

Everett

One year prior—

After three missed connections, two delayed flights, and sleeping on an airport floor, I finally arrived in Central Oregon, feeling exhausted and frustrated. I've lost an entire day of my week-long leave traveling, I smell like stale airplane air, and I've missed out on a few wedding shenanigans that Charlie and Hayes are getting into. Two of my very best friends, who have been through hell and back to make things work, are finally getting married. Hayes' mom, who practically raised all of us, as well as my sister Odessa, arrived a few days ago. A few buddies I've met over the years who were SEALs with Hayes when he was in the Navy arrived yesterday, and they've all been flooding the group chat with pictures. The only person yet to arrive is Drew, Charlie's older brother and the third key member of the H-E-D trio.

Getting off the small plane, I step into the crisp winter morning air. The smell of dirt and juniper greets me as I make my way towards the terminal, eager to see the people I call family. Between my deployments and military career, as well as everyone else's busy lives, we haven't all been together in years.

Fully expecting Hayes and Charlie to pick me up at the airport, I made my way to baggage claim, praying my bags actually made it. My phone vibrates as I walk, Hayes caller ID popping up.

"What's up, Groom? You outside? I'm—" I begin, but my words are abruptly cut off by the sight of a woman nearby, leaning back to capture the perfect shot of a laughing family at their reunion. As I steal a glance at her, I nearly trip over my own feet. She's stunning in a subtly enchanting way, her honey-brown hair billowing like warm sunlight down her back, framing her delicate features with a soft glow. Her slate blue eyes seem to shimmer with warmth, growing brighter as a beaming smile unfolds across her face, revealing a cute button nose and soft pink lips that seem to invite conversation. The urge to sweep her up and tuck her safely in my pocket flares within me, but I push it aside, shaking off the distraction and refocusing on my conversation with Hayes.

"'Bout that. There's been a major incident involving a dress button coming loose and the girls had to drive to Bend. I intended to get you myself, but then the caterer called and needs me to meet them at the resort," he replies. I can't help but steal another glance at the woman, not even caring what he has to say.

Her smile practically radiates through the room as she hands the phone back to whomever she was taking a photo of. They match her energy, thanking her profusely. She says something back before turning and walking in the other direction. Her hips sway in skin-tight jeans with a confident grace, leaving me momentarily stunned and flustered.

I have to shake my head to get out of the lust filled stupor she put me in so that I can respond to Hayes. "No worries, man. I'll grab a cab or something."

"What? No. Charlie's assistant, Isla, is on her way to the airport already. Might even be there already. I'll text you her number, but it's in the group chat too. See ya soon, brother!"

He hangs up before I can respond. My gaze naturally swings around the room, looking for any sign of the illusive Isla. I've visited Three Sisters a few times, but she's always been out of town, so we haven't properly met. Quite the disappointment, considering Charlie has told me she's beautiful and fun.

The baggage carousel beeps loudly and whirs to life, spitting out luggage onto the conveyor belt. I keep one eye on the bags while scanning the terminal for Isla. She could be waiting in her car, but I can't help but look for her here. As the last few bags tumble out, I finally spot my suitcase, snatch it up, and head straight for the exit.

Once again, the sight of denim jeans has me stumbling over my feet. This time, the dream-girl is bent over, pulling luggage off another conveyor belt and delicately setting it in front of an elderly woman. She beams that same smile, pats the blue-haired woman's shoulder, and then walks away. *Apparently, she's the Mother Teresa of the Redmond airport.*

Rather than walk outside, I step off to the side and find the text with Isla's number. It rings an ungodly number of times before going to voicemail. I keep it short and sweet, letting her know I've arrived and want to know where to meet her.

When I hang up, I look around the airport once again. It's small but clean and bustling with travelers. The holidays may be over, but you wouldn't be able to tell standing here. Out of the corner of my eye, I catch something falling toward the ground. A woman pushing a stroller failed to notice her toddler drop the teddy bear he was clutching. My feet start moving on their own accord to help, but the teddy bear is quickly snatched up and handed back over to the crying toddler. *That damn smiling woman treats helping others like it's a full-time job.*

She turns around and then digs in her purse, pulling out a cell phone. Her eyes widen a fraction before she mumbles something and then puts the phone up to her ear. Before I can realize what's happening, my phone starts vibrating, and I answer it on autopilot. "Hello?"

A sweet, melody-like voice responds, and I swear she's saying the same thing as the girl I've been staring at. "Everett? Hey! Hayes asked if I could pick you up at the airport, but I haven't seen you yet." I quickly looked around, searching for any other woman on the phone who could be Isla. No way is the beautiful girl I've been eye-stalking through the airport Charlie's assistant.

"Appreciate it, uh," I say, trying not to stumble over my words. "I'm near the south side of baggage claim, toward the front doors."

Her eyes immediately find mine and I can see the recognition in them as she starts walking towards me, her smile widening.

"Isla, right?" I ask, feeling an unexpected rush of adrenaline.

She nods, her eyes sparkling with amusement. "The one and only. Sorry if I kept you waiting," she says, gesturing toward my bag, the corners of her mouth lifting in a playful smile.

My hand instinctively rubs my stubbly jaw, trying to hide my surprise at how stunning she looks in person. "No worries; I figured that Mom would have lost Teddy if you hadn't swooped in to save the day," I reply, grinning as she steps a bit closer.

Her laugh is like music, light and infectious. "Oh, she definitely had her hands full. You'd think she was trying to wrangle a herd of cats," she says, her voice warm and inviting. "Come on, I parked this way."

She guides me toward a sleek BMW X6, popping the trunk and gesturing for me to toss my bag inside.

"Fancy car you've got here," I comment, keeping my tone casual, even as my heart races.

She huffs out a slight laugh, rolling her eyes good-naturedly. "Yep. Jeff insists on having the best of the best. It's, uh, a 'thing' of his." The mention of another man pulls the air from my lungs.

We open the car doors and climb inside. I can't help but ask, "Is that your boyfriend?" *Say brother. Please, say brother.*

Her hand falters for a moment before she says, "Yep," and slams the door shut. My heart sinks at the confirmation, but the way she said it—a hint of reluctance—makes me wonder if she's as thrilled about it as I am about her. For now, I'll file that under "potential future possibilities" and "proceed with caution."

Chapter One

Isla

Present day—

I watch from the second-floor balcony of the Cascadia Property Management building as the sun sinks behind the Cascade Mountains. I've been off work for nearly an hour, but I can't bring myself to go home—not that it feels like "home" anyway. Jeff, my boyfriend, insisted we rent one of the nicest houses in Cascadia County, which devours almost my entire paycheck. He offered to cover utilities, lend me one of his cars, and pay for our golf course membership. At the time, it felt fair, but now I realize my mistake: he doesn't pay for anything—his parents do. I'm living paycheck to paycheck, wondering every day why I lack the courage to end things with Jeff.

So instead of going home and facing reality, I contemplate life. It certainly has a way of throwing unexpected curveballs directly at your face, doesn't it? One day, you're a brazen five-year-old telling off a bully for pushing you down. The next day, you're twenty-six and in a toxic relationship that you can't seem to escape. I can't help but wonder what the hell happened to that courageous little girl. How on earth did she lose every ounce of confidence she ever had? Was it the move to a new state? Was it the lack of friendships starting over? Was it the childhood cancer? Or was it simply the lack of parental support she's received throughout the years? Who the fuck knows? At this point, does it even matter? I'm still dating an asshole to please my parents, who don't even care how I'm treated.

The wind rips through the trees below me, sending the distinct smell of an impending Central Oregon winter storm wafting up to me. It smells like fresh pine and smoke from a nearby fireplace, a reminder of the harsh yet beautiful winter to come. The cold air stings my cheeks, but I snuggle down deeper into the Canada Goose down jacket that Jeff's mother, Christy, purchased for me. Normally, I donate all the "hush-money" gifts I receive, but this one is the exception. She left the wrapped box on my doorstep after the first argument Jeff and I had. Stupid me assumed it was an "I'm sorry" gift from him because he genuinely felt bad about yelling at me. It wasn't until months later, when several more gifts appeared, that I understood Jeff had nothing to do with the designer items. Christy was doing what she does best: buying forgiveness for her son. I fell for the whole charade. Since then, I haven't kept a single gift.

Two knocks sound from the door to my right, and I laugh when Everett opens the door, his signature cheesy grin already showing. "Do you mind if I join you?" he asks with his best Austin Powers impression.

A small smile forms before I nod and scoot over on the small loveseat, making room for him.

Everett may not work in my office or even in the adjacent suite for EFSC, but he's here more often than not. His best friends, Hayes and Drew, started the Elite Forces Security and Contracting business a few years ago and take up residence in the building now. Ev worked for them for a little while until he was offered a position with the Cascadia County Sheriff Department. Now, he's formally a sworn in deputy, but his main position is Rotary Wing Pilot.

"What brings you into the CPM/EFSC building today?" I ask, already feeling a little more at ease with his energy around me. He has a contagious lightness about him that makes me want to stick to him like a leech, sucking out all that positive energy.

"Wanted to see my favorite people and then get a workout in." Hayes created a state-of-the-art gym on the first floor of our building for himself and the guys on their team. I hadn't noticed the black joggers and running shoes when he walked out, but that's because I tend to avoid looking directly at him. He's the definition of sex appeal, and he doesn't have to try. His smile alone does things to me that it absolutely should not. He looks like a clean-cut Charlie Hunnam, and I'm not the only one that thinks so—he offhandedly mentioned that his call sign during his days in the Army was Teller, after Jax Teller from Sons of Anarchy.

"Is everyone still in there? It's been ten levels of awkward all day." My boss, Olivia and Everett's friend, Drew, ended their months' long fling last week despite obviously being in love. To say the turmoil in the building is nearly palpable would be an understatement. The entire office building is downright dreary, and it doesn't help that the suites are open to each other and only divided by large glass partitions.

"Drew, Delta, and Liam were in the gym, punishing each other with their workouts. Don't think they'll stop until I send their asses home. Drew's really going through it, trying to figure out how to get out of this promise thing with Heather before it's too late with Olivia."

With a heavy sigh, I nodded. "Olivia's in business mode. She won't talk about anything else apart from properties and clients. On the work side, it's incredible how much we've gotten done in four days. However, on the personal side, it must be *really* bad." It's a little reminiscent of a few years ago, when her husband, Dan, died. She became hyper-focused at work, not allowing herself to think of anything else.

"Is that why you're out here freezing your ass off? My little empath was avoiding the depressing energy inside." I can't prevent the chuckle that escapes, but I at least attempt to shove down the giddy feelings that always arise whenever he calls me "his" anything or shows me the slightest bit of attention. Everett is one big, complicated situation that I don't have the faintest idea what to make of. He's become my closest friend, yet no one knows about it. Everything we do is in secret—texting, phone calls, sitting on this balcony. He's done nothing more than treat me like he treats everyone else, yet the massive crush I've developed on him makes it difficult to see things clearly. Would things be different if I wasn't in a relationship? Does he only treat me this way because he feels bad for me? Is all of this one-sided, or could I actually be the girl who gets the perfect guy?

His shoulder nudges me, reminding me that he asked me a question that I needed to answer. "Sorry. No. I mean, yes, it was exhausting in there. But that's not why I'm out here. Jeff is having 'colleagues' over tonight. I wasn't ready to go play hostess to a bunch of drunk men who expected me to cater to their every need." I'd rather listen to an angry Jeff reprimanding me for working late than deal with his obnoxious friends.

"Isla—" He says my name with a hint of his own reprimand coming, but I cut him off before it could start.

"I know, Ev. I know..." I attempt to settle my head on his shoulder, but he places his arm around me before I can get comfortable. Once I feel the slight pull as his hand settles, I sink into his embrace, my head resting against him. "I know that I need to end things with him. It's going to be catastrophic, though. My parents aren't going to understand, and they will be upset." Our families are so intertwined that I know they will all choose his side. They always do. Jeff could scream at me in front of my parents, and it would somehow end up being my fault. It's happened before, and if I don't end it soon, it will surely happen again. They think he walks on water because of who his parents are and what they've done for our family.

"Let it be catastrophic then, La. You have so many people in your corner, ready to support you. If your parents can't do that when they know how he treats you, then they don't deserve a place in your life."

My head nods in agreement, but the words coming out don't match—a constant battle of logic and emotion. "It doesn't feel that simple. They're still my parents. Before we moved here, they were good parents—devoted and caring throughout all my treatments. They weren't these high-class people who only cared about money and what the Walton's thought."

When I was seven, I was diagnosed with A.L.L. or acute lymphoblastic leukemia. Everything was different before that; my dad had just finished law school, and we were barely scraping by financially. About a year after my initial diagnosis, my dad was offered a position by Jeff's dad, Cyrus, at his firm, in Three Sisters. When Cyrus found out we were struggling financially because of the treatments, he paid off all the medical debt. He didn't even tell my dad he did it, but one day we got a call that it was paid in full. Still, to this day, he hasn't fully admitted to being the one to pay it, but there isn't anyone else who knew we were having trouble and could have afforded to pay it. My parents still feel like they owe the Waltons and hold it over my head from time to time.

He stays quiet for a moment, lost in his thoughts. His hand on my shoulder doesn't move, but I can see out of the corner of my eye that his thumb is tapping on his index finger in a slow, rhythmic pattern. His little anxious habit that he always has when he's feeling uneasy or unsure about something.

"Is it about the money still? I could write a check to cover the cost so that you don't feel indebted to them." The seriousness of his tone clenches my stomach, making me realize just how much my situation is weighing on him.

"With that massive Astor Trust fund that you refuse to touch?" I poke at him, trying to lighten his sudden, dark mood. He likes to throw his knowledge of my history in my face, but two can play at that game. Everett comes from a very prominent family. His trust fund is well beyond the millions, but he hasn't spent a dime. He had the courage at eighteen to do what I still can't do at twenty-six—cut off his parents, consequences be damned.

"For you? I'd personally hand it all to them." He pulls me in a little tighter, and my head involuntarily turns to catch a glimpse of his expression.

He's already looking at me, his eyes filled with concern and something else. My heart hopes it's admiration but knows it's probably only pity. Either way, I place my hand on his chest and feel the steady rhythm of his heartbeat beneath my palm.

"I don't want your money, but I appreciate the offer. Olivia and I had a massive talk a few weeks ago—about some things that Jeff has said." A small line between his eyebrows forms, but apart from that, he keeps his expression neutral. "She told me not to worry about anything and that she would have a condo in town available soon. Once I have the keys, next week, I'm going to end things with Jeff." No one, not even Everett, knew about what Jeff had been holding over my head for the last few years. He's been working for his dad in the mayor's office since he moved back to Oregon. Any time Olivia needs a permit or license approved, Jeff threatens to deny it. At the time, it felt easier to appease him so that Olivia didn't suffer from his sabotage. Now that she knows, it feels like I'm finally one step ahead of him.

"Good. La, you deserve the world. You're the best woman I know, and I know countless good ones." His head dips back, and he turns to look at me with those electric blue eyes piercing into mine. His tone becomes icy when he says, "Call me before you talk to him. I'm dead-serious, Isla. Guys like him... I don't trust that he'll willingly let you go."

I nodded as my eyes turned misty all of a sudden. He doesn't know that I've tried to leave Jeff before, and I ended up with a broken windshield and a lecture from my parents. If he, or any of our friends, found out, Jeff would have had his ass kicked more than once. Everett spent over a decade in the Army as a helicopter pilot, and Drew and Hayes are both former Navy SEALs. The guys they work with are all Special Forces as well. It's probably the only reason Jeff isn't as aggressive as he used to be, and why he hates that I work for Olivia and Charlie in a suit next to alpha males.

"I would rather not drag you into my mess. I'll be okay." I don't know how much control he has over the sheriff's department, but I'd hate for Everett to get caught up in Jeff's bullshit. It's safer if he stays out of it.

"It's not dragging if I'm jumping head first. I *need* to be there for you. To make sure you're safe. Please." He wraps me back up in his arms and I let myself sink into his embrace.

"Thanks, Ev." It's easy to forget about all of tomorrow's worries when someone like Everett is there to hold you together.

Without intending to, he weaved his way into my life and changed everything.

Without intending to, he helped me find the confidence that I lost all those years ago.

Without intending to, he made me fall in love with him.

Chapter Two

Isla

Everett held me until I absolutely had to leave, neither of us saying much after my big revelation that I was leaving Jeff. It was like he knew I just needed to be held at that moment, not questioned or judged.

During the entire ten-minute drive home, I could sense Jeff's simmering discontent over my late arrival. He wouldn't show any hint of it around his friends—that would come later, once everyone had left or, if I were lucky, in the morning.

The driveway appeared before me, a ribbon of asphalt snaking through the trees and illuminated by the solar lights below. From the main road, the house was hidden from view, nestled away so that our front yard remained mostly untouched nature—a major reason I agreed to this sprawling home in the first place. Jeff could revel in his pristine country club backyard while I basked in the beauty of Central Oregon.

In summer, bursts of colorful wildflowers fill the space, and the tall Western Larch trees transform into a glorious shade of gold in the fall. I imagined this would be my private oasis. Instead, it's become my own personal hell.

As I drive up the path, the imposing facade of the house looms ahead, taunting me as if it knows I don't want to be here.

Tonight, seven cars are parked in front of the house and the garage off to the side. Most I recognize as "friends" who love to party on weeknights, while the few unfamiliar ones are likely "associates" Jeff is trying to impress. For being the "elite" of Three Sisters, they're all a bunch of losers.

With a sigh, I park Jeff's BMW beside the house so I'm not blocking anyone in, something I'm sure I'll hear about tomorrow. *How dare I park his car out in the open? Ungrateful, inconsiderate, blah, blah, blah.*

My hands tremble slightly as I stare at the dark windshield, my gaze unfocused. An uneasy feeling wraps around me, and I can't tell if it's guilt from letting Everett hold me or some instinct warning me that something feels different tonight.

Taking a deep breath, I let a few curse words slip before finally stepping out of the car. The cool night air hits me like a slap, jolting my senses as I hurry toward the house. It's only the first week of December, but the temperatures have already dropped into the low teens at night.

When I open the door, the familiar scent of the cleaning products our service uses fills the air. As grateful as I am that Christy provides us with such a luxury, I can't shake the feeling that I live in a hospital rather than a home. I'd much prefer to be greeted by the comforting aroma of a vanilla candle or the smell of wood burning in the stove.

Laughter rings out from the dining room but the rest of the house appears to be quiet. Stifling a groan of annoyance, I place my purse in the cubby of the sideboard and hang my jacket on the mahogany coat rack in the entryway. The expensive decor looks beautiful but lacks any real personal touch. The whole house resembles a staged showroom more than a lived-in home.

I long for the day when I can fill the walls with memories and warmth.

Shaking off the dread that settles in my toes, I plaster on a cheery smile and step into their domain. This side of the first floor features the dining room at the front of the house, the kitchen opposite, and a set of stairs leading upstairs to the guest rooms.

Jeff in his usual seat at the head of the table, the farthest spot from where I walk in, allowing me to gauge his mood before he sees me. He's casually rolled the cuffs of his purple button-up shirt, and his tie is long gone, indicating he must be comfortable. His messy pompadour is as full as ever, showing no signs that he's been nervously running a hand through it. To the side, there's a glass half-full of amber liquid, which ideally means he's been sipping it rather than guzzling. *Here we go.*

"Hi, everyone!" If a record could've skipped with my sudden appearance, it would have.

The heads of seven drunk men snapped toward me, as if they didn't hear me coming in. The surprised faces quickly turn into genuine smiles and friendly greetings as they all welcome me into *my* house. Everyone, except Jeff, that is. His smile looks as forced as mine feels, and those dark eyes look ready to scrutinize anything I have to say.

"Working late again? Olivia can't seem to let you go, can she?" The way he says it, more like a statement than a question, already has me on the defensive. His tone alone anchors my feet to the tile by the doorway— my body refusing to go to him.

"Nope—not working. I actually finished up a bit early and remembered we have the Saints Gala coming up. But I don't have a thing to wear! I became fixated on finding the perfect gown." Giggling, I glance around at the men.

Without missing a beat, Jeff raises a dark eyebrow. He laces his fingers together slowly but remains silent.

"I'm sure you gentlemen know how that goes," I say with my best bravado, playing the role of a bimbo housewife as if I were a full-time cast member on Bravo.

"No, I don't believe we do. Can't say I've ever been 'fixated' on finding the best dress. Have any of you?" His eyes roam around the men sitting around, daring them to disagree with him.

"Dress? Not really my style." Cameron Bushnell responds with a chuckle before adding, "However, I wouldn't dare disrupt my wife when she's on the prowl for a new dress, especially when it's for a black tie event. A lion doesn't interrupt a lioness during the hunt." It takes all of me to not smirk, even though I want to do nothing more than bless every hair on that man's body for standing up for me.

"She does have impeccably good taste. I should've asked for her advice before wasting away behind my computer screen all evening." I say, refashioning that fake smile on my face like I'm Mrs. Potato Head. *Over my dead body would I ever ask that horrendous woman for anything.* Cameron may be great, but his wife is pure evil.

Jeff's gaze bounces between Cameron and me, the silence growing heavier with each passing second.

"Well, I won't disagree that Amber is certainly the most beautiful-ly dressed," he gives me a pointed look before continuing, "at every event. I won't say I'm not disappointed that we had to endure take-out rather than one of your famous home cooked meals, though."

"Endure?" one of the men I've never met challenges. "I'd hardly say anything that comes from the Ponderosa Pine kitchen is something we have to endure. Don't go givin' your beautiful woman a hard time for not cooking for us. My first wife, Bethanne, couldn't cook for shit, but she fucked harder than the IRS." *So close to earning my gratitude, old man, so close.*

The table erupts in laughter at the crude humor—Jeff included, as he raises his glass to the man sporting a huge grin.

"Well, gentlemen," I declare to the table, "I'm going to let you finish this rousing game of poker without any more interruptions from me."

Jeff doesn't even spare me a glance, but Cameron does. Pity practically oozes from his expression as he watches me turn and leave. I ignore it, just like I always do, because if I dive too deep into how that pity makes me feel, I'll burn this house down and ruin my relationship with my parents forever.

The imperial staircase in this house is as extravagant as the rest of the house. The bottom steps wide and growing more narrow toward the half-landing. Each step feels like it's leading me further away from the suffocating atmosphere of the poker game and closer to the peace and quiet of my space.

As I reach the top, I can already feel the weight of the evening lifting off my shoulders. The hard part is done; the mental game of verbal tennis is over, and I feel like I may have won by default. A win is a win, though.

My only hope now is that Jeff drinks until he passes out somewhere downstairs and I don't have to deal with him until tomorrow. The countdown until I'm able to move out has already started. If I can just pretend for a few more days, this nightmare will be over, and I'll be out of this house.

Chapter Three

Everett

Isla left the office building over an hour ago, her eyes burning with a mix of despair and resolve. I can't shake the worry gnawing at me about her relationship with Jeff. Does she even realize how unhappy she is? I'd give anything for her to see what I see in her—the strength beneath her soft exterior and the light that draws people in.

I've wanted to tell her how I feel, to let her know she deserves so much more than what Jeff offers, but my worry is that it would only confuse her more. She needs to be the one to decide about Jeff with a clear head—not because someone she cares about drops a bombshell of feelings in her lap.

At this point, I'm shocked she hasn't figured out how I feel about her. It seems like everyone in the group knows about my obsession, but thankfully, they're not giving me too much shit about it. I'm sure they can see I beat myself up over it more than they ever could.

The only way I can clear my head is by hitting the gym, so after sulking for a while, I finally head down the stairs. The guys have been down here for hours, pushing their bodies to the limit, each one driven by the need to silence the turmoil within.

Drew, especially, has been pushing himself harder than normal the last few days. Olivia's ending things with him sent him into a spiral. He's always been removed, not allowing himself to grow close to someone so he doesn't get heartbroken. Olivia, as well as her kids Ben and Ellie, broke down those walls in a way no one else had before.

Delta and Liam are surely working out as penance for whatever demons they're battling. With the line of work these guys were in, it's not impossible to guess what eats away at them. All of us, really. But I mostly flew high and fast, firing from the sky with the precision only a semi-active laser (SAL)-guided missile can offer.

I've known Delta since boot camp, back when he was Colton Thatcher, the 18-year-old kid from Colorado wanting to play Army. He looked like the rest of us—buzz cut, skinny, and full of nerves. Now he's covered in tattoos, in a constant state of bulking, and hardened to the world, same buzz cut, though.

Liam was on the same SEAL team as Hayes and Drew, but apart from that, I don't know much. A trustworthy, six foot eight, giant mystery of a man. The conspiracy theories about where he's from have run rampant among the group, but no one has been able to confirm anything. Despite his imposing presence, Liam's unwavering loyalty is enough to keep us from asking too many questions. *I still think Russian Mafia, though.*

None of us spoke, only letting the sound of weights clinking and grunts of exertion fill the air for another 45 minutes. I kept my focus on the mechanics of the workout, making sure my form was perfect. The last thing I need is a torn hamstring from attempting to keep up with these maniacs.

Delta gives up first, collapsing to the ground and laying like a starfish on the mat. His cheek smashed on the rubber mat while his chest heaved dramatically. Liam, on the other hand, pushes through until the very end of the set. He's probably one of the biggest men I've truly ever seen and an absolute machine in the gym, but I swear, a goldfish has more of a personality than him.

Drew doesn't even give them a glance as he does a battle rope circuit that leaves sweat pouring down his face. The ropes hit the ground with a rhythmic thud, each movement deliberate and powerful. The intensity in his eyes is unsettling as he pushes himself to the limit, showing no signs of slowing down.

Grabbing my water bottle, I chug half of it down before tossing it into my bag. Delta and Liam stretch in silence, not bothering to do more than necessary to cool down. I can't imagine it would help them tomorrow if they had, though. These guys are used to pushing themselves to the limit, but by the looks of it, they hit their limit tonight.

They both look up at me as I step toward them. I gesture with my head toward Drew, making a slicing motion over my throat while raising an eyebrow in question. I need to know if they think he's at his limit, like I do.

When they both nodded without hesitation, I let out a long puff of air, anticipating that this wouldn't be easy. Drew is clearly struggling, lost in his inner world of pain and exhaustion. It can be a dangerous place to be when you feel alone.

At least I have Liam and Delta with me as backup. I've been through my fair share of combat training, but Drew was practically bred into the SEAL team. He's a force to be reckoned with on a normal day. Amped up like he is tonight, with that razor sharp focus, will be like taking down a grizzly bear shot up with steroids.

He doesn't even flinch as I stalk up behind him, still whipping the battle rope like it's as light as a feather. Liam and Delta flank my sides preparing to step in before I can get my ass seriously kicked.

My arms lift out to wrap around Drew's chest, but before I can make a move, he spins around, fists clenched. Green eyes of rage lock onto mine, and I can see the fire burning within him. "What the hell are you doing?" he growls, his voice low and dangerous.

My hands instinctively cover my face while I try to show surrender, stepping back. "Woah! Take it easy, man."

"Seriously. The fuck are you guys doing?" He looks between the three of us like we are the crazy ones.

"Will you just take it easy?" I ask again while motioning downward with my hands.

For a second, it looks like he may snap, then he scoffs loudly. "I'm calmer than you are."

"Say it again," I goad as he places his hands on his head, taking long, deep breaths.

I didn't hear Liam ask, but Delta says "The Dude" and then follows it up with, "Come on, The Big Lebowski!"

Finally, Drew repeats louder, "Calmer than you are."

"That's a good boy. You ready to talk about why you're hulking out in here?"

He shakes his head, the defiance written so clearly across his face that I want to knock it off him.

"Fine! I'll talk because none of these pansy ass men will look you in the face and tell you that you're a dumbass. I had to do it the last time; guess it'll be me again!" My huff turns into a shout, and when I see his eyes widen, I know it's working.

"What the hell are you doing, Reynolds? You should be on a flight to South Carolina! Not throwing a goddamn pity party for yourself in the gym. You want to honor your stupid ass promise to stupid ass Heather, well, do it! She hasn't answered her phone? Get on a goddamn flight and show up on her doorstep!" With each word, his jaw drops slightly lower. I'm probably taking too much satisfaction in yelling at him, but damn does it feel good to get it off my chest.

He splutters over his words, but I cut him off. "The conversation goes like this: 'Hey Heather, I'm honoring my promise and letting you know, in person, that the break we had has, *in fact,* turned into a breakup. I wish you the best in your evil, wicked life. Goodbye.' End of story. If Kara doesn't want you at her wedding after that? Then so fucking what? Move on, you big dumb idiot. You have better, more important relationships here—with Ben, with Ellie, and with Olivia. Olivia, the woman with whom you are so enamored that you have to spend five hours in the gym to avoid thinking about.

He scoffs, grumbling, "They were here too," as he side-eyed Delta and Liam, trying to divert some of my wrath.

"They were babysitting you! We have a goddamn group chat devoted to making sure you make the right decision. Well, time's up, buckaroo. You either book a flight, or we hog-tie you and I will personally fly your ass to South Carolina. I've got access to a helicopter and stainless cable ties. Weather be damned, *you are* going there."

Rather than argue, like I thought he would, his head nods in agreement. "You're right."

Without another word, he turns around and walks toward the locker room.

Liam and Delta remain silent, watching him walk away like he wasn't just chewed out.

"Did it work?" Delta looks between the door that Drew went through and me.

We all stood there, waiting, wondering what kind of uno reverse Drew just threw at me. I was ready for some pushback, maybe even getting cussed out. Instead, he agreed but stormed off. Delta gestures with his thumb, his voice growing more confused. "Were we supposed to follow him?"

It isn't until he walks out, phone in one hand and credit card in the other, that we realize my outburst did, in fact, work.

Without looking up, he sits at the end of a weight bench, scrolling on his phone. "Booked. The earliest flight is Saturday morning, so I'll need a ride."

For the first time all day, I let out a relieved breath and sat down on the rubber mat to do my own post-workout stretch. One problem down. If only it were as easy to throw a tantrum with Isla.

Like a bull to a red flag, Drew looks up and locks his eyes on me. Instant regret of sitting directly in front of him hits me. A sick smile starts working its way across his face. "Now, let's talk about Isla. What the hell are you doing, Astor?" *Is it even legal to drop a Uno reverse card on top of a Uno reverse card?*

Rather than fight it, I throw my upper body back on the mat and stare up at the ceiling. "Isla may be the death of me."

The guys remain silent, but apparently choose to get comfortable while they wait for me to spill my guts. I catch a glimpse of Delta taking a seat on an open bench while Liam leans against the squat rack, his massive frame nearly as tall as the pull-up bar.

"Jeff's a fucking asshole. I'm reading between the lines of what Isla isn't saying, and my gut is telling me it's bad. Or *could* be bad?"

"Could?" Delta's question comes out through clenched teeth.

Letting out a heavy breath, I sit up on my elbows. "Isla's leaving him next week. She told me she'd let me know before she did it, but knowing her, she probably won't."

The three of them shift in sync, going from relaxed to rigid.

"No fucking way is she doing that alone." Delta sounds incredulous at the mere thought of Isla facing Jeff on her own.

"Didn't Linc help her with her security system?" Drew asks before immediately dismissing his question with a wave of his hand. "Doesn't matter; he can hack in and keep an eye on things."

Liam huffs through his slightly crooked nose before shaking his head. "Not good enough."

A brief moment of relief comes over me, knowing that I'm not the only one who feels like her doing this alone is a bad idea. Isla is fiercely independent for someone who is stuck under the thumb of a deadbeat boyfriend. She'd carry the weight of the world on her shoulders before she asked for help. It's been frustrating as hell to watch her struggle trying to find her identity, but I know firsthand how important it is to let someone come to their own conclusions. No amount of yelling from the finish line will help if the person isn't close enough to hear you. I learned that lesson the hard way with Odessa and our parents. I took on the big brother role as well as the protector role, sheltering her from the vile words and actions of our parents. So much so that the first time she saw our father throw a baccarat tumbler at the wall behind our mother's head, she was in middle school and completely shocked. She remained oblivious to the toxic relationship our parents had—their weird foreplay in a volatile marriage—until I couldn't shield it from her any longer. A bitter realization hit her hard: the almighty Astors, who may have more money than most developing countries, severely lack emotional intelligence and stability.

A wet bundle hits me, yanking me out of my derailed thoughts. The sweaty towel that Drew threw at me landed to the side of me, causing me to gag at the sight.

"I asked you a question, dipshit." Drew chastises me, his

eyes narrowing in annoyance. "What do you want to do? She may not be your girl *yet*. But we all know it's bound to happen. We'll follow your lead—we just hope it involves 24-hour surveillance, a bodyguard attached to Isla, and a bodybag for Jeff if he *even fucking* tries."

A bitter laugh escapes before I can stop it. That sounds like a pretty damn good plan to me. Locking her up in a secure tower would be the only thing better. The problem will be convincing Isla to have someone there with her.

"I'll talk to her this weekend. I can—" Fuck, I don't know how to finish that sentence. Words momentarily evade me before I finally say, "I don't know. Lay it on thick, I guess. Persuade her to have one of us with her when she tells him."

Delta's tongue pushes his cheek out before he sighs. "What about recommending Hayes? He's the most neutral to her, and Jeff won't feel threatened because he knows he's married to Charlie. Any of us go— Jeff will make it a bigger deal and throw out accusations to hurt Isla. The town thinks Hayes walks on water; no way would they believe his bullshit if Hayes is with her."

Drew, Liam, and I nod in unison. That's the best plan we've got so far, and we only have a handful of days to convince Isla to go along with it.

Chapter Four

Isla

Wet drops hit my cheek, waking me up from a deep sleep. I drifted through hazy dreams, where everything felt safe and familiar; echoes of laughter and warmth enveloped me, temporarily shielding me from reality. But now, the sensation jolts me back to the present, harsh and unwelcome. My eyes fly open to a mostly dark room, with only the light from the hall illuminating Jeff standing over me.

Why is he hovering over me? What time is it? The questions swim through my disoriented mind as shadows dance along the walls. My elbows try to push me up, but they feel weak and shaky as I try to figure out what's going on.

What is happening? "What—?" I can't even begin to question what's going on before a slimy, cold substance is slammed into my cheek. Pain streaks across my face like a lightning bolt, causing me to gasp in shock and confusion.

My hand instinctively reaches up to wipe it away, only to come into contact with something sticky and foul. The smell is what hits my senses next, but I can't make sense of the light metallic aroma that lingers in the air.

"Good, you're awake. Let's have a chat about time management." Jeff's voice is cold and menacing as he leans in closer, his eyes filled with malice.

My jaw feels unhinged as I stare at him, trying to make sense of what he's holding. The breath I try to draw in feels ragged, jolting my entire chest with each puff I attempt to inhale. "Did you just slap me across the face with a steak?"

The corner of his mouth twisted into a familiar, mocking smirk. "If you had bothered to come home on time, I wouldn't have had to embarrass myself ordering takeout." He waved the meat in front of me, his tone dripping with sarcasm. "Honestly, this could've all been avoided."

My stomach churns, and I can feel the tension coiling in my shoulders as the pungent scent of raw meat fills the air, its slick surface gleaming just inches from my face. Despite the sheer shock of it, a part of me isn't even surprised anymore. Jeff's antics know no bounds; he will go to any extreme just to make his point known.

He cruelly lets go of the steak, letting it fall onto my lap. The curl of his lip in disgust is a stark reminder of his lack of empathy. With a shake of his head, he turns and starts pacing the bedroom in front our walk-in closet. "What's your fucking problem, Isla? Huh? I don't think I ask for much in this relationship."

I stay silent, but quickly shove the covers down to the end of the bed and sit up on my knees. It's not much of a defensive position, but Jeff clearly isn't done with this conversation. When he turns his back, I fumble for my phone on the nightstand with one hand, ripping it from the charging cord. I have it slid into the pocket of my joggers before he turns around again.

"Come home at a decent time. Make fucking dinner once in a while. Be the good little housewife you so desperately want to be. Instead, you humiliated me in front of my associates. All night, they asked where you were, giving me crap about how you're out with one of those so-called elite special forces guys." He lifts his chin, his nostrils flaring as he studies me, a hint of disbelief in his expression. "Is that really what's happening? You cheating on me with one of those washed-up wannabes?"

The anger inside begins to boil until I can't handle it anymore. "Fuck *off*."

He turns on his heels, the moment frozen as shock flickers across his face. I can't remember a time I've ever yelled at him, let alone stood my ground like this.

But then, in the blink of an eye, rage twists his angular features into something unrecognizable. Every muscle in his body seems to coil with tension, as if he's a predator, ready to pounce.

Instinct kicks in, and I scramble backwards off the bed, heart racing. My feet hit the cold floor, sending a jolt of adrenaline through me, and I make a dash for the primary bathroom.

I can hear him behind me, the heavy thud of his footsteps closing in, each one a relentless reminder of how fast he's gaining on me. In a desperate burst of speed, I hurl myself toward the bathroom's open door. I barely manage to slam the door shut behind me, the sound echoing against the walls like a warning bell.

My fingers fumble to lock it just as he crashes into it, the force rattling the frame. I can't catch my breath, my pulse pounding in my ears, but for now—at least for this moment—I'm safe behind the barrier, shaky and terrified.

With trembling hands, I yank my phone out of my pocket and unlock it. It isn't a thought of whom I should call—I know who I should call. A deputy would be here in a matter of minutes to arrest Jeff. If I called any of my friends, they'd be here just as quickly, and Jeff would disappear longer than Houdini.

Instead of calling who I knew I should, I called the only person that Jeff is truly afraid of—his father.

The door vibrates as Jeff pounds on it, trying to break through it.

Three drawn-out rings, and despite it being nearly two in the morning, Cyrus answers his phone. "Isla," the powerful voice of someone I looked up to growing up, suddenly doesn't sound as powerful—it sounds disappointed.

"Jeff's drunk. He just hit me. Come get him, or I'll call the police."

"Fine." The hiss in his voice shows his annoyance, but I have a hard time caring. This isn't the first time I've woken him up in the middle of the night; however, I'm counting on it being the last.

The door has since stopped rattling, but the sound of items being thrown about in the room is still audible.

With a deep breath through my nose, I open the security app on my phone and click the camera for our bedroom.

Jeff is throwing everything that isn't glued down toward the bathroom door. Glass shatters as loud thuds hit the wood. I've learned not to keep anything valuable in this house, only things that I can buy a dozen of—or at least, Christy can.

I watch through unfazed eyes as he stomps about in our room, muttering to himself. He couldn't care less that he's acting like a toddler throwing a tantrum.

A notification that someone is pulling down the driveway snaps me out of my trance. Cyrus made it in less than four minutes, a record. I wouldn't be surprised if he somehow knew this was coming. Knowing Jeff, he probably already called his dad when the guys left and ranted to him about my short-comings.

Cyrus walked through the front door like it was any other day, pausing in the entryway. I kept my eyes trained on the bedroom camera, waiting for Jeff to realize I called his dad. When he heard him, I could see the sneer he sent me through the camera.

His dad didn't even wait for him to start down the stairs; he simply turned and walked back out the front door. The same song and dance we've done one too many times. That doesn't stop me from switching through the cameras throughout the house until he's out the door, though.

With a heavy sigh, my head haphazardly fell forward. The weight of everything falling solely on my shoulders.

For the hundredth time today, I'm left questioning why the hell I ever put myself in this position. How did I get here? I held on to memories of the good times we had for years, but now they feel tainted—like snapshots faded by the harsh light of reality. When we first moved here, he was the only friend I had, the only one not afraid of the little girl who didn't have much hair and wore a beanie every day. I remember the way he laughed at my silly jokes and didn't flinch when the kids at school stared. That version of him feels like someone else entirely.

Things started to change gradually when he started middle school, and slowly began to drift away from me. By the time I started high school, he was a senior and wouldn't even glance my way in the halls.

Still, every now and then, he'd give me a glimpse of the guy he used to be. There were moments when he'd invite me to watch a movie in their theater room—just the two of us. The dim lights made it feel cozy and intimate, like I was the only one he'd share this with. Then there were the times he would suggest we stroll around the golf course after one of our parents' dinner parties—where we could chat about everything and nothing. In those fleeting moments, it felt like we could pretend everything was still the same, as if the distance between us didn't exist and our bond was still there, hidden just for us. Those nights were a mix of comfort and nostalgia, but they always ended too soon, leaving me unsure of when there would be more.

Then he left for college, and I honestly didn't think he'd ever come back. I had grown used to and savored those small moments of connection, so when he was gone, it created a huge void that made me question my worth. Did I mean so little to him? Was I just a passing moment in his life?

Years later, after I'd started working for Olivia, I unexpectedly ran into him at the grocery store. He had moved back home and looked genuinely happy to see me, as if the time and distance hadn't mattered.

We caught up briefly, exchanged numbers, and started "seeing each other casually." It felt like my freshman year all over again; I was the center of his attention, but only when he chose for me to be. Looking back, I see that I should have questioned that label—how casually can you date someone who once meant the world to you? But I was naive, holding onto hope like a lifeline, as if the boy who once defended me could somehow become the man I needed now.

Before long, our parents found out we were seeing each other. They weren't just happy; they were elated—as if it had been part of their plan all along for us to be together. They insisted that we move in together, claiming it would look good for our families if we did. I agreed, thinking it would be a fresh start, a chance to recapture what we had lost.

But I was blissfully unaware that it was all a carefully crafted manipulation. I allowed myself to be swept up in his charm, convinced that our connection was real. The truth hit harder than any slap could: I realized he never truly cared about me; his primary concern was always about keeping his parents happy.

Still, even knowing that, I didn't want to let go. I kept slipping back into this cycle of misplaced loyalty and nostalgia, convincing myself that the boy I once knew was still buried beneath the façade of anger and resentment. *Then again, it wasn't just me doing the convincing—my parents have always been very persuasive.*

Chapter Five

Isla

"Don't worry about it! Olivia and I almost have everything wrapped up for the week anyway. It's supposed to be a snowpocalypse out there this weekend. Stay safe if y'all go out at all! Let us know if you need anything." Charlie offers before hanging up the phone.

Calling her was the first thing I had to do this morning. I came up with an excuse about a migraine and not wanting to drive in the imminent weather to avoid going into the office. Thankfully, Mother Nature blessed me with a snowstorm that is supposed to blow in sometime today. After everything that happened last night, there's no way I could face the inquisition at work. It's the sad, pitying eyes that get me every time. I could barely stand the looks when I had cancer. Now, knowing it's because of the situation I put myself in... I just can't.

Instead of sleeping all day in bed, like I want to, I'll be packing my bags. Jeff is at work until this evening, so I'll have plenty of time to get out of this godawful house. I don't even have a plan for where I want to go yet. All that I know is that I need to get out of here and go somewhere where I can be alone.

Let the bruise on my cheek heal a bit before I have to dive into a game of fifty questions and convince my friends that Jeff isn't worth the jail time.

The second thing on my "get the hell out of here" to-do list is taking a shower. I need twenty minutes of reprieve to wash away the emotions from last night, scrub my tear-stained face, and cleanse the lingering scent of meat that my brain refuses to let go of. After Jeff left, I took three showers and removed all the bedding, swapping it out for clean sheets and blankets. I'd hoped that would be enough, but each time my mind flashed back to the memory of myoglobin dripping on my face, I could smell it all over again. After two hours, I finally rubbed Vicks vapor rub under my nose and fell into a fitful sleep.

For the last time, I step into the large walk-in shower. When the temperature hits somewhere between scalding and hell, I immerse myself, relishing in the burn that is surely removing a few layers of skin. This shower was everything I thought I wanted when we moved in. Enormous, with multiple shower heads and enough space to dance around in. But now, it's nothing more than a big shower that wasn't worth the trauma of living here.

As I scrub my skin raw, I let the notes in my favorite body wash of rose, jasmine, and bergamot purge my brain of the horrors of last night. I'm letting it all go because today I have a plan. Today, I'm choosing me.

With a new attitude, a mission, and a sense of empowerment, I step out of the shower feeling refreshed and determined. I dry off, get dressed, and start making my way through the six thousand square foot house.

Most of the rooms are relatively empty and sterile, so it only takes about thirty minutes to get through the majority of the house. The box I carted around between rooms ended up carrying nothing. Not a framed photo, candle, or knick-knack of mine in sight. I knew that I had been careful not to leave anything cherished in Jeff's wake, but to not have a single personal item left around the house seems impossible to even me. Instead, Christy bought only expensive decor items to "liven up" the space. *Because black, gold, and white sure are lively.*

The primary bedroom is much the same. Last night, staged photos adorned the dresser and nightstands. They ended up in shattered pieces on the floor when Jeff threw his fit, though. After he left, I picked up the broken pieces and removed the photos from the frames. They currently lay in a pile on the dresser, and the frames are in the garbage. Within a few days, new frames holding the same photos would be placed where they had originally been. *Rinse and repeat.* It's asinine to me; we don't even look happy in the pictures. A matching couple posed at a charity gala, looking miserable next to each other. People in photos from the 1820s look happier than us. Yet, without fail, they receive beautiful frames and a permanent spot for everyone to see. No wonder Jeff tosses them around like the sight sickens him. I'd do the same, but I know he wouldn't be the one to clean up the mess.

I clean out the bathroom in record time, tossing the few cosmetics and toiletries that I still have into the empty box. The thought that I have even more things crammed into the tiny cubby of my gym locker at work almost makes me chuckle. Everything I hold dear is probably at the office, including a quilt my late grandmother made for me.

The closet holds more of my things—dresses and shoes that I'll never wear again but shouldn't leave. Instead of putting them into boxes, though, I start a donation pile off to the side of the large countertop in the middle of the closet. The donation pile ends up filling higher than the few boxes I had, but there's no way I'm bringing negative sentiments into my fresh start.

Like a sixth sense, I can feel the energy in the house shifting. I haven't heard a sound, yet I know he's here. If I could get away with it, I'd hide somewhere and hope he thought I was at work. Unfortunately, I can almost guarantee he's seen the car outside.

I wasn't mentally prepared to have this conversation, but I know that it needs to be done. This needs to end. He has to be sober and see me leave to understand that it's finally done.

Only it isn't just him that enters the bedroom. With him comes the reek of gin, like he's been bathing in it. He's still in the same clothes he left in last night, and it's well after noon.

"Isla." His low growl sends a chill down my spine. Crazed out of his mind, Jeff is one thing. I can handle the screaming and throwing things. Enraged, detached Jeff is a different monster. His eyes are bloodshot, but they look empty, like the anger has consumed him and he can't even see me.

I watch from the closet as he glances around the room, taking note of the few boxes and things I've been packing. When his gaze snaps back to me, his head tilts to the side in question.

I keep myself rooted to the floor, hands frozen on the shirt I was folding.

A maniacal laugh rips up his chest and his entire body doubles over. "You think you can leave me?"

My breath feels caught somewhere between my chest and throat, but at least this is a version of Jeff I recognize. Arrogant, egotistical, and an asshole.

"Jeff... We aren't happy together."

"That wasn't my question, Isla! Do you think you can leave me?" My focus shifts between his exaggerated hand movements and his face.

It feels futile to argue with him, so instead I remain stark, still, and expressionless. Unfortunately, all that does is enrage him more.

"You're *not* leaving! I'll kill you before you can leave me. No one would even know. I own this town. No one will bat an eye when we tell them you killed yourself." He sounds so convincing, I almost believe him. My brain knows he's wrong, though. Between Charlie, Olivia, and Everett—they'd never let him get away with it.

"My friends would never believe that. Hurt me and they'll kill you. They'd actually get away with it, too. Unlike you." I spit at him with as much venom as I could lace in it.

A wicked smile crosses his face as he steps into the closet to stand in front of me. "I'm not worried about your little gang of friends, Isla."

He grabs the back of my head and pulls me closer to him, the smell of gin assaulting me once again. "I'll pick them off one by one, too. Think I'll start with that nosey boss of yours. "

Chuckling in his face, I give him my best mocking smirk. "Good luck with that. Touch her, and you better start praying that Drew doesn't find you first."

I can see the first spark of fear dancing in his eyes, but he quickly masks it with a sneer. "Fu—"

Cutting him off, I continue with a snarl, "Pray for Hayes. He's the most merciful of them all—a quick death. Meanwhile, I'll be praying it's Liam, and he skins you alive before disposing of you like the trash you are."

He yanks my ponytail backward, and I stumble while trying to regain my footing. Before I can comprehend his plan, he's slamming my head into the granite counter and then immediately yanking me back.

My arms instinctively flail, reaching for any leverage to fight back, but his grip on my hair is relentless. The pain shoots through my skull, but it's the least of my worries right now. I can already feel the forward motion as he thrusts my head back toward the hard counter. This time, I'm able to anticipate it and at least get my hands up to take some of the blow.

The next time he yanked me backward, he let go, letting the momentum send me flying backward into the shelves that once held my shoes.

The slanted wooden shelves crumble when I hit them, which only seems to infuriate him more. Most of them caved under me with the impact, but the few high ones began falling on top of me like dominoes. The pain barely registers in my brain because I can't focus on anything apart from that Jeff looks possessed as he grabs each shelf and throws it behind him.

Slowly, my head shakes as I try to understand how he could have just thrown me into the shelves but is now trying to help me out of them. The warm blood pouring from my head clouds my vision, but I don't miss the sinister expression that grows on his face as he looks between me and the last shelf.

His nostrils' flair with each threatening breath as he raises the shelf above his head. I can't tell if time has slowed, or he's taunting me, but neither of us move for what feels like an impossibly long time.

My eyelids begin to grow heavy as the pain finally starts to settle in. He must have sensed my imminent loss of consciousness because, with a bone-chilling grin, he brings the shelf crashing down toward me.

Instinctively, my body curls in on itself, making myself as small as possible, while my arms attempt to cover my face.

Pain radiates through my body with each blow, my cries mingling with the sound of wood splintering.

The last thought I have as I succumb to what can only be described as "The Darkness" isn't one of bravery; it's overwhelming grief.

Jeff's right; I'm never leaving this house.

Chapter Six

Everett

F at snowflakes began to fall as I drove into the department today, splattering against the windshield of my 4Runner and creating what should have been a peaceful ambiance. Instead, each flake felt like the ticking of a clock. I had hoped to see Isla at the CPM/EFSC building, but when I arrived, Charlie told me she had called in sick—a migraine. Instantly, red flags began waving in my mind. Isla had come to work with a 102° fever and a migraine before, but now she was calling in sick? *The math ain't mathin'.*

That's why I truly appreciate my new position at the sheriff's department. As a sworn deputy, I'm not chained to a desk when I can't be in the air. I can circulate through town, attend community events, or just chat with locals. When Luke hired me, he told me that each department is like a different breed of dog. The office staff are like Corgis—friendly but yappy. The dispatch team consists of border collies, highly intelligent and herding everyone where they need to be. The patrol deputies are the German Shepherds, and the detectives are the Bloodhounds. But me? I get to be the friendly Labrador, ready to work at a moment's notice, but generally just a friendly face around town. As long as I'm carrying my weapon, wearing a vest, and showing my badge, Luke said my time wouldn't be micromanaged. He may be a hardass sheriff, but he values community over everything else. If I'm not needed in the air, he wants me to cultivate a good rapport on the ground—my supervisor, L.T. Will feels the same. Essentially, I do my job when it's needed and smile for the town when it isn't.

The Cascadia County Sheriff Department office is a sight in itself. Pulling in feels like entering a fortress of justice. Olivia's grand-aunt, who was more like her mother, left behind a significant fortune when she passed away, and the county voted to build this new station. It's not just huge; it's modern and impressive, equipped with state-of-the-art technology. Each department has its own assigned office space based on size. The Search and Rescue team is the biggest, thanks to its high volunteer rate; even though only two of us are employed full-time, we take up most of the building.

We don't have much crime in the county, but we do handle plenty of rescues—missing hikers, injured climbers, and the occasional body recovery. People often underestimate the Cascade Mountains, forgetting that Mother Nature can be an unforgiving bitch.

Lieutenant Will coordinates all SAR missions, making sure we have the necessary resources and personnel in place. I may be the only full-time employee he sees regularly, but he manages a team of nearly a hundred volunteers.

Our section is on the first floor, just to the right of the front desk, which allows volunteers and the community to feel part of the team without delving too deep into the department. It also means Jill, who's worked the front desk for over forty years, is always in our business. She's not part of the dispatch team on the second floor, but she somehow knows everything going on in town before the deputies do. She's also become one of my favorite people here. With no shortage of tea to spill, she makes the long, slow shifts bearable.

I set my stuff down at my desk and grabbed a cup of coffee from the break room when I caught wind of something brewing. Jill was loudly talking on her cell phone about a car accident that occurred just a few minutes ago. I'd grown accustomed to tuning her out, but the moment I heard her mention the intersection of Johnson and Whitemore, my hackles rose. That's the road I take to get home, and it's not just me—Drew is my roommate, Charlie and Hayes live within a few miles, and Olivia and her kids are right next to them. *Almost* all of my people have to cross that intersection to get home.

I find myself rising from my desk chair before I even realize it, my heart pounding as I make my way to Jill's desk. I'm not one to break out in a cold sweat from anxiety, but right now, that fight-or-flight response is taking over my body.

Jill glances at me, her eyes instantly filling with empathy. Her voice shakes as she explains, "The hit-and-run. It was Olivia's car. Lucas called it in." She's one of the few who calls him Lucas, not Luke or Sheriff Haynes.

Nodding, I try to swallow the lump in my throat so that I can speak. "What do we know?"

Her head vibrates as she rolls her lips together, and tears fill her eyes. She's known Olivia for much longer than I have—everyone in this town has, but we all love her the same.

Her lips part as she inhales quick breaths before letting them out. "Hit and run. Medics are on their way; they should be there soon, and we will know more." As soon as the first tear streaks down her face, I know that I can't leave her here alone.

Without thinking, I pull her into a tight hug before quickly releasing her. Jill needs to be comforted right now, but unfortunately, it can't be me who does it. Olivia needs me first, and Drew needs me second.

"Mary!" I hollered over my shoulder toward one of the SAR volunteers sitting in the conference room. Some volunteers come in before shit actually hits the fan, so they can be ready to go at a moments' notice.

She stumbles out of her chair, her chocolate eyes wide as she stutters, "Me?" *Shit. I scared her.*

Instinctively calming my tone, I put on the most charming smile I can muster. "Your name is Mary, right? Sorry, there are a lot of volunteers, and I'm still kinda new around here."

A red blush creeps up her cheeks as she nods, a small smile forming on her lips. "No—I mean, yes. I'm Mary."

I start talking as I walk back to my desk, grabbing my radio, gun, and keys. "Great. Mary, I'm going to need you to sit with Jill while I go help at the scene. If she hears anything that isn't reported to the station, I need you to call Luke or me." Another perk of still being a sworn-in deputy is that I can help wherever I'm needed and have lights and sirens to get me there faster.

Without listening to her response, I took off toward the back of the building. The patrol vehicles are all stored behind the building in a secure lot. The shift change happened about thirty minutes ago, but the vehicles from the last shift still aren't back. Hopefully, that's a good sign and they're already working on a perimeter.

As I jump into my patrol SUV, I turn the volume up on my personal radio. It hasn't been more than sixty seconds since Jill told me about the accident, and my blood hasn't stopped racing since. All I want to hear are the facts directly from the scene or Luke's mouth.

The radio is in chaos right now, but the second I hear someone say, "Single female passenger, Olivia Turner, alive and responsive," come through, my body relaxes a fraction.

Luke began shouting orders to everyone on the team next, trying to get a solid perimeter set-up.

Before I start driving, I message dispatch that I'm leaving the premises and will be heading to the scene. They'll let Luke know I'm on route and give me more direction.

I peel out of the parking lot, sliding on the fresh snow, while yelling at Siri to call Drew. It rings an ungodly number of times before going to voicemail.

"Fuck!" My fist pounds on the steering wheel after the second call to him goes to voicemail.

"Siri, call Hayes Carrington!" This time it's answered on the second ring.

"What's up, Ev?" My chest involuntarily rakes at his tone. He hasn't heard about the accident yet, and as much as I would rather not be the one to tell him, I have to.

"Olivia's been in a car accident. I don't know much. Tried to call Drew, but he isn't answering."

"What?" He asks incredulously, like I'm making it up. "Olivia? No—she just walked out the door."

An involuntary growl comes out of me. "Hayes! I'm not fucking around. It was Olivia. It was confirmed on the radio."

His intake of breath is the only sound I hear while the human side of him processes what I just said. It should only be a matter of seconds before the SEAL side kicks-in and starts problem-solving.

Like a switch flipping, his tone changed with it, growing stern and laser-focused. "I'll find him. He just left with Heather." *What in the fucking Mercury in retrograde is happening today?*

"I don't have time to process that. Call me when you find him," I demand, ending the call abruptly. I knew it was going to be a shitty night, but even I couldn't have predicted it would go this badly.

Chapter Seven

Isla

The sound of glass breaking in the distance breaks me out of the sleepy haze I was in. My eyes attempt to pop open, but I immediately wince at the motion. It hurts; everything hurts. From my head to my toes, pain laces through my body.

Gingerly, I touch the tips of my fingers to my cheek. Each touch reveals a new, swollen, tender spot. With as little touch as I can, my fingers graze upward to what feels like a golf ball covering my right eye. I knew it would be bad, but at this point, I can't even fathom recovering from an injury like this. I can't open my eyelid, let alone see anything out of that eye.

Through blurry vision, out of my left eye, I see the destroyed closet. Shoes and clothes are thrown everywhere; shelves are broken and lying on the floor; and reddish brown streaks cover every surface. The haze I feel grows with each small movement as I attempt to look for my phone, but I refuse to let it pull me under again. After a minute of searching, I gave up the dream of finding it. Of course, nothing can be easy. Guaranteed, Jeff took it and smashed it into oblivion anyway.

This feels like a real life horror movie, and I'm the star actor. I can practically hear the audience yelling at me to hide. The problem is that I have no idea where Jeff is. I don't even know what time it is or how long I was out for.

Rather than attempting to stand, I stiffly move so that my knees are under me and my hands are on the ground, supporting me. I'll crawl through broken glass and fire if it means getting out of this house.

The sharp pain in my rib cage is enough to take my breath away, but it's nothing compared to the overwhelming waves of nausea I feel.

My hands push through the ruins of garments, sliding toward the exit of the closet. It's evident now that I should've installed a panic button, like Lincoln recommended when he put in the cameras. I could've had an entire squad of Special Forces swooping and rescuing me. But nooo, Three Sisters is sooo safe. *Stupid, Isla.*

It's then, with my hand grazing over a chiffon dress, that the realization that I'm being filmed sinks in. Everything that's happened in the last twenty-four hours has been recorded and is sitting in a cloud somewhere the guys can find it. A morbid sense of relief overcomes me. No matter what, if I had died in this closet, Jeff wouldn't have gotten away with it.

If I wasn't on my hands and knees, fumbling my way through the pain of crawling, I'd probably laugh. A sick sense of justice, but dang, it feels good to know that he won't win.

Through slow movements, I finally find my way to the door frame and even more slowly pull myself up to stand. The first baby step I take is laced with pain, but I wouldn't say it hurts any more or less than crawling. My only hope is that it's at least faster.

Rather than stepping, I shuffle my way along, my palm firmly placed on the bedroom furniture. At this pace, I won't make it to the front door until the morning. At least it's quiet; there's no sign of Jeff upstairs or downstairs. With any luck, he's already gone, and I can at least get to my purse and keys before he gets back.

The pain and nausea start to fade, but in their place is a new, disoriented feeling. Everything spins—the room, the floor, my hands. I know that I need to devote every remaining brain cell to staying alive and getting out of this house, but my body wants to betray me.

Stumbling and panting, I move through the hall toward the stairs. I practically slam into the wall next to the stairs, my arms flying out to brace myself against it. My cheek rests on the smooth surface for a few seconds—probably too long—but I'm not ready to give up the feeling of being steady.

Slowly, I let myself down so that I'm sitting on the top step. There's no way I'm about to walk down that flight of stairs without falling and breaking my neck.

One step at a time, I scoot my way down, wincing with every move. The urge to take a break, take a nap, or just give up entirely is overwhelming, but I push the thoughts out of the way and try to think of what I should be doing to overcome this. Unfortunately, my thoughts only lead to what the guys would think if they saw me now. They've all been to war and endured physical combat, often making life altering decisions in a split second. Here I am struggling to make it down a flight of stairs because I moved in with an abusive asshole. *Stupid, stupid Isla.*

By the time I get to the last step, my head feels like it weighs a hundred pounds, swaying from side to side. The rest of my body feels close to the same, screaming at me to stop. I can't stop, though. I know I can't stop. Stop and you die.

The front door is merely twenty feet from where I sit on this step. I made it out of that stupid closet and down an entire flight of stairs without passing out. Surely, I can make it to my purse and out the door. *Right?*

Or, maybe I should take a break; it's been quiet since I heard the door slam. *No, do not stop.*

I'm in the open, exposed, and vulnerable. I shouldn't stay here and risk falling asleep, but I can't fathom how the heck I'm supposed to get to that door.

Somewhere, deep in my brain, someone is shouting "mind over matter, La," to me. *But how do I do that?*

I can't think, I don't trust myself or my decision-making right now. I need to figure out what the guys would do. *Kill Jeff.*

Okay, not what the guys would do. What would Everett tell me to do? *Move.* Don't stop until I'm in his arms.

My right hand reaches up, gripping the railing from the inside, attempting to pull myself up. With a groan and a lot of force, I stand and plant my feet, trying to gain some sense of balance.

Unfortunately, the movement causes the spinning to turn into lightheadedness. Before I realize it, I'm plunging back into The Darkness again—only this time my thoughts are of Everett.

I can't give up—he's waiting for me.

Chapter Eight

Everett

The lights and sirens on the SUV clear the path of traffic that is already starting to back up on Johnson. Deputies are beginning to direct traffic, but now that it's becoming dark, and the snow is coming down harder, it's chaos.

A cruiser with lights on pulls out right as I'm pulling in, so I snag its place. The SUV is off and my door thrown open before I look at the scene. Grabbing my winter gear from the back is my priority right now. If I see the damage or Olivia on a stretcher, there's no guarantee I'll give two fucks about protective gear.

I don't notice the adrenaline coursing through my veins until I have all the winter gear on, besides my gloves. Only then do I notice my hands shaking. A first for me, considering that having steady hands under pressure is kind of a requirement for being a pilot.

Rather than walk out there, amped as all get out, I choose to do something I haven't done in far too long. My fingers lace together, I close my eyes, take three controlled breaths and say a prayer for Olivia's safety. It's easy to forget your faith when you're trying to play God, but nothing brings you back to reality quite like the reminder of how mortal we all truly are.

The familiar sense of calm washes over me, long enough that I can get my gloves on and shut the rear door. I'm normally good under pressure—the best, actually. My mind and body can be completely separated. It's a tactic you have to learn when flying or else your hands will surely follow wherever your eyes go. A tactic that I need to tap into to get through this shift. *Except, that gut feeling is back, and it's telling me this is only the beginning.*

My feet start moving toward the central point of the accident, but my eyes scan the full extent of the scene, taking in every detail. The Cascadia County Fire Department is blocking some road with one of their trucks, but not the scene. Another fire truck is parked on the side of the road behind an ambulance. The smell of gasoline and smoke fills the air; people shout orders from all directions; and red and blue lights are the main sources of light. I wouldn't say it's tunnel vision, but rather an out-of-body experience where I let my instincts take over. I'm no stranger to carnage; hell, I've been the one to cause it, but this is different. This isn't me, hundreds of feet in the air, raising hell on terrorists. This is me, up close and personal with the horror that one of my best friends recently had to endure, and it's fucking devastating.

A white pickup truck is off to the side of the road, the front end completely smashed in. A large man, assumingly the driver, has a medic checking him out right now. It's dark, and the snow hasn't let up, but even from here, I can see the shock and devastation on his face. I'd only been partially listening to the radio, but I know he's a victim in this as well.

Without realizing it, my feet stopped moving as my gaze swept to Olivia's SUV. It lay on its side in a field, the undercarriage the only part visible from where I stood. Firefighters swarmed the scene, their faces set in grim determination as they carried equipment and worked to stabilize the vehicle. The flashing lights of emergency vehicles illuminated the carnage, creating a surreal and eerie atmosphere. Knowing that Ben and Ellie could have been in that vehicle brought a newfound terror rooting deep inside me—twisted metal and shattered glass, the mangled structure a grim reminder of the fragility of life.

"Astor!" Luke shouting my name snaps me out of my trance, and I trudge the rest of the way through the muddy field toward him. He looks massive and formidable out here, like he's Thor about to summon lightning down upon us.

The closer I get to him, the more I notice the tension etched on his face. His fair skin is flushed from the cold night air, and his eyes are wild with determination. Fury radiates from him like he's one second away from snapping.

He begins to explain before I even have to ask, his voice unwavering as if he's given this speech a hundred times. "Fire got her out without any issues. She was responsive but kept mumbling about her hearing. Bus pulled out right before you got here—Levi's got her. He wouldn't let anyone else touch her."

Shit. I can't help but flinch at the mention of her late husband's twin brother being the one to treat her. Small towns seem great until you have to be the one to save the people you love.

One beat passes, then two, neither of us speaking. His body becomes so tense he could be a statue. His voice, in complete juxtaposition to his rigid state, is soft when he says, "I was on the phone with her when the person following hit her."

"Following her? " I ask, my heart beat seemingly hitting harder once again. "This was intentional?"

The raw intensity in his gaze tells me everything I need to know. "When she left the office, she said someone was tailing her, playing stupid games. Ended up hitting her into oncoming traffic when she stopped on Johnson."

I sense the tremor in his voice, the way his hands clench into fists at his sides as he fights to steady himself.

"Fuck! Who the hell would go after Olivia?" She's practically Three Sisters royalty, beloved by the entire town. Anyone trying to hurt her must be dumb or not from around here. Even without knowing she's been with Drew, no one in their right mind would target someone who is best friends with the owner of an Elite Forces company. Everyone on Hayes's team is a trained killer, tracker, and expert in combat tactics—men who have faced truly evil people and emerged unscathed from the chaos of battle. Whoever thought they could go after Olivia must have a death wish.

His back molars grind together, teeth flashing white in the dim light of the room, a stark contrast to the deep shadows forming under his eyes. "Not sure yet. I need to interview the driver of the F-350 and see if he has a description of the vehicle."

I nod, the knot in my stomach tightening as dread pools there. I let out a heavy sigh, forcing my lips to twitch into a semblance of calm. "Tell me where you want me."

"All hands on deck tonight. I want that asshole found. Tonight. Go door-to-door if we have to for security footage," he instructs, his determination a thin veneer over the simmering frustration beneath. It isn't hard to see the cracks in his facade the way his jaw works as he fights to keep a level head.

"I'll call Hayes," I offer, eager to do something, anything. "The office building might have caught something."

"Good. That's good." But even as he speaks, a look of profound sorrow crosses his face, deepening the lines of worry set in his brow. "You talked to Drew yet?"

When I shook my head, I watched as his shoulders

slumped just a fraction, and his eyes closed tightly, as if trying to block out the weight of the world pressing down on him. For a brief moment, he got lost in his own memories, a flicker of anguish crossing his face before he masked it with indifference.

His steely reserve is back, cold and impenetrable, when he finally says, "Let me know when you do."

Trudging back through the slippery field is harder than it was getting down there. My legs feel like deadweight, and the cold wind cuts through my jacket, sending shivers down my spine.

I shed my wet outer jacket, gloves, and beanie, tossing them onto the back seat to hopefully dry out a bit. Winter hasn't officially started yet, but it's already being a real bitch.

Once I have the heat on full blast, I call Hayes. He's got access to every security camera at the CPM/EFSC building, and they're always recording. If whoever hit her was waiting around for her to leave, he'll have them found before she gets to the hospital.

He answers before it even rings, this time, "Ev."

"Need you to look at the security footage outside. Someone was targeting Olivia. Luke said they were following her from the office." A muffled sob sounds from the phone, and I realize I'm probably on speakerphone and Charlie can hear me.

Softening my tone, I add, "I'm sorry, Char. Luke said she was banged up but awake. Levi's the medic who's with Olivia tonight. They aren't at the hospital yet, but they should be soon. He'll make sure they take care of her."

More sniffles sound from the other line, but Charlie doesn't say anything. Olivia's been her best friend for a few years now, and the two of them have gone through some heavy things together.

Hayes clears his throat before saying. "Silver, Nissan Xterra. I'd say early 2000s edition, but I'll need some time to find an exact year. No license plate is visible, but I'll call Lincoln."

"Thanks, man. You heard from Drew?"

A huff comes from Charlie while Hayes grumbles out a "no."

Shit.

Chapter Nine

Isla

"Wake up! You dumb bitch! Wake the fuck up!" Jeff screams at me, shaking my shoulders violently. My brain rattles in my head in protest, and I struggle to open my eyes, but they refuse to cooperate. Instead, my body gives out completely, sending me spiraling back into The Darkness.

Chapter Ten

Everett

As I navigate the relentless snow, my thoughts drift back to the accident and the mangled wreckage of Olivia's car. The scene impacts me more than I ever thought it would. Drew nearly lost Olivia tonight. The kids nearly lost their mom. We all nearly lost one of our best friends.

It's a miracle she's alive, that she was responding and awake when leaving the scene. Hayes has sent a few updates, but I haven't heard from him in at least an hour.

My fingers itch to call Isla. I don't even know if she's heard about the accident yet, and it's killing me that I haven't received any word from her. I need to hear her sweet voice give me the reassurance I'm craving: that Olivia and Drew will be okay, that we'll find the car, and that she's safe.

Rather than dwell on my feelings for Isla, I try to envision the Xterra that caused Olivia's accident. Hayes sent us a high-quality photo showing the car, providing every detail we needed, down to the brand of tires and the bumper guard. The only thing missing was the license plate number, likely removed by the perp before he hit Olivia.

At least it's enough for us to go on right now. The department made a Facebook post after the accident, alerting the community. Over five hundred people in the area have already commented and will be watching for the vehicle once the storm has passed.

A call from Hayes brings me out of my thoughts and I answer without formalities. "How's Liv?"

"She's beat up pretty good—minor concussion, some broken ribs, and cuts and bruises," he replies, sounding exhausted. My shoulders slump as if a fraction of the weight has been lifted. I knew she would be okay, but hearing it unravels a few knots in the pit of my stomach.

"I dropped her off at her house with Drew and Levi. Not sure if the two of them will survive the night with all their bullshit."

"Liv and Drew?" I ask, squinting through the flurries that dance in front of my windshield.

"Nope. Drew and Levi. Think Vi's ready to kick Drew's ass for being a dick to Olivia about Heather. And Drew—"

"Wait, let me guess," I cut in, already knowing where this is going. "Drew's being a jealous brat because Olivia doesn't want his help." Drew may be like a brother to me, but he can be a real dumbass sometimes. If Levi actually stood a chance, I'd have no problem with them duking it out a bit. They've always had that tension over Levi's loyalty to Dan, but now, with everything that's happened, they're practically a pressure cooker ready to explode.

"Yep," Hayes grumbles. "He was already knee-deep in it. Then the devil showing up unannounced didn't help either. Drew's going to be kissing ass for the next year. At this point, he's going to have to build a goddamn greenhouse so he can grow peonies year-round for her."

"Not sure that's possible, my man. But I'm sure she'll

forgive him. Hopefully not before making him eat some humble pie, though. If anyone needs a dose of humility, it's him." I can't say I fault him for his unwavering commitment to his promises, but I'm not sure I could be that honorable if Isla was on the line.

Hayes chuckles at the thought. "Think Charlie may already be brainstorming ways he can pay penance for all his wrongdoings. Thank god we live close to Olivia; she raged the whole way home. I thought she was going to send herself into early labor."

"She doing okay? All things considered, and with her being as pregnant as she is?"

"She's better now that everyone is home safe." Then he adds, "Oh, almost forgot. She got ahold of Jeff while we were at the hospital. He said Isla's been sleeping most of the day and is extremely light-sensitive. She hasn't even turned her phone back on."

Tiny tingles dance across my skin as he talks, igniting a nagging sense that something isn't adding up.

"Something feels off," I say, frustration creeping into my voice. "I don't know what it is, but this entire day has my spider senses going haywire." I may not have known Isla for that long, but I *know* her. Not once has she mentioned migraines to me before any of this. I have no way of knowing if it's a fluke or if the entire story is bullshit, even though every fiber of my being is screaming the latter. It's not like I can storm the castle right now to check on her, though.

Hayes grunts in agreement. "You and every single guy on the team. Half went into the office to see what they could figure out, and the other half is out on patrol."

Relief flows through me. I trust the guys at the department to track this guy down, but having Hayes's team doubling down means it'll happen quicker. It's damn near impossible to slip anything by them—*unless you're Charlie and have a nearly two-year head start, that is.*

"Mind starting a group chat? I'll send whatever we have on this side if anything pops up."

"Yep. Talk later." He ends the call, and I try to regain the same focus I had before.

So far, even with all my military training, it's still my Grandma Astors advice that I lean on: "Use that intelligence of yours to find evidence that will support your intuition." Her little words of wisdom always stick with me in situations like this, when my gut is telling me to stay on course.

She used to say I was like a metal detector, always picking up on energy that others couldn't. Odessa and I tried to stay with them as much as possible, especially before we moved to South Carolina. It wasn't long after they passed away that we realized we had inherited a fortune that rivaled those of royalty. They chose to skip over my mother, leaving it all to Odessa and me. Our parents were left with only what my mother had received from her grandparents—most of which they'd already blown through—and a few estate items. A small fortune to most, but never enough for them. Thus, the reason less than a decade ago they wrote us off, realizing neither of us would ever give them a dime.

Odessa may have dipped into her account more than I have, but even she has always been careful with how much she spends, trying to prove herself based on her hard work rather than her wealth. We both know firsthand the dangers of being frivolous with that kind of money; it can twist relationships and erode moral compasses. That's why I've only ever purchased one thing with it—something I know my grandfather would have approved of.

He wasn't an extravagant man; he worked too hard to spend his money on nonsense, but when he did spend, he went big. He sought out the most unique, rare items he could find. If only four were made of something, you could bet that he owned one. That's when I knew my dad truly only cared about money—when he sold the Packard Panther my grandfather had cherished.

My mood sours even further the more I think about my parents. They're cut from the same cloth as Isla's boyfriend, Jeff. I had him pegged from the moment I saw his slicked-back hair and smarmy smile. I know I'm projecting some feelings, but there isn't a single thing I trust about him.

The more I drive, the tighter the worried knot in my stomach grows. I'm ready for this shift to be over, for the car to be found, and for Isla to return a damn text.

Chapter Eleven

Isla

Raised voices come from somewhere around me. I can tell one of them is Jeff, but the other sounds muffled, like they're not actually here. I haven't moved an inch, trying to gain some sort of recognition of where I am.

My body is curled into the fetal position, with cold, smooth tile beneath me. Any movement is sore, but my head feels the worst—like I have a debilitating migraine. *Is that why I'm on the floor?*

"Fuck them! They're trash. No one would think it was me who hit her." Of course, Jeff is screaming. *He's such a baby.*

I can't make out what the other voice is saying, but they're clearly pandering to him and talking in soft tones, trying to calm him down. It doesn't work, though; whatever they say sets him off again.

"No! I hid the fucking car!" *What car?* The sound of a glass bottle hitting the granite countertop in the kitchen snaps me out of my confusion. Everything from the last however long comes rushing back like I hadn't forgotten it all. My only functioning eye struggles to open through the crusty, dried tears gluing it together. But when it does, I'm face-to-face with the black tile on the edge of the stairs.

"It's fine. It's in dad's shipping container out at the property. Once things die down, I'll part it out." I don't know what he's talking about, but it's now evident he's talking to his mom. He's using the same whiny voice he always uses when he talks to her.

Placing one hand firmly on the bottom step, I push up and transition into a crawl, getting onto all fours.

I need to get out of this house now. Silently, I start moving my knees along the tile. Thankfully, the leggings I'm wearing muffles the sound while also allowing me the give to slide.

I'm halfway to the entryway when I hear, "Olivia didn't die, mom. Chill the fuck out."

My body stiffens, like a deer caught in headlights. *He. Hit. Olivia. With. A. Car.*

I should've known he'd go after her. I should've warned her that he was impulsive and dangerous. Never did I think he would actually try to kill her, though. Postpone a few proposals, sure. Talk a lot of crap around town, definitely. But this? Who the hell have I been dating for the last two years?

A new source of energy pulses through my body. The adrenaline hit I needed. I make it to the front door, my gaze searching for my purse. It's gone, though. The only thing around is my jacket, lying heaped on the ground, like it was torn off the coat rack and thrown down.

My hands shake as I try to find the opening and slide it on. It's all I have, but at least it's something.

Using the door to pull myself up again, I slowly turn the handle, trying to be as quiet as I can be.

Jeff is still complaining loudly to his mom, so I pop open the door and stumble outside into the cold night air.

My feet hitting the cold bricks is the second I realize I

forgot shoes. It doesn't halter my steps, though; I'd choose frost-bite over dying any day.

The small set of stairs is slick with inches of snow as I hurry down them in the darkness. The long driveway is too open for me to run down, so I stumble to the side of the house toward the tree line. Jeff's BMW is still parked to the side, taunting me like a forbidden fruit just out of reach. The only light guiding my way is from the house behind me.

Snow falls softly in small flakes, making it hard to see but not impossible. Hopefully, it's enough to cover the tracks my feet are leaving behind—but at this point there's not much I can do about that.

Each step stings as the cold snow bites into my feet while I stumble between trees and sagebrush, trying to move slowly and conceal myself despite the intense pain. I know where the road is, but it'll be a miracle if anyone is driving at this time of night.

What time is it? It was midafternoon when Jeff first attacked me and I haven't seen a clock since.

The edge of the road appears but I stay in the tree line, where I'm out of sight of Jeff but close enough to see a car.

I settle my back on a thick Larch tree and pull my knees up into my jacket, tucking my feet in and sealing them from any more cold exposure. This jacket may be rated for -30 degree weather but that doesn't necessarily mean my toes will warm up. My only hope is to cocoon myself like I'm in a sleeping bag and not let any skin be exposed to the biting wind.

Surprisingly, I feel pretty insulated in here. My hot breath creates a small pocket of warmth around my face, providing some relief from the freezing temperatures.

I don't know how long I hid there for, but I most likely dozed off because the sound of Jeff's booming voice startled me awake. He's off in the distance, probably still at the house, yelling my name. Staying as still as possible, I pray that the black jacket offers another layer of camouflage in the dark night.

Chills roll through me from fear and the cold weather as the voice grows closer and more angry. The realization that I don't have any more fight left in me hits hard. Even if I did, I could barely move. My muscles are stiff from the beating they endured and from hiding in this position for so long.

It isn't until I hear the very faint sound of a car engine that hope finally courses its way back through my veins.

Chapter Twelve

Everett

My shift is nearly over and there still haven't been any signs of the Xterra.

I've driven the same slow route almost a dozen times. Each time I try to focus on a new thing, from tracks in the snow to potential buildings that could fit a car, but so far, I've come up empty-handed. The snow dumping down has created a safe haven for whoever targeted Olivia's SUV. Any tracks they may have left behind are covered with layers of fresh snow every few minutes. I'm looking for a needle in a snow-covered haystack, but that hasn't stopped me from looking.

The SUV lights mix with the red and blue flashing in the dark as I drive. The effort may seem futile, but Drew would be out here doing the same thing for me. He wouldn't give up until he found whoever hurt my girl. I'm not about to do it either. Everyone on the EFSC team is still out looking. I have two group chats between the deputies on duty and the team guys that I've been trying to keep up with. The EFSC guys have more training and skills, but the LEO's have home court advantage and know the area better. Both sides are utilizing every resource they can to figure out who was driving that Xterra. Me, though? I still let my instincts lead the way, driving the same loop over and over again.

Reaching over, I turn the heat down with a heavy sigh. My eyes are drying out from the warm air blasting out and it's only making me more tired. The snow has slowed down in the last hour or so; it's no longer dumping, but instead comes down in small, fluffy flakes. In any other scenario, it would be beautiful to look at. Currently, though, it's just as ominous as it was on my drive to work, sending my overly active sympathetic nervous system into overdrive. It's like my body knows something my mind doesn't. *That, or I've developed a small form of PTSD to literal snowflakes.*

My foot barely pushes on the gas as I drive down the familiar road next to the golf course near Isla's house. She hasn't responded to any of us since Charlie spoke to her this morning. If Charlie hadn't spoken to Jeff to see what was going on, I'd be knocking on her door. He told her he'd let Isla know what was going on when she woke up; apparently, the migraine was worse than we thought. On one hand, it makes sense, and that could truly be why she didn't come into work today. On the other hand, I don't trust anything Jeff says. I do, however, trust my gut, and anytime I approach her driveway, I swear I can physically feel my adrenal gland ramping up.

Like clockwork, the small adrenaline spike surges through me when I round the corner on Cloverdale, but I can't tell if it's because Isla needs me or simply because she is near me. Rather than ignore the feeling, I take extra time to scan my surroundings. The SUV is barely moving as I try to look through the hazy air. *For what, though? A sign? A tire-track? I don't know.*

On the left side of the road are tall trees and brush; during the day, you can see a small meadow beyond them, but it's mostly all public land on that side. On the right side of the road, it looks mostly the same, but houses are tucked back in on that side, unable to be seen from the road. An occasional paved driveway is the only way to tell where the houses are hidden.

Another adrenaline spike hits my bloodstream like a lightning bolt. My breathing shallows, turning into slow, quick breaths, like if I breathe too loudly, I'll miss it. The tingle in my fingers sets me on guard as I search the tree line for whatever has me on high alert. The SUV continues to roll through the fluffy snow, my foot keeping the same amount of pressure despite my inner turmoil.

The shadow that passes through my peripherals has me slamming on the brakes, the tires sliding through the slick snow. My attention locks on the dark mass crawling from the ditch into the road, about thirty feet away from the entrance of Isla's driveway.

With one touch of a button, I inform dispatch of what I'm seeing. "Unit 38. East on Cloverdale Road, near the 2500 block. Be advised. There's something entering the road, moving slowly." Through narrowed eyes, I watch the black figure from the comfort of my SUV. It looks too small to be a bear, yet too large to be a wolf—simply a black blob with no head, neck, or legs visible.

I don't have any time to process the response broadcast back into my ear because the blob thrusts itself forward, like it's using the last of its energy to reach the middle of the road. The front half remains covered, but black legs extend behind it, exposing a set of pale, bare feet.

"Unit 38. Possible injured person. Requesting medical assistance to the 2500 block of Cloverdale Road." I shout into the radio as I haul ass out of my SUV. Like its second nature, my right hand covers my 9 mm, unsheathing it.

Walking slowly, I start to yell at the person to get their attention. The body doesn't move, but I keep yelling, hoping I'll get a glimpse of the person so that I can figure out what is going on. It isn't until I'm within ten feet that I see the fur at the top of the coat and realize my gut instinct was right.

"ISLA!" My legs groan in protest as I push myself toward her, shouting her name. The way my feet slide across the road, ten feet away seem like a hundred.

It isn't until I hear another shout mixing in with mine that I realize my mistake—Jeff is looking for her too. With the way that my vehicle is parked, most of their driveway is dark, but I practically have a spotlight on us.

Sheathing my gun, I scoop her into my arms, like she weighs less than a bag of flour. The puffer coat conceals most of her face and body, but it's already covered in dried blood. Before I let myself succumb to the new rage building inside me, I focus on getting her safely to my patrol car.

The shouts behind me grow louder as I trudge back with her back to the SUV. The passenger side is closest to me, but that means it's also closer to Jeff. I already know that I'm going to need the distance, even if it's not much, and the cover that being on the driver's side gives me.

I set her as gently as I can in the back seat, murmuring softly that I've got her and she's safe.

Once the door is closed, I radio in again. "Requesting backup. The victim is Isla Mitchell. Immediate medical attention is required." Jeff once again shouts Isla's name as he walks toward the road, reminding me to also mention him. "Victim's boyfriend Jeff Walton is a potential suspect; he's approaching Cloverdale now. "

Unsheathing my gun once again, I use the SUV as a shield and start working. As much as I want to kill Jeff with my bare hands, I know there's a protocol to follow.

The driveway is mostly unlit but the snow reflecting off the moon allows me to see enough to know that Jeff is now three-fourths of the way down the driveway, carrying a shotgun.

"Cascadia County Sheriff Department! Stop walking! STOP WALKING! Put your hands up." Keeping my gun in my right hand, trained toward his slow advancement, I use my left hand to radio in. "Suspect is armed with a shotgun. Code 99."

Rather than listen, Jeff continues to approach slowly. His tone is surprisingly steady for someone who just beat up his girlfriend and now has a gun pointed at his face. Coolly, he states, "Back off, deputy. This is above your pay grade." Even from here, I can see the pompous smile he wears on his face when he asks, "Do you know who I am?" *Yeah, an asshole.*

"Jeff Walton. Stop walking! Now! Put the gun down."

His chuckle sends a shiver down my spine. "Isla's coming with me. My dad's already on his way. If you want to keep your job, you'll forget this ever happened," he remarks, continuing his leisurely pace. The gun he's carrying is lowered to point at the ground, but that doesn't mean he couldn't raise it and fire a shot in under three seconds.

"Put the gun down, Walton." My finger settles on the trigger, as I continue shouting at him. "It doesn't have to go like this!"

His feet falter for a second when he's close enough to realize who I am. "Fuck you, asshole! You think you belong in this town, but you don't." He's perfectly illuminated in the headlights by now, so I don't miss the change in stance—the raise of his right arm while the left moves to support it.

Adrenaline surges through me as training kicks in, and I squeeze the trigger. One shot after the other echoes into the night until the magazine is empty.

Chapter Thirteen

"Code 99. Shots fired. Suspect is down. Requesting medical assistance." As the words leave my lips, I don't take my eyes off Jeff's unmoving form.

My free hand moves to replace the now-empty magazine, the motion feeling almost automatic despite the gravity of the situation. I yank a new magazine from the case the familiar harsh scrape a balm to my fraying nerves. With a practiced flick of my wrist, I push it into the grip of my firearm, feeling the satisfying thud as it clicks securely into place.

Dispatch begins to relay information, voices buzzing through my earpiece like an urgent hum, but I stand behind cover, waiting for backup. *Protocol.*

The first cruiser arrives within thirty seconds, pulling in from behind me.

"Astor." A hand squeezes my shoulder, snapping me out of my trance. Lieutenant Will. Sweet mercies, considering he's got at least two dozen more years of experience.

Nodding my head, I say. "Let's go." We slowly approach Jeff, calling out orders. He doesn't respond. Once we get to him, I grab the shotgun and move it while Will begins life-saving measures. It's clear he's gone, but protocol is protocol. Another cruiser flies in, Captain Ellis is out and running toward us before I can turn around.

"Isla..." I glance back to Lieutenant Will, and he gives me a nod, "Go." Then he returns to Jeff, shouting over his shoulder, "Cap! There's no..."

Captain Ellis and I pass without looking at each other, both sprinting to where we are needed.

Isla lays perfectly still as I throw open the door. The interior lights illuminate the black parka as I try to find the zipper.

My throat tightens when I finally expose her face. It's worse than I ever could have imagined. She's unrecognizable right now. Her normally honey colored hair is dark and matted to her face. Blood has pooled and dried on her eyebrows, creating a stark contrast to her pale skin. Her nose has swollen to three times its normal size, like it was broken repeatedly. Shades of color I've never seen before on a face. One eye is so puffy and swollen that there's no way she can see out of it, but her eyelashes flutter when my cold hand gently touches her cheek.

"La, baby..." My voice comes out sounding more like a plea than anything else.

Her eyes don't open but she starts mumbling what sounds like incoherent gibberish. The racing of my heart and labored breathing don't help me understand her, either. I can't stop scanning her face in the dim light, trying to make sense of what she's trying to say.

Each word made out with labored breathing, and I only make sense of a few.

"Cyrus."

"Property."

"Jeff."

"Hit Liv."

"Shipping container."

"Cyrus."

The words I can comprehend start to land like grenades, each one blowing up my understanding of the situation.

"Jeff? Cyrus? Did Cyrus do this to you?"

"No. Jeff hurt me. Caught me—packing. He hid a car." It takes a second for me to remember why I was even out here in the first place. Jeff was the one that hit Olivia, and he's hidden the car.

"Jeff hid the car with Cyrus?"

She slowly nods, but I can see her dimming again. "Okay, you're okay. Medics will be here soon."

"Love you, Ev." I don't have a moment to digest or respond before I hear someone approaching behind me.

"How is she?" Luke asks. He must have arrived at some point in the last few minutes, along with medics.

"Not good. She has a pulse; she was conscious and talking, but—" I look down at her again, the beautiful girl I fell in love with, beaten to unrecognizable. "She's in bad shape, Luke." My voice trembles with each word.

"It'll be okay, we've got her. Let's get her loaded up, alright?"

I slide my hands under her again, pulling her out as gently as I can. The stretcher is already set up behind the SUV, and I ease her onto it.

Bill, a seasoned medic that I've seen around a few times, straps her down and starts giving orders. I move with him as he goes, keeping my hand on her at all times. It isn't until we get to the ambulance that I'm forced to stop with a hand on my chest.

"It fucking kills me to say this, Everett. I can't let you go with her right now." Pain radiates through my neck as I snap to look at Luke, my jaw and fists clenching at the same time.

I only lose steam when I get a good look at him. The man standing before me isn't the same one from the scene I saw at the start of my shift. The heaviness of the last few hours is weighing him down so much that he isn't even standing at his full height. The God of Storms, looks like the storm went after him instead of his enemies.

"We have to follow protocol. You need to ride with me to the station for an interview. The agency that will do the investigation will be on its way as soon as they can."

I gave him one nod and looked back into the ambulance before stepping back. *Protocol.*

Through unfocused vision, I watch Bill start working. The one small reprieve is that I know he's close with Isla and he's clearly skilled at what he's doing. Isla is already hooked up to an IV, wires, and cords hanging from her delicate body.

Luke says something to Bill, and I see the muscle in his jaw flex before he nods.

With a heavy sigh, Luke closes the door and motions for me to follow him back to his cruiser. "Need you to give me a quick debrief." *Protocol.*

I don't move from my spot, though. I watch through the dark night as the ambulance takes off, lights and sirens blaring.

When it's completely out of sight, I keep my vision trained at the spot where I last saw it and start telling Luke everything that happened. The route I was on when I saw Isla, carrying her to the back seat, to when I heard Jeff's shout from the driveway. I go over the commands I gave him, the shotgun he waved around, and finally discharging my weapon.

He listens intently, nodding along but remaining silent. When I finish, the only thing he asks is, "Did Isla provide you any information on what happened?"

My eyes rapidly blink as I try to remember what she said, and then it hits me and I turn toward him. "Jeff was the driver of the hit-and-run. He hid the car in a shipping container, somewhere, with Cyrus."

"Ellis!" Luke shouts. "Get a search warrant for all of Cyrus Walton's properties! Start with the one on Whitemore—see if there's a shipping container. Send one of the guys starting shift to make sure no one goes onto the property." *Protocol.*

He dismisses Captain Ellis and then looks back at me, waiting for me to continue. "She told me Jeff caught her packing today. I knew she was going to leave him, but she said she would let me know before she did." I should've known she wouldn't ask for help. *Why did I let her leave the office that night?*

Luke's hand lands on my shoulder, squeezing. "You could not have prevented what Jeff did tonight. But you did save her."

I wish with every fiber of my being that were true, but the weight of the guilt won't let me believe that.

"You okay with waiting in the truck for me to wrap things up?" After a single nod, I walk to Luke's truck and sit in the passenger seat while he works his way through the scene. Talking to L.T. Will, making sure the scene remains untouched. *Protocol.*

Time feels meaningless as I sit in a daze, staring at the dashboard awash in red and blue lights. The image of Isla crawling out of that ditch haunts me. If I had been a few minutes earlier—or later—everything could have been different. The unknown of what could have been collides with the reality of what did happen, nearly overwhelming me.

Isla's injuries didn't occur recently; they were far too colorful and swollen for that. She must have been hurting for hours—maybe since she left work. *Was that when it started?*

Did he find out she was with me before she left the office?

Did she make it to the hospital yet?

Will Isla ever recover from this physically? Mentally?

Does Mayor Walton know his son attacked Isla?

Do her parents know he was abusive?

Why did he go after Olivia?

The questions whirl and spin in my mind, one after the other, each more frantic than the last, but none offer any answers.

The slam of the driver's door snaps me out of my daze, and I look at the clock on the dashboard. 02:00 exactly. My normal shift is officially over.

I don't have to see Luke's expression to know how fucked up this entire situation is. The energy surrounding him already encompassed me, bringing me even further down than I thought I could be.

Halfway to the department, his phone rings, and with an audible swallow, he answers. "Sheriff Haynes."

The caller doesn't say much, but Luke visibly relaxes as they talk. His only response to the caller is an occasional "good" before he thanks them for calling and hangs up the phone.

"I called Hayes on my way to the scene. They went back to the hospital to be with Isla. She's going to be okay. That's all I can say for now." That should comfort me, but it doesn't. I'm too flustered to think about anything besides being mad.

Mad that I didn't get into that ambulance with her.

Mad that I'm not there holding her hand and making sure she's okay.

Mad *as hell* that I didn't tell her I loved her too.

Chapter Fourteen

Everett

Luke leads the way through the department building toward his office, his phone ringing incessantly since we left the scene. My thumbs spin in calming circles on my index finger, a trick I picked up in third grade when I struggled to focus. Before fidget spinners became popular, a teacher taught us that repetitive motion can help regulate emotions and reduce anxiety. This habit stuck with me; back then, it would calm my pre-test jitters. But now, after discovering Isla battered on the side of the road, I'm not so sure it's working the way it should.

He goes over the list of things I need to turn in while I'm on paid leave, as well as the names of the people I'll be talking to for the investigation. Occasionally, I nod when he pauses, but I'm barely half-listening. If I could push Isla from my mind, I'd probably be paying more attention, but the longer I sit here, the more anxious I become. In my mind, I can only see Isla's flawless face, marred by dried blood and bruises, as if the image is attempting to punish me for not being there to protect her. *And, it's working.*

The loud knock on his door was the only thing snapping me out of the trance I was in.

"Sheriff Haynes." The raspy voice of a woman in her late fifties enters the room. Her graying hair is tucked neatly into a low ponytail. The black blazer has seen better days, but you can tell this isn't her first rodeo.

Luke greets her with a terse "hello" but stands to shake her hand.

When his left-hand motions toward me, I stand on autopilot to shake her hand.

"Deputy Astor," I introduce myself without any real emotion. Her shoulders sag a fraction of an inch, her eyes turning from hardened to sorrowful.

"I'm Detective Smith, with OSP. I'll be conducting your interview and writing the report. Not today, though. It's to my understanding that your shift was almost over when the incident occurred."

Luke answers for me. "That's correct. I've advised Deputy Astor on what's to come in the following days. As soon as you're ready, he can submit to a blood test and visit a doctor. Thereafter, he's been told to go home and get some sleep. Refrain from talking to anyone about what happened and check in at 0900 Monday morning." With schooled features, I pretend that I am aware of all that. It's not Luke's fault that I wasn't paying attention to him.

"Feel free to have a seat. I have an exam team already on their way. Unless you'd be more comfortable going to the hospital in Redmond." If she had said Bend, I probably would've opted for the thirty-minute ride just to maybe catch a glimpse of Isla. Redmond is the same distance, but north of Bend, and ultimately a waste of my time.

The knot in my throat won't go away as I clear my throat, so instead of saying anything, I simply shake my head no in response.

"Okay. As Sheriff Haynes mentioned, we won't be conducting a formal interview for a few days. You need time to rest, recover, and process everything that has happened. Have you been assigned a peer counselor yet?"

I look to Luke, hoping he'll take the lead once again.

"An independent contractor will be here as his advocate and to provide emotional support. Our department is small, and most of the deputies are involved in some way. I thought it'd be best to bring in someone from outside to help with the counseling process."

"That makes sense," she replies. "Will he be here for the physical exam?"

"Not unless Deputy Astor wants to wait," Luke says. "He's on his way, but the roads are still icy."

I shake my head. I don't need a peer counselor, and I definitely don't want one. I'm just going along with it so it doesn't interfere with the investigation.

The exam team arrives within five minutes and starts to set up in Luke's office. The room stays quiet, with only the sound of the medical professionals working. Detective Smith scrolls through her phone while Luke observes the exam team closely, ensuring everything is done properly.

After I've been poked, prodded, and tested for any signs of drug or alcohol use, they let me know I'm free to go.

Luke follows closely behind me, snatching my keys from my desk before I can grab them.

My eyebrows raise in silent question as I watch him pocket the keys. "Hayes is almost here to pick you up. You can get your vehicle tomorrow after you've had some rest," he explains.

Normally, I'd be annoyed that he confiscated my keys, but I'm more confused about why Hayes is picking me up. He should be with Isla, not me. A wave of anxiety courses through me, making me feel like I can't catch my breath.

Luke takes pity at the sight of me, clarifying once again before I have to ask. "Charlie is still there—with Delta. Hayes is your peer counselor. He's already worked as a consultant for the department, so he's in our system. You can talk to him about anything you need to, including the case."

I nod, grateful for Luke setting that up for me. I would've told Hayes everything anyway, but at least now I don't have to worry about it jeopardizing anything.

As stoically as I can, I choke out a thanks to him. I don't think I've said more than a handful of sentences since my initial report to Luke, but I know he understands and doesn't hold it against me.

Hayes walks through the front door of the building only a matter of seconds later. There aren't many people around in the early hours of the morning, but everyone's head snaps in his direction. He may not be much taller than me, but when he's in a bad mood, he exudes a truly menacing presence. Currently, he's giving Thomas Shelby in an episode of Peaky Blinders.

Luke gives me one parting pat on the shoulder before I walk out of the building. Hayes waits for me to pass him before turning to follow me, like he's my bodyguard rather than my best friend.

Outside, the first rays of sunlight are starting to peek through the sky, but the snow has stopped falling, creating a beautiful, sparkly winter wonderland. *I hate it.*

I slam the passenger door of his truck as soon as I hit the seat. Any reluctance I felt about speaking dissipated the moment I turned to confront Hayes. A flood of questions burst from me before he even had the key in the ignition. "Is she okay? Did she wake up?" His hand hovers in the air, suspended mid-motion. "What did the doctor say? Did she tell you what happened?" I notice his mouth opening and closing with each question, but I keep firing them off before he can respond. "What the fuck happened to her? Did she—"

"Everett!" His thunderous voice cuts me off." Shut the hell up so that I can tell you what I know." *Tough love, but necessary.*

I nod, hanging on to every word he says, like he's the only lifeline I have in this storm.

He drew in a long breath as he placed the key in the ignition. Letting it out slowly, he squared his shoulders toward me. "They had her pumped full of fluids and pain meds by the time she got to the hospital. Bill did everything the right way and stayed with her until we arrived."

I felt my heart race as he continued, "She was in and out of it, but she was talking to Charlie when I left. Other than a few broken ribs and a shit-ton of bruises, her body is fine."

He paused, glancing away as if collecting his thoughts. "Her right eye is swollen shut, she has a broken nose, and she has a severe concussion. The hospital admitted her and is keeping her for a few days. She needs a plastic surgeon, but apart from that, she's going to be okay physically."

He scratched at the five o'clock shadow that looked like it had been there for days, his eyes tired and bloodshot. "Mentally, I don't know how she will recover from this. From what I gathered, she and Jeff got into a fight the night before. She was packing her bags yesterday when he walked in on her. He attacked her and left her in the closet."

His words gut me. I can almost feel the weight of Isla's fear, the desperation in that moment when he turned on her. The thought of her confined, terrified, and injured sends a wave of guilt crashing over me. *I should have been there. I should have done something.*

"She managed to make it down the stairs and overheard

him talking about Olivia. The only thing she doesn't know is how long she was outside."

"Me either," I reply with a long sigh. "All I know is that she was so damn cold when I picked her up that if I hadn't seen her chest rising and falling, I would've thought she was dead."

"What do we do next? I can't fucking go to the hospital to check on her. I'm essentially under house arrest until they conduct my interview."

"Right now," he says as he puts the truck into drive, "you need to go home and take a massive dose of sleep aids to crash once the adrenaline fades. I'll grab my computer and head back to the hospital."

I understand his reasoning, but it feels like a messed-up plan. He should be sneaking me into her room so I can support her, not tucking me into bed like a child.

Sensing my frustration, he places a reassuring hand on my shoulder. "I'll send you updates and won't leave her side. I'll check on her security system, and if we don't have access, I'll have Linc hack in. I'll get all the answers you need while you sleep, but you need to sleep."

Reluctantly, I nod in agreement. If it were anyone but him or Drew, I'd never accept this arrangement. But I trust them both implicitly, and I know Hayes will do everything possible to keep her safe and keep me informed.

Just as I'm about to step out of his truck, he stops me. "Hey, what happened to 'Alibi and hide the body?' This would've been the perfect opportunity."

A long time ago, Drew, Hayes, and I made a pact: if any of us ever needed it, we'd cover for each other. Back then, it was about my fucked-up dad potentially hurting Odessa during one of his drunken benders. That was long before any of us were skilled enough to kill anyone.

I huff at him, letting out a snort. "Of all the things, that's what you're going to say about it?"

He shrugs, looking unapologetic. "We can all agree that asshole deserved a hell of a lot more than a few bullets in his chest."

Slightly offended, I grumble, "You're one to talk." Hayes knows all about the injustices of mercy killing. Charlie had a stalker who met the same fate as Jeff. At Hayes' hand, nonetheless.

"Can't argue with that," he concedes. "But I still wish they'd suffered a bit for all they did to our girls."

If only that last part were true. It's no secret to my friends that I have feelings for Isla. I've had them since the first time I saw her at the airport. I've always been a romantic at heart, a firm believer in love at first sight. Most people see me as a player, believing I never go on more than one date with a girl. But the truth is, I was waiting for the girl who captured my heart in an instant. The moment our eyes met, I knew Isla was the one I had been waiting for, and I was right to hold out.

Yet that day, karma cruelly reminded me that while Isla may be my one and only, she already belonged to another.

Chapter Fifteen

Everett

My phone pings with an alert that someone is pulling down my driveway, but I choose to ignore it. The guys wouldn't let anyone past the gate unless it was someone they trusted. Since yesterday afternoon, it's been a media frenzy, and Hayes sent Liam, Delta, and Cooper to babysit me. So far, they've been taking turns walking the perimeter, scaring the hell out of reporters—or, from the sound of it, eating everything in the fridge.

The sound of the front door opening and wheels rolling across the hardwood floor makes me groan. *Odessa is here.*

I hear Delta first, greeting her like he has for the last fifteen years. Whatever he said has her laughing as she introduces herself to Cooper and Liam. A quiet chuckle escapes my lips when I hear Cooper and Liam stumbling over their words. Two bumbling idiots who can't seem to form a coherent sentence in front of a supermodel. Not many people know that *the* famous Odessa Astor is my younger sister—at least, not until they see us together. With only a fourteen-month age gap, we look like twins—same ash-blonde hair, blue eyes, and symmetrical features.

My bedroom door creaks open slightly, and I peek through one eye to see her head poking in.

Rather than greet her like a decent brother, I groan and mumble, "Who called you?" I'm already exhausted from everyone fussing over me, and it's barely been twenty-four hours.

One perfectly manicured eyebrow raises as she purses her lips. The slight flare of her nostrils is the only warning I get before her signature eye roll explodes. "Fucking everyone except you."

She shoves the door open further, stepping through the threshold and crossing her arms over her chest. "Thank God Mom got ahold of me before the five thousand reporters calling me nonstop did." She doesn't mean our biological mom; I know she's referring to Hayes' mom, Connie. Dess and I spent more time at their house than our own.

As I sit up, a grimace forms on my face. I'd forgotten that the repercussions from the other night won't just impact me. Odessa is a public figure, constantly traveling the world for her career. Any hint of scandal involving her family will get blown out of proportion. This whole situation could jeopardize her credibility and tarnish her reputation—potentially harming her career.

"Shit! Dess, I'm so sorry. Your campaigns—"

She recoils at my sincerity, giving me a piercing look. "Everett Astor! I'm not mad at you because of the media attention. I'm pissed off because I'm your sister and you didn't call me. I'm only here to make sure you're okay."

"I know, but—"

Her hand shoots up, palm facing me, as she glares. "Don't even start! I couldn't care less about what anyone thinks of me.

Next time a major fucking thing happens, you call! You'll tell me you're fine, and I'll ignore you while I hop on a plane to check on you. That's it. That's what family does—it's what we've always done."

She's right about that. We've always been a tight-knit group, ready to drop everything for each other. *Unless, of course, someone decided to withhold vital information because they're stubborn—fuckin' Charlie.*

"Thanks for coming. I'm glad you're here," I say genuinely. Then, louder, I add, "Even if it means I have to kill my babysitters for checking you out."

A loud, distinct chuckle comes from the kitchen, and I can guarantee it's Delta mocking the guys for getting caught.

Odessa rolls her eyes again but cracks a smile at my taunt. "Unless you got one of those fancy shootin' helicopters around, I don't think you can take down the big one."

This time, it's Liam who laughs. It's low; it almost sounds more like a cough, but it's definitely a laugh.

My eyes widen at Odessa and I whisper, "Holy shit. I've never seen that guy smile, let alone laugh."

"Fuck you, Astor." He grunts out with a thick, possibly Russian, accent. His skillful mafia enforcer mask slipped back on.

Odessa smirks and uses her thumb to gesture behind her. "I think he's my new favorite."

"Gird your loins, man!" I shout to Liam while Odessa scoffs at me.

"Miranda Priestly? Best comparison I've ever had." With a smirk, she lets my insult roll off her shoulders.

Her eyes bounced around the room before they finally settled on me again. A look of sorrow fills them before she blinks it away.

"Mom and I stayed at Olivia's last night. Drew filled us in on everything."

I nodded while trying to swallow the lump that had formed in my throat.

"You saved her. That's it. Don't dwell on the what-ifs, what could've beens, or what should've beens. She's alive, you're alive, and the bastard that did this has already started decomposing."

A strangled guffaw comes out. "Always so eloquent, Dess."

She lifts one shoulder and drops it. "You raised me." *Point taken.*

Ignoring her, I dramatically flop back down on my bed.

"You've got a little over an hour before Mom, Drew, and Olivia will be here. I'll make the coffee while you shower." She steps out of my room and then yells over her shoulder, "And do something about that shit on your face! It's a sad excuse for a beard, and you're not in a biker gang."

"Glad to have you here, Dess!" I holler back. She might be a pain in the ass, but at least she's honest. It's one thing I've always appreciated about her, she doesn't beat around the bush.

By the time I make it into my packed living room, it's been over an hour since Odessa first got here. It took more time than normal to make myself presentable, worry about how Isla's doing, and stew over the possible repercussions of my meeting tomorrow.

The guys and Odessa are still perched at the dining room table, scarfing down the brunch that Connie is making before she can even plate it. Drew is next to Olivia on the couch, his arm tenderly around her, who, after being in a flip-over car accident, looks better than Isla had the last I saw her. Liv still has plenty of dark bruises covering her face, but the swelling seems to have gone down tremendously. The only good thing to come of this so far is that at least they're back together.

Rather than greet them first, I knew I needed to see Connie. She's been through more traumatic events in her life than anyone I've ever met—losing her husband at a young age, two of her best friends dying in a car accident, all the deployments she endured, Charlie's stalker situation, and now all of this.

"Hi, mom." She turns toward me, abandoning her cooking to wrap me in a hug. Sympathy and worry pour from her as she pulls me into her. Connie treats all of us like she does Hayes. Every bone in her body is maternal, even when she's only making us breakfast. Simply having her here brings a sense of comfort and warmth that I didn't know I needed.

"Love you always, sweetheart." She pats my cheek tenderly, tears filling her eyes, before she turns around and starts cooking again.

Grumbling from the living room has me turning and making my way in there.

The closer I get to Drew, the more I see the exhaustion etched into his features. He was already struggling before Olivia's accident, barely eating and sleeping. It hasn't been more than 36 hours since Olivia was in the car accident, but I can bet he hasn't slept since.

My feet stall as soon as I cross the threshold. For the first time, I feel awkward in my own skin. Do I hug them? Comfort them? Do I make a joke to lighten the mood? Should I ask them how they are?

Drew's the first one to look up, his eyes narrowing on me. I can't get a read on him, though, whether he's angry or simply analyzing my every move. Olivia follows his gaze; a low gasp escapes her when she sees me—like this isn't my house, where I should be.

"What's wrong?" I ask, self-consciously touching my face to

make sure I hadn't nicked myself while shaving and that blood isn't spontaneously pouring out.

Olivia gingerly stands up and walks toward me, tears spilling down her cheeks. "No, nothing's wrong." She gives me a hug, and I make sure to be gentle around her bruised ribs. "It's just..."

Drew quickly intervenes, standing up and saying, "You look like shit."

With a gasp, I clutch my chest. "Damn! Can't a man catch a break? Odessa said the same thing!"

Odessa, overhearing from behind us, bursts out laughing and shouts, "You're one to talk, Drew. You look like the walking dead." *Siblings: the first to insult you and the first to defend you.*

He rolls his eyes dramatically before yanking me into a hug. "I don't doubt it," he shouts back at her. Then, in a quieter, more grumbly tone, he adds, "I've come back from fighting wars more mentally unscathed than I have been after this week."

Olivia chuckles softly, wiping away her tears as she watches our banter. "You guys are ridiculous," she says, smiling through her tears. "We can't stay long—we just wanted to check on you and say thank you."

Without answering, I raise my eyebrows in question, hoping she'll elaborate.

But it's Drew who jumps in before she can. "I owe you, man. Hunting down that car in a snowstorm, saving Isla, and putting a bullet in Jeff? There wasn't anyone more deserving of it than him." *Few bullets, if my aim is as accurate as I know it is.*

Olivia gives Drew a slight side-eye before commenting, "Right, but mainly the saving Isla part." Her chest trembles slightly before she adds, "We're going to see her now. I'll call you as soon as we get there and let you know how she is. I know Hayes and Charlie have been keeping you updated, but I have a feeling you want as much information as you can get."

I nod, acknowledging her words. "I appreciate it. If I thought I could get away with it, I'd be there in a heartbeat."

"I'm sorry, but I know Isla would want you to follow what Luke says. Cyrus is already spewing some pretty hateful things; he's not going to let this go easily. You toeing the line may be the only way to avoid any more damage."

Drew interjects, "What a fucking asshole. How he ever got elected as mayor is beyond me."

Stuffing my hands into the front pockets of my jeans is the only thing keeping me from clenching them into fists. "I know, but I did everything by the book," I reply, trying to keep my voice steady despite the anger bubbling inside me. "It'll blow over. This town is pro-police, and half of them already hate Jeff."

Olivia immediately finds a spot on the floor to stare at, avoiding my gaze. Drew's eyes shift behind me, silently communicating something to one of the guys standing there. *Shit.*

"What is it? What aren't you telling me?" I ask, a sense of dread creeping up my spine.

Drew finally meets my gaze, his expression hardening as he says, "He's already started doing nationwide interviews. Police violence is a hot-button topic right now, and according to him, your military background is proof that you're a threat to society. Big Media picked it up, and they're running with it, digging into every mission they can tie you to. He's painting you as some dangerous vigilante and hoping people buy into it."

Olivia shifts uncomfortably, her silence speaking volumes. Drew's expression remains unchanged as he analyzes my reaction. It feels like everyone is waiting for my response—or perhaps my breakdown.

Instead of feeling more angry or upset, a laugh bubbles up inside me—so hard that I double over, struggling to catch my breath. "The goddamn arrogance of that family. What the hell are they thinking? Everything was recorded! Let him say what he wants; he's only going to look like a dumbass in the end."

Drew lets out a heavy breath and shakes his head. "I agree. But don't turn on the news for a while."

I shrug; it doesn't matter what he says. I knew he'd target me and dig up whatever he could. "Not to be cocky, but I'm a decorated war hero with a squeaky clean past. He can say whatever the fuck he wants about me, and as long as he leaves Isla out of it, it won't even faze me."

That's when I notice Olivia still won't look at me, nervously biting her lip. The realization hits me like a punch in the gut. "Oh, shit. He's going after Isla too, isn't he?"

One tear slowly rolls down her bruised face. "Saying you two were having an affair."

"Her parents are okay with that? What a fucking joke!" The surge of anger is overwhelming, but I try to rein it in. I've always known they were terrible people who only cared about themselves. I shouldn't have expected anything different from them now.

Olivia quickly swipes at her face. "I hate them. All of them. Mr. and Mrs. Mitchell, the Waltons. I don't understand why Isla thought she owed them anything."

My shoulders sag under the weight of knowing exactly why she felt she owed her parents and the Waltons. With a resigned sigh, I explain, "Cyrus paid her medical debt when she was younger and had cancer. Her parents practically groomed her to believe she owed them her life—not the doctors who saved her."

She looks shocked, her eyes wide with disbelief. "No, they didn't," she whispers, her voice filled with betrayal rather than surprise. My head rears back in surprise at her reaction. Olivia's fists clench at her sides, her whole body trembling with anger. "Lovey did," she seethes, her voice dripping with venom.

"How do you know that?" I ask, just as Drew chimes in with, "Wait, Isla had cancer?" I try not to roll my eyes, but Drew really has a knack for sticking his head in the sand.

Olivia lets out a ragged breath. "I need to sit down to tell this story, but then we need to go." She slowly backs up and sits on the loveseat where she had been, and Drew follows her, sitting at the edge of the seat with his body turned toward her. I remain rooted in my spot, arms crossed over my chest, trying to process the bombshell that just dropped.

As Olivia begins to recount Isla's heartbreaking childhood battle with cancer, I feel the weight of everyone behind me, who had been sitting, now moving closer to listen.

"The Mitchells moved here when I was in fifth grade, and I believe Isla was in second. Cyrus offered her dad, Marcus, a low-paying position at his firm but with amazing benefits. He had just finished law school and was buried in debt along with Isla's medical bills, so he took it willingly. Isla had finished her treatments, but they practically kept her in a bubble." She pauses, looking at each of us. "Seriously, they only allowed her to be friends with Jeff. She couldn't play sports, go to birthday parties, or even attend school regularly. At the time, I thought it was weird, but I assumed it was just because she had been so sick. Looking back, though, I remember Lovey huffing about how controlling the Mitchells were. When she found out Marcus was working eighty hours a week to cover the debt, she went directly to the hospital and paid it off."

I try not to interrupt, but I can't stop myself. "Are you sure? Isla is convinced that Cyrus did it."

"Yep. I know because I went with her. Lovey never wanted anyone to know about her good deeds, so we never talked about it. But I remember it clearly. She wrote a check for over two hundred thousand dollars. It was the first time I realized she wasn't just well-off; she was rich."

Olivia's grandaunt, her grandmother's sister, had been involved in Central Oregon real estate since before it became a popular destination. Most locals attribute the growth of the area to Lovey and her business ventures—she was a pillar in the community who chose to reinvest in the place and people she loved most. She passed away before I moved here, but I haven't heard anything but glowing praise for her generosity and impact on the community. It's not surprising that she would be the one to help Isla's family while remaining anonymous. The frustrating part is that it's equally unsurprising that the Waltons were ambiguous about the situation so they could take the credit.

"So, what do we do? How do we tell Isla that it was Lovey and not the Waltons without causing more harm than good?" Odessa asks from next to me. I hadn't even realized she was now standing shoulder-to-shoulder with me. Despite her concerned words, anger is etched on her face. She's always been fiercely loyal and ready to defend everyone she cares about—the problem is, she tends to pick fists over words. It's hard to believe she has a heart of gold when she's knocking grown men out with a left hook—even if they do deserve it.

"I think Olivia should be the one to tell her after things have calmed down. It won't change anything whether she finds out today or in a few weeks, but she needs to hear it from the source to understand why Lovey did what she did." I respond, aiming to set things right while knowing this isn't the right time.

With a nod, Olivia stands up to give me another hug, and Drew grabs their coats. "Love you, Ev. I'll send you updates as soon as I get there."

I watch them leave, feeling a mix of pressure and anxiety about what's to come.

Odessa must notice my apprehension because her shoulder bumps into mine. "You know who has more power and would drop everything to defend you?"

"Don't go there, Dess." I already know who she's talking about, but I'm not willing to involve them in this mess.

"Everett. Don't be a stubborn ass. They're the best person to have in your corner right now." Odessa's voice is low so that no one else can hear, but her tone is anything but subtle.

A bit too frustrated, I snap, "For fuck's sake, Dess! Drop it."

With a huff and a glare, she turns around and heads back to the dining room table, where everyone else pretends to ignore our conversation. I'm not trying to take my anger out on her; this is my problem, and I need to handle it myself. The only thing I can do is tell the truth tomorrow during my interrogation—I mean, interview—and have faith that justice will prevail in the end. My only concern is Isla and how she's feeling, both mentally and physically. Worrying about anything else is a waste of time; I can't control it. Follow orders, keep a clear head, and focus on what I can do to support Isla from a distance. That's all that matters right now.

Chapter Sixteen

Isla

"Charlie? You here?" I asked while trying to see through my blurry vision. I can barely see through one eye, and the other is completely swollen shut. However, I don't think Charlie's left my side since I got here. Every time I ask, she always responds and comes to stand next to me.

"Yeah, I'm here." The tips of her warm fingers gently touch my left forearm before she slides them down to grab my hand.

"Is anyone else in here?" Doctors and nurses have rotated so often that I don't even attempt to remember their names, not that I could anyway. The migraine I had felt like someone used a pickaxe to give me a lobotomy and then left it in there as a souvenir. Thankfully, the throbbing in my head has dulled a bit, and only a few concussion symptoms are still present.

"No. Just me and you right now. Hayes is getting some sleep at the hotel. Lincoln is on guard duty, but he's outside the door." My heart sinks when I hear Everett isn't here, but it isn't long before I recall why he can't be. He was the one who found me on the road. He was the one who shot Jeff when he was hunting me down. It's all surreal. The memories may be fuzzy, but they're all terrifyingly there.

I try to swallow the emotion, but it's overwhelming. My voice comes out in a rasp when I ask her, "What's going on with the investigation?"

A heavy sigh comes from Charlie as she squeezes my hand. "Everett is under a standard officer-involved shooting investigation. His interview is tomorrow morning, and an outside agency is reviewing the case. For now, he's not allowed to talk to anyone who was involved that night. It's..." She pauses, her voice trailing off as she struggles to find the right words.

When she doesn't continue, I can tell that the situation is more serious than she wants me to know about. "It's what?"

"It's becoming more complicated than we initially thought. Cyrus has the media involved, trying to get it picked up by national news outlets. It's adding a lot of pressure to the investigation," Charlie finally admits, her hand quivering in mine.

The weight of it all settles into my bones like a heavy anchor, pulling me down with the realization that my worst fear is coming to fruition. Everett has been dragged into the mess of my so-called life and is now the one paying for my consequences.

She must sense my overwhelming guilt because she squeezes my hand tighter, offering silent support in the midst of the chaos.

"Isla. Everett will be okay. The situation is complicated, but it's not anything we can't handle. Cyrus can say whatever he wants and no one that matters will believe him." I wish I could believe that, but she doesn't know him like I do. The lengths that family will go to get what they want; the people they have protecting them. Even my parents are on their payroll, and I wouldn't be surprised if they chose a paycheck over me.

"What are my parents saying? Have they even been here?" I don't know exactly how many days I've been in the hospital, but long enough they should have by now.

There's a hesitancy in her voice when she says, "Yeah, yesterday evening. You, uhm, you insisted they leave. They asked to speak to you alone and after a few minutes, you were yelling at them. I don't know what they said, but you were really upset."

The repressed memory of confronting them in my room starts to come through. I was admitted some time in the middle of the night, but they didn't show up until after the staff brought dinner in. "My dad tried to convince me to tell the police an intruder attacked me. Clear Jeff's name." Fresh tears begin pouring down the sides of my face, dripping over my ears and onto the pillow.

A low gasp gets caught in her throat before she breathes out in disbelief, "They didn't."

The soreness in my upper body intensifies when my shoulders shake with grief. "I don't understand, Charlie. So what if his parents paid for my childhood medical bills? He tried to kill me, and now they want me to lie for him? What kind of parents ask their child to do that?"

"Shitty ones," she replies instantly. Hardly anyone knows about my never-ending indebtedness to the Waltons, but Charlie is one of the ones that does.

A soft knock sounds from the right of me, assumingly where the door is, so I sit back, trying to compose myself. "Hey, honey. Not sure if you remember from earlier. I'm your nurse— Cynthia. How are you feeling this evening? Can you rate your pain level on a scale of one to five? One is mild discomfort, and five can't breathe normally because it hurts too bad." I'm too tired to look at her, but her voice sounds nice— gentle and soothing.

"Three. It all hurts, but my head hurts the worst."

"I'll have the doctor get you some pain meds ordered so we can get that under control. Are you hungry? Thirsty?"

I shake my head while saying no.

A few minutes later, a woman comes in, introducing herself as Doctor Beach. I hear wheels rolling and feet shuffling, but besides that, it's silence. When I glance over, Dr. Beach is sitting on a stool beside me, looking at my chart. Her auburn hair is pulled into a low bun, and a white lab coat is thrown over blue scrubs. Even through blurry vision, I can tell she's naturally beautiful and full of sorrow.

"You know, I was the one who did your initial intake. My shift was almost over, and in you came, beaten, nearly hypothermic, and barely alive. You were completely out of it, yet the moment anyone apart from Bill touched you, you fought like hell. He was the only one who could keep you from being combative long enough that we could get you sedated. I've worked with him for the last decade, and not once have I ever seen him shed a tear or stay with the patient past the necessary procedures. But for you, he did both." Tears filled my own eyes. Bill's wife, Gwen, was the first teacher I ever had in Three Sisters. I think I spent more time with her that school year than I ever did with the other kids—she even let me eat my lunch with her. Then every summer from my freshman year of high school until I started working for Charlie and Olivia, I babysat their four boys. Eight summers of chasing after those energetic kids, making sure they were safe and having fun. It was exhausting, but I spent so much time with them that they became family. A new guilt forms thinking about how difficult it must have been for Bill to be the one to work on me that night.

Dr. Beach cleared her throat and let out her own ragged

breath before continuing. "He filled me in on the history between you and his family. Mentioned you were the best babysitter they ever had. When I started to ask him if he knew about your relationship and that you're a victim, he cut me off. Tears streaked down his face, but he turned to me and angrily said, 'That girl has a heart big enough to care for everyone in the world, and believe me, she does. The only person she didn't seem to care about was herself. When she finally decided to fight back, *this* is the outcome.'" The raw emotion in her voice as she recounts her version of that night makes it almost unbearable for me to listen to her speak, but I don't stop her.

"I thought he was going to say something about how unfair it was that you were here, but he..." She paused and took a deep breath, letting it out slowly. "He surprised me. He looked back at you, and he simply said, 'She's no longer a *victim* in this scenario. The second she chose to care about herself, she became a warrior. She may still be fighting for her life, but she's going to come out of this as a survivor. Don't ever treat her like she's still that victim; she doesn't need your pity. She needs your admiration.'" I don't wipe away the tears that stream down my face, letting them fall freely as I absorb the weight of his words, spoken by Dr. Beach.

She smiles sadly. "He wasn't emotional because he felt sorry for you. He was emotional because he was proud of you. You should be proud of yourself."

I nod my head, but words fail me as I try to express the overwhelming gratitude I feel towards him. The strength and empowerment in his simple statement washed over me, filling me with a newfound sense of resilience and pride.

Charlie replies for me: "He's a good guy—Bill. A good dad and a good medic."

Quietly, I acknowledge their sentiments: "He's the best."

The nurse, Cynthia, administers the next dose of pain medication and then she and Doctor Beach excuse themselves, so I can rest.

Right as the drugs start to hit, Charlie's phone rings, and she answers quietly. "Hey, Liv. Oh, uhm, I'll ask her."

She softly says, "Olivia and Drew are here. Do you feel okay enough to see them?"

More tears immediately spring into my eyes, but I nod. Within two minutes, Olivia is rushing into the room and Drew is right behind her.

Before they reach the side of my bed, I start sobbing. "Olivia, I am so so..."

"No!" She interrupts me with such urgency that I stop mid-sentence. "Don't you dare apologize for anything he did. You have nothing to be sorry for."

"Are you okay? Do the kids know? Are they okay?"

She lets out a strangled sounding laugh. "I'm okay. Sore today, but feeling incredibly lucky to be alive and have the support of everyone around." Her tone grows more terse when she asks me, "How are you feeling? Emotionally and physically?"

"Well you just missed the pep talks of all pep talks from my doctor, so I'd say emotionally, somewhere between damaged and good. Physically, they're pumping me full of meds, so also somewhere between damaged and good.

Drew actually chuckles at that, his hand reaching out to squeeze my arm. He keeps his voice low and quiet when he says, "We just left my house. Connie and Odessa are there, as well as most of the guys. They're *all* worried about you."

Olivia adds, "We'll let them know you're doing okay, or you can if you'd like."

Charlie clears her throat but doesn't say anything, prompting me to ask, "I can? How?"

She places something in my hand and when I tip my head just so, I can see it's her phone. Technically, I'm not supposed to use a cell phone because of the concussion, but I really don't care.

I place the phone next to my ear and hear that it's already ringing.

The breathy voice of Everett answers, like he ran for the phone. "How is she?"

With the first smile and laugh I've had, I respond. "Doing great given the circumstances."

"La?" The sound of relief from Everett when he says my name has me instantly choked up.

"Hey, Eh..." Olivia's finger touches my lips before I get the rest out.

"Shh" *Shoot. The investigation, duh.*

"Hey, uh, Hayes?"

A low, strangled chuckle comes from the phone. "Any other circumstances, and I'd be pissed you're calling me another man's name." His normal jovial voice sounds too thick; the impact of everything is clearly affecting him.

"Are you okay? I'm so sorry. I can't believe that you're involved. I tried to keep you out..."

"Isla, stop. I wish you wouldn't have. I'm sorry I didn't find you sooner. How are you, really?"

"I'm okay." Loud sniffles sound from next to me, mixing with my own, reminding me I'm not alone.

"I'll be there as soon as I can. If you need anything, call me or call Hayes, and he can call me."

When we say our goodbyes, Olivia takes the phone back and quietly whispers, "It's okay to love him. The people that matter will support you, regardless of what timeline you choose to follow. Don't hold yourself back because of anyone else's opinion. You've fought your way out of hell; don't stop fighting until you have everything you want."

With a shaky breath, I nod in agreement, feeling a sense of relief wash over me. The exhaustion mixing with the meds takes me under before I can think of how to respond. As I drift off to sleep, I hold on to Olivia's words, finding comfort in the idea that I have the power to choose my path.

Chapter Seventeen

Everett

Monday morning, eight thirty a.m., and I get a call from Luke letting me know that my meeting with Detective Smith will be moved to a "safer location."

"I'm sorry, Sheriff Haynes, are you telling me that the sheriff's department isn't the safest place in Three Sisters?" I ask, feeling a little more cheeky now that I've had a decent night of sleep and was able to speak to Isla last night.

Luke grumbles on the phone something that sounds a lot like "Fucking hell," but immediately covers it with professionalism. "You'll be meeting Detective Smith at her office in Bend. Normally, they want you to feel comfortable and interviews are held in the department in which one works, but it's starting to become a zoo around here." As he's talking, loud voices can be heard in the background, emphasizing that he has a lot to handle today.

Luke quickly adds, "Detective Smith moved the appointment to 09:30 so that you can get there with the extra drive time. Just... Answer everything as you remember it to be. Don't worry about trying to make things sound better or worse than they were. Honest and straightforward." Luke's tone is firm but understanding before he hangs up without saying goodbye.

I'd heard from Lincoln that things were getting tense in town, but based on how terse Luke was, it must be worse than I thought. He has to deal with the locals who are standing up to the media that has officially descended on Three Sisters. Cyrus' smear campaign is doing exactly what he intended—bringing in outsiders to stir up trouble and complicate the investigation. What he doesn't realize, or perhaps doesn't care about, is the backlash he's facing from the community. This town loves Isla and Olivia, and most people are rallying behind them to offer support and shield them from the negative attention. Restaurants, shops on Main Street, and even some hotels are refusing service or simply closing for the day. With each brazen move he makes, Cyrus is alienating himself further, and it's only a matter of time before the truth comes out.

Gathering my thoughts, I stand by the front window and gaze out at the peaceful landscape. The snowstorm from two days ago has begun to melt and refreeze, creating a beautiful icy glaze over everything. The house is set far enough back from the road that I can see cars slowly passing by, but not so close that anyone can spot me without deliberately looking. Still, I'm sure that's exactly what they're trying to do. Liam and Cooper have been scaring people away left and right. It feels like every media outlet is hunting for photos of the cheating deputy with a history of killing bad guys—*or whatever the headline says about me today.*

"Change of plans, gentlemen! I need your help." I hollered toward the guys eating in the kitchen before turning and walking in there. Liam and Cooper both look up at me, but where Cooper's eyes go wide, Liam's remain unaffected.

As seriously as I could, I quoted Doug MacRay, "Can't tell

you what it is. You can never ask me about it later, and we're gonna hurt some people."

Liam responds without missing a beat, "Whose car are we gonna take?"

I smirked at his response, a new appreciation developing for him. It doesn't take much to win me over, but nailing a movie quote is foolproof in my book.

Cooper runs his hand down his perfectly groomed mustache, shaking his head when he realizes I'm joking. "Hate you guys," he mumbles. "What are we really doing?"

"Need a ride into Bend for my interview. It sounds like the same looky-loo's around here are also in front of the CC department."

Cooper's eye's light up mischievously, understanding the situation. "With pleasure," he says, heading towards the door and pulling out the keys to his new Durango. "Everyone mocks the Rango 'til they need the hellcat."

"Oh, we'll still mock it. It'll always be a mom car." I confirm with a smirk, before adding, "but not like a regular mom, a cool mom."

Cooper may chuckle, but I don't miss the way his stance changed the second he got out the door. Liam and he both go completely rigid, looking for any potential threats in the distance. They walk in perfect sync, shielding me from the road as they walk me to the passenger side of the Durango.

As soon as we pull out of the driveway, cars begin following us, tailing us closely. Cooper allows it for a few minutes, leading them on an alternate route to Bend that doesn't involve the main highway. It won't add much time to our trip, but the winding roads provide the perfect opportunity for us to lose our pursuers. In a blink, Cooper floor's it, utilizing that supercharge hemi like a pro. Before they even had a chance to speed up, we were already out of sight, flying down the road like a bat out of hell.

A tiny spike of adrenaline hit me, and I couldn't help but grin. Even Liam had a smirk on his face by the time we made it to town. He pulled into the Bend department without any further issues, and the second he shut off the engine, nerves rattled through me. I'm confident that I did everything in my power to follow the Cascadia County department's protocol, but that doesn't mean I'm not anxious about the investigation.

With one nod, I say to the guys, "I'll text you when I'm done."

Cooper shakes his head, his eyebrows drawing together tightly. "We'll be right here. No chances are we leaving."

Steeling my spine, I take a deep breath and step out of the car, ready to get this over with.

Detective Smith stood at the front desk, waiting for me. She looks the same as she did when I first met her. Professional, composed, and intimidating.

This time, I reached out my hand first to shake hers. "Detective Smith. I apologize for my lack of manners the other night. I don't think I properly introduced myself. Deputy Everett Astor."

Her eyes soften a touch, but she keeps her lips pressed in a thin line. "No offense taken. I understand you were in a difficult situation. Let's sit down in my office and go over everything."

I follow her into her office, trying to keep my nerves in check as we sit down. It's much smaller than Luke's, but she has more personal touches— family photos, a potted plant, and a mug that says, "Stupid people keep me employed."

Detective Smith wastes no time getting straight to the point: "Alright, Deputy Astor. I'm going to go over the formalities with you, and then we can begin the interview process."

She begins her small spiel, saying that the conversation will be recorded and used to further her investigation. When she's finished, she looks me dead in the eye and admits, "I want you to know that I've already reviewed the footage from the camera on your SUV as well as the security footage that we received from Isla Mitchell and Jeff Walton's place of residence. I *am* allowed to give you the option of watching the footage first or proceeding with the interview. Just let me know your preference." Her serious tone and direct approach emphasize don't give me any clues on how I should navigate this.

Clearing my throat, I admit, "I'd prefer not to watch the footage if that's alright with you. I wouldn't say I have a photographic memory, but I trust my recollection of events. Let's proceed with the interview." I respond, trying to sound confident. Hayes warned me against watching any of the footage of Isla being attacked, knowing that it would completely derail my focus during the interview. Currently, I'm choosing to trust his advice and keep my focus on only my recollection of the night.

She nods before hitting record on her cell phone. After she states her name, mine, the date, and the reason for recording, she begins, "Let's start with your version of events leading up to the incident."

I take a deep breath and quickly let it out. "Okay. I think it would be best to start with the minute I clock into work. It might be the long version, but I want to make sure all the details are included for accuracy." As I begin to recount the events, I try to emotionally detach myself from the events.

"From the minute I clocked into work, I felt in my gut that something was off that night. I know that gut feelings aren't reliable or always accurate, but for context, I need to mention it. Within about fifteen minutes of clocking in at 16:00, I was made aware of a roll-over car accident in which a friend of mine, Olivia Turner, was involved. Sheriff Haynes radioed that it was all hands on deck to find the driver of the car that was involved in the hit-and-run." I continue my recount of the mundane events of my shift and explain that Luke didn't give anyone orders on where to look or how long they could or should stay out. Due to the snowstorm, he left it up to the individual deputies to decide how to approach the search for the driver. Some deputies chose to canvass nearby neighborhoods, while others focused on the rural areas. Besides Luke monitoring where we radioed in, it was basically a free-for-all based on everyone's comfort level of driving in the snow.

Occasionally, she asks me a question or to elaborate, but she mainly just lets me talk.

"I thoroughly understand that, to most, it doesn't make sense as to why I would drive the same loop, despite not finding anything. I don't understand it either, but I've grown to trust my gut first and find the logic after."

My breath comes out shaky when I get to the part about driving down the familiar road Isla lives on. "My ten-hour shift was nearly over, but I remember feeling wired, like my body could sense something in the air before my brain could. The snow had finally started to let up, allowing me to see a touch further than I had been able to all evening. I still drove at the same slow, steady pace, heading east on Cloverdale. But something felt different, as if my body knew I needed to pay more attention to my surroundings. Then, out of nowhere, a black mass flung itself into the road. I slammed on my brakes so hard that I slid a few feet through the snow. I immediately radioed in my location and informed dispatch that I was unaware of what it was."

Detective Smith inhales deeply—clearly the footage she saw replaying in her mind as well. "When I saw the extension of legs and bare feet, I knew it was a person distressed and again radioed in for backup."

My throat starts to feel tight as I remember the fear and urgency I felt at that moment. The image of Isla's desperate struggle in the snow is seared into my memory. Swallowing doesn't seem to help the tension building in my chest, but Detective Smith takes a small form of pity on me, pushing one of the water bottles toward me.

I nod, downing half of it in one gulp. "I got out of my vehicle and unsheathed my 9mm while shining my flashlight on the mass. I took tentative steps at first, shouting at the person, but they were unresponsive. When I was about ten feet away, I recognized the hood on the top of the coat to be a friend of mine's, Isla Mitchell."

Staring at the plastic water bottle, I roll it between my hands, trying to calm the overwhelming emotions flooding my mind. "I ran to her, sheathed my gun, and tried to assess her wounds visually. The black puffer coat concealed most of her, though I could only make out dried blood and light brown matted hair. When I heard a male voice shouting her name from a distance, I recognized it to be her boyfriend, Jeff Walton. I picked her up and carried her to the back of the passenger side of my SUV."

"Did you suspect he was a threat at the time?" Her question almost catches me off guard, but I quickly respond, "I didn't have time to consider the possibility that he wasn't a threat. My priority was getting her off the road, out of the snow, and to what I considered a safe place to wait for medical attention."

The beating of my heart only intensifies with each sentence, like it's reliving that night as well. "I radioed in once again, alerting dispatch who the victim was and that she needed immediate medical attention. Then I unsheathed my gun once again and used my vehicle as cover to determine if it was, in fact, Jeff shouting and if he was a threat or not."

"Can you describe the scenery playing out before you? How far away was he? Where he was at in location to your vehicle." I thought it was hard before, but the questions are only getting harder.

Closing my eyes, I try to focus on that night. "My vehicle was still facing east, and the shouting was coming from the north, from where I knew Jeff and Isla's house to be."

"How did you know that was their home?"

"Isla has been a friend of mine since we were both in the wedding party of our mutual friends. We've worked in the same office building, we've gone to the same birthday parties, and we hang out in the same circle of friends. Moreover, it's a small town. I could probably tell you where half the residents live, or at least in which area of the county."

She nods, approving my answer like I passed a test, before asking another question. "Could you see the suspect from your position?"

"Not at first, but the closer he got as he walked down the driveway, the easier it was to spot him. The first thing I noticed was that he was carrying a shotgun in his right hand, pointed at the ground. I shouted out my credentials and ordered him to stop walking. I radioed in once again to update, but he continued toward me. He began shouting that I needed to back off, give him Isla, and that I needed to forget this ever happened."

"Without backing down, I continued to order him to put the weapon down, but when he recognized me, he began to raise the gun. I discharged my firearm, aiming for center mass."

"How many rounds did you fire?" she asked.

"18," I replied, "17 in the magazine and one in the chamber." *All of them.* I couldn't tell you how many hit their mark, but I hope every single one.

She moves on to the next question, "Did you render any medical aid?"

"No. I radioed in once more and waited for backup. When Lieutenant Will arrived on scene, we approached the suspect, cleared the firearm, and he began administering first aid." *We both knew he was gone by then, but protocol is protocol.*

"What did you do while Lieutenant Will was working on the suspect?" *Prayed his ass was being dragged to the depths of hell.*

"Captain Ellis had arrived to help Lieutenant Will and I went to check on Isla." She nods, encouraging me to go on. With detail, I describe Isla's injuries, what she said to me about Jeff, and Luke's arrival. Detective Smith nods along, listening to everything I have to say without asking any more questions. Then she shuts off the recorder and lets out a massive breath, her cheeks puffing out with it.

"Thank you for your thorough account, Deputy. I'll make sure this information is included in the report." Her tone sounds as serious as it had throughout the interview, but I notice her shoulders relaxed a fraction. *Is that good or bad?*

"I'll walk you out," she says, standing.

I stand as well, extending my hand across the table to shake hers again. "I appreciate it. Thank you for your time."

When she grips my hand firmly, she yanks me forward. Her words were low, but not quite a whisper: "I watched every single video of that night. Between you and me. You did the right thing, the correct way. It may not feel like justice is served, but believe me, the world is a better place without the likes of Jeff Walton."

With a nod, she releases my hand and heads towards the door. I followed behind, slightly stunned that she broke character and admitted what we all knew to be true. It doesn't guarantee that this will all go my way, but it's a damn good start.

Chapter Eighteen

Isla

"Isla, Isla, Isla!" Doctor Chipper walks into my room, singing my name and smiling with a cheeky grin, like I'm his favorite patient.

"Doctor Chipper," I say, mimicking his vibrant energy. His name isn't actually Dr. Chipper, but every time he walks in, he has a smile plastered on his face and uses the same singsong tone when he talks to me. His real name is Doctor Porter, and he looks somewhere between my dad and my grandfather's age. It's difficult to tell because he's absolutely benefiting from the free pharmaceutical samples to keep himself looking young. Not that it matters how old he is; he's been my favorite doctor so far. Except for Dr. Beach, he's the only one who isn't treating me like a victim of domestic abuse. He treats me like Isla—a plastic surgeon patient who wants a new nose, or at least a nose to match my old nose. Either way, he's the breath of positive air that I need in this situation.

"Today's the day, princess. Doctor Monroe agreed that you're in a much better position for surgery." Dr. Monroe is the head of neurology and the one who had me admitted because of the severity of my concussion.

Scuffling sounds come from the other side of the room as Hayes sits up to listen to what's going on. Charlie left last night, per his and my insistence, to get a full night of sleep at the hotel next to the hospital.

"Does that mean I'm out of here today, too?" I ask, genuine excitement bubbling in my chest.

"Not exactly." He sits on the round seat of the rolling chair and scoots it to the edge of the bed. "In normal circumstances, yes. With the grade of your mild TBI, we want to keep you overnight. If everything goes as planned, you can go home tomorrow or the next day. That is, as long as you have someone to help you out and monitor for any concerning symptoms."

The excitement I was feeling instantly began to feel more like dread. I hadn't thought much about where I would be going after this. The house Jeff and I shared is obviously out. I would rather not step foot in there again. My parents are still upset with me for kicking them out of the hospital. I know that I could ask Charlie and Hayes, but they've already done so much for me that I feel bad for asking for more.

Before I can dive too much more into a plan, Charlie waddles her seven-month pregnant belly back into the room and starts talking like she's been here the entire time. "Got that covered. Hayes picked up her stuff and got it set up in the guest room. Between the two of us and the gaggle of guys he keeps around, she'll be in good hands."

My jaw must hit the floor because she looks at me and rolls her eyes while shaking her head. "What did you expect, I? You're family. You'll stay with us until you're all healed up, and then you can move into the apartment that Olivia will have waiting."

Tears fill my eyes and I quickly close them. My emotions

are all over the place because of the concussion, and I swear I've cried more in the last few days than I have in my entire life.

"Great! Let's get that nose looking as beautiful as it did before. The pre-op nurse will be in to get everything started soon. I'll be in town for the next two days, and we will remove the packing and nasal drop. Then I'll be back right before it's time to remove the splint, usually about a week." With that, Doctor Chipper is off to do whatever doctors do in their spare time.

"What else did I miss?" Charlie asks as she settles onto the couch next to Hayes. His right arm automatically wraps around her, drawing her into him, while his left hand rests on her baby bump.

The corner of my mouth tips upward. "That's it, so far. Oh, Hayes had to escort some reporter that snuck in this morning."

"If by escort you mean 'physically shove out the door and call security,' then yeah." Hayes says through with a smirk.

Charlie gasps before shrieking, "I knew I shouldn't have left! I hate when I miss the 'stoic' but 'ruthless' Hayes."

With a grumble and a sigh, Hayes replies, "I'm always ruthless, Sunshine."

Ignoring his comment, I thanked them for being here. "I appreciate everything you guys are doing. I'm just so sorry this is all happening. Everyone is giving up so much right now for me."

Charlie groans as she stands up, placing her hand under her belly as she walks to stand by me. "Don't worry about that. We know how hard it is to ask for help, but that doesn't mean you shouldn't. Like I said a few minutes ago, you're family. I know that typically means a blood relationship, but to us, it's always been more than that. It's about who shows up when we need it, even though we didn't ask for it."

Hayes stands up, putting his arm around Charlie. "Especially when we don't ask for it. Life can be really fucking hard sometimes, Isla. No one gets that more than we do. But that doesn't mean you need to suffer through it alone."

A small smile grows on Charlie's face when she turns back to me. "Even when I was at my lowest..." She shakes her head, trying to stop the tears welling in her eyes. After a second, she lets out a breathy exhale. "I didn't want to have anyone around me, but Dan and Olivia wouldn't let that happen. They barely knew me, but they brought me into their family and treated me as such. Including me, crying with me, even protecting me. Then, when Dan died, we did the same thing for Olivia. She didn't have to grieve alone, worry about getting groceries, or make sure Ellie and Ben still had fun. *You* were a part of that. You showed up every day, working beyond overtime to make sure everything at work ran smoothly. Then you would leave work to help out with whatever we needed. You've been a part of our family for so long, helping us all through different heart-breaks or struggles. It's unfortunate that it's your time to lean on us, but no one deserves to have our help more than you do."

Tears streak down both of our faces as I nod my head. Charlie and Hayes, Olivia and her family, Drew and Everett, even the guys that work for Hayes and Drew—they've all treated me better than my family ever has. There were so many times I felt like a little sister to them, but I couldn't accept it—or maybe I was just too afraid that once I did, I would lose them.

Hayes' phone ringing breaks the moment, pulling me out of my thoughts. He glances down and then looks at me with a smirk, turning his phone, so I can see it.

Butterflies take off when I see it's Everett. He's still under investigation for rescuing me and shooting Jeff, so we aren't supposed to talk. Which only makes me more desperate to talk to him and make sure he's okay.

"May I?" I ask nervously, looking between them.

Hayes does his best to hide his smile as he hands it over. "We're going to walk to the vending machine down the hall." His face grows serious when he says, "I'll be able to see everything. But if anyone besides a nurse or doctor walks through that door, you scream."

I nod my head, staring at Everett's name on the caller ID.

As they walk out, I hit the green button. "Hey…" I say, trying to sound casual.

The inhale of breath is the only sound I hear for a second, before finally he chokes out, "La?"

"Yeah, I hope it's okay that I answered. I know the whole…" My voice trails off before I gather my thoughts and think of how to say this without getting caught. "Thing? Is messy."

Feigning offense, he lets out a gentle gasp. "Are you kidding? I hope he never picks up the phone again. Your voice is far lovelier than his." I can tell he's aiming for a casual tone, but the hint of his voice breaking gives me hope that this whole thing isn't one-sided.

With a slight grin, I ask, "How are you? Is everything okay?"

I hear the low chuckle of disbelief as he waits for me to finish asking. "You're laying in a hospital bed, asking me how I am? Only you would be more concerned about someone else over yourself. I'm fine. I had my interview, and I said everything exactly as I remembered it. They have my body-cam footage, footage from the car, and thanks to the guys, footage from every inch of your property. The case is pretty cut and dry from a legal standpoint."

My body relaxes each second he talks, until I finally feel normal again. His voice could calm a raging storm, soothing even the fiercest winds.

"That's enough about me, though. How are you? That's actually why I called Hayes. He normally texts me every few hours, but I hadn't heard from him." I'd be lying if I didn't say the butterflies soared with that tidbit of information.

"I'm good," I reassured, before adding, "The only update is that they're going to do the surgery today."

Concern drips from his voice when he asks, "Is that even safe? Going under when you have a concussion?"

"I guess so. Dr. Chipper and Dr. Monroe signed off on it. I'm mainly worried he'll make me look like 'Ms Piggy' with a bad nose job. How vain is that?" I let out a nervous chuckle, trying to lighten the heavy atmosphere with a touch of humor.

"Nah, you could never look bad. Plus, he's one of the best in the world. We made sure of it," he reassured confidently over the phone, his voice calm and soothing.

My jaw drops as his words sink in. "What do you mean?" I inquire, disbelief evident in my tone.

Nonchalantly, he elaborates, "I had Odessa make some calls. Her friends have undergone more plastic surgery than a Kardashian. They all vouched for Doctor Porter as the best, so we flew him in."

You what?!" I exclaim, unable to fathom the potential expense of such a decision.

"Technically, I didn't. Odessa made the calls, moved the mountains, and footed the bill—despite my attempts to pay for it." My head spins a little with the new information as tears fill my eyes. I had wondered why it felt like I was Doctor Porter's only patient, and he was treating me like royalty. For Odessa to do that for me, it feels overwhelming. She's always been a friend to me, but this feels like an entire new level of care and generosity that I never expected.

"I don't know what I did to deserve you all." I tell him truthfully.

His voice grows incredibly soft when he explains, "You've got a heart of gold, La. We're all just happy that you're okay.

Me, especially." He pauses for a brief second and then, through shaky breaths, he says, "Seeing you like that on the road, I don't think I've ever been that terrified in my entire life."

"Me either, but I'm thankful it was you and not some random person. I'm only sorry that it ended the way it did, and now you have to deal with the fallout."

"Don't be. It's nothing I can't handle." There's so much conviction in his voice, I almost believe him.

A nurse knocks on the door, smiling, and then Hayes and Charlie follow behind her.

"Looks like it's time for surgery." I know that it's one step closer to getting out of here, but I wasn't ready to be done talking to him yet.

"Already?" He asks with a hint of disappointment in his voice. "Damn. Okay, well, I'm so fuckin' glad I got to talk to you. You're gonna do great, baby."

I do my best to cover the shock and utter elation at his unexpected term of endearment, but that doesn't stop my heart from racing with excitement. "Thanks. I'll talk to you later?" Before he can respond, Hayes motions toward his phone. "Oh, wait, I think Hayes wants to talk to you."

I passed the phone back, my mind still processing his revelation. I want nothing more than to live in this moment, where there's a potential future with Everett. Yet, each time I attempted to contemplate it, my mind recoiled, as if protecting itself from the prospect of another heartbreak.

Chapter Nineteen

Everett

Drew's text flashes on my phone screen.

Instead of replying, I unlock the front door and return to preparing dinner for myself and Liam—more like reheating one of the many casseroles that someone has dropped off. He's the sole member of my security detail and hasn't taken a break in the past few hours. His time has been consumed by monitoring security feeds and patrolling the perimeter; I believe he's even brought out the binoculars a few times. Should I be worried they're not telling me something? Probably. Do I care, though? Not really. I'm still riding my high from talking to my girl before she had surgery today.

Drew barrels in like a tornado, slamming the door behind him. "So, for today's briefing, I have bad news, good news, really bad news, worse news, and then hopefully a happy ending." He starts his spiel before I can even take a breath.

"Bad news: Protesters from out of town have taken control

of the CPM/EFSC property's border," he says without any emotion, like he's reading off a grocery list. "Good news—"

"Wait! Protesters? What the fuck are you talking about?" I interrupt, feeling a surge of panic.

Drew pauses, his thumbs tapping on the edge of the counter. "Against police brutality, excessive use of force, and, uh, cheaters," he adds before huffing. "They started at the department. Luke, with the help of the fire department, had an epic winter water fight. First responders—of course—won. But all those protesters decided to move to public ground at the next most offensive place—the CPM/EFSC building."

"Because Isla works there?" I ask, trying to connect the dots.

He nods, his expression serious. "And because you're an investor in EFSC."

"Fuck." They're targeting the only place that ties us together, even though neither of us have any ownership of the building. It's also the perfect place to linger; open and large sidewalks surround the entire property. The guys also make sure to shovel and salt the entire property so that it's clear of snow. Unfortunately, I can see how that would make for an easy landing spot for protesters.

"So the good news is—Luke gave us a heads-up and we got the team in the building before anyone noticed." Drew explains, his tone a mix of relief and tension.

"And now for the worse news... or wait, are we diving into the really bad news next?" I interject, trying to remember what the hell he said.

"When the locals saw them trying to graffiti the building, they decided to stand guard and create their own human shield." I stare at him, blinking, waiting for him to continue because I know the next thing will be worse. Instead of looking at me, he opens up his laptop and starts typing while he talks.

"Luke was then called because some protesters and locals were starting to fight. He now has deputies in between the two groups, and things are getting tense."

I have to stuff my hands into my pockets to keep my thumbs still. "What's the plan?"

He smirks and I swear I see a sparkle glinting in his eyes when he says, "Psychological warfare in three phases." He gestures toward his computer screen for me to see, so I grab the chair next to his and sit at the kitchen counter.

His screen has 12 security monitors displayed, covering every inch of the outside building and a few of the inside. At least a hundred protesters lined the sidewalk around the CPM/EFSC building, some holding signs and others shouting chants. Luke must have requested backup from our neighboring department because there are about thirty deputies that I don't recognize standing between the protesters and the inner area of the locals.

I lean in closer to get a better look at the community that is guarding the building. The protesters outnumber them by at least three to one, but it doesn't deter them from standing their ground. Seeing them protect the building like this feels a hell of a lot more symbolic than simply protecting the building Isla and I have a connection to, though. This is the town showing their loyalty to us and making it known which side they are on.

Taking a deep breath, I feel a surge of gratitude toward this town. I haven't been here long enough to feel like a local, but their unwavering support makes me feel like I belong here.

Out of the corner of my eye, I glance at Drew, who is also watching the cameras. He at least looks better than the last time I saw him. I'm surprised he left Olivia at all with everything going on, but I'm appreciative he included me in this. Clearing my throat, I ask, "So, three phases?"

"Yep. Phase 1 is to lure our people into the building with an enormous pizza delivery so that they are out of the way and content in the building, or give them the option to leave." He points toward Luke, who walks through the line of deputies, like Moses parting the Red Sea. He's carrying a stack of enormous pizzas that make even his large frame look small. "Once they're inside, and they've made sure that no protesters have slipped in, they'll start Phase 2."

We both watch as the locals begrudgingly follow Luke through the front door. The CPM/EFSC is two stories and built like a fortress, so it should keep them safe until the situation is resolved. The second floor is set up with two business offices as well as two common spaces that will be perfect for the locals to hang out in.

"Phase 2 is what Will is working on." He points toward Lieutenant Will, who is handing something out to the deputies standing between the building and the protesters. "Ear plugs for when we turn on the speakers."

"What's going on with the speakers?" I questioned, leaning in closer to the live feed. Some protesters are already starting to look weary, while others are growing agitated.

"Linc is going to blast a high-frequency sound that will piss off the protesters and make it difficult for them to stay in the area. It's our attempt at a non-violent way to break up the crowd and prevent any potential violence." I can tell there's a hint of excitement in his plan, knowing that this tactic was probably only to appease Luke.

My eyes narrow on him. "And when that doesn't work?"

"Phase 3 is Luke dismissing the deputies and waiting for them to clear, so the guys can fire pepperballs along the border of our property. As long as they don't hit the sidewalk, which is considered 'public', they can cover every inch of our space without causing any legal issues. Going to turn the parking lot into a cloud of PAVA." The grin he had plastered on his face widened as he explained the plan, clearly confident in its effectiveness.

I respond with a chuckle, "It's a good thing y'all busted your asses to clear the snow." There won't be anything to dilute the smoke from the pepperballs. It hasn't snowed since the night I found Isla, but there are still a few feet of packed snow sticking around.

I looked back at the live feed, watching the disgruntled people chant. Drew's phone lights up and when he reads the text, his energy shifts to full on diabolical. "Can you call Linc? I want to keep my phone open."

Nodding, I lean back to pull my phone out of my pocket. Lincoln answers on the first ring, "We ready?"

"Yep. Give the warning." Instead of responding, we hear through the speaker on the phone and then, slightly delayed, the same words come through the computer speaker. "This is your warning to vacate the property. This area will undergo controlled security measures in two minutes. I repeat, you have two minutes to vacate the premises. Please leave immediately, or you could be subject to potential harm." Lincoln's voice is firm and authoritative, emphasizing that there is no room for negotiation. None of the protesters heeded the warning, aside from a few wearying exchanges. If anything, it fuels them. The shouts become louder, the banners are raised higher, and the crowd seems to grow in defiance. It's clear that they are not going to back down easily, no matter the consequences.

"You now have one minute to vacate the premises. Please exit the area immediately to ensure your safety. Failure to comply may result in further action being taken." Lincoln's voice remains unwavering, but I can tell he's secretly hoping they stay where they are.

The protesters continue to stand their ground, showing no signs of backing down as the tension in the air thickens. After another thirty-second warning, he gives the final. "This is your last warning. Leave immediately."

When no one moves, I hear him chuckle through the phone line before counting down. "Three, two, one." A god awful squealing sound comes from the computer speaker, and Drew reaches out to turn the computer volume down a few levels.

"Shit, man. That's awful!" Within less than a minute, at least half of the crowd had already started to disperse. Those remaining were able to put headphones on to block out the noise, determined to hold their ground. The standoff continued for another four minutes before Linc cut the sound.

"Please leave immediately or be prepared to endure controlled security measures."

The crowd remaining all joined in front of the building, linking arms in solidarity. Without realizing it, they started falling perfectly into position for the guy's plan. The deputies surrounding the back and side of the building were able to leave their posts and get back in their squad cars.

Shouts of "Stand strong!" and "We won't be silenced!" filled the air as they prepared to face whatever security measures were to come.

Out of nowhere, Luke and five other men wearing Cascadia County Sheriff gear, equipped with gas masks and respirators, take the place of the remaining deputies at the front of the building.

Lincoln's voice blares through the speakers once again: "This is your last warning. Leave immediately!"

With perfect synchronization, Luke and his men take three large steps back so that they put distance between themselves and the protesters.

Through one of the cameras facing the building and not the street, I watch as Lincoln, Cooper, and Delta walk out onto the second floor balcony. I can only guess which one is which based on size and gait, with Lincoln having a slight limp, Cooper being the tallest of the three, and Delta being the shortest. They all carry the same model pepperball launcher and wear bandanas, sunglasses, and hoods. When one more person walks out in the same gear, I look at Drew with raised eyebrows. "Who's that?"

He huffs, "Levi," but leaves it at that. I had heard he was taking a small leave of absence after being the medic to help Olivia, but I wasn't aware he was down to play vigilante.

Like a scene from a movie, white powder begins exploding on the ground in a perfect line, about a foot from the sidewalk. The sound of pops filled the air like a fireworks show, causing most of the protesters to scatter, confused and fearful, before they even came into contact with the airborne PAVA. I don't know how many pepperball rounds they use, but the guys don't stop shooting until the entire area is filled with white smoke, hovering in the air. By the time the smoke starts to clear, the sidewalk is void of any protesters. Besides some trash left around, you'd never know anyone was out there.

Across the road, the protesters, who didn't move in time, are coughing and squirting water into their eyes.

Captain Ellis slowly pulls down the road in between the protesters and the building. Over the PA system, he shouts his orders for the people to leave town, stating that if they aren't from here, they aren't welcome here.

Drew lets out a deep breath, relieved that everything went according to plan. "I should get back to Olivia's. The kids and Zeke got back yesterday, so I felt okay leaving for a bit, but I'd rather not be gone too long." Zeke is Levi and Dan's father, as well as Luke's predecessor.

"I take it they're okay with you moving yourself in?"

He smirks back. "As far as I know, they've yet to mention it. I talked to Ben a little about wanting to be near them as much as I could while we navigated through what's going on. They don't know the extent of everything, but—"

"He's a smart kid." I finish for him. Ben is a third-grader who has the maturity of a high schooler.

Drew's smile only grows prouder. "Yep. Thankfully, they seem happy to have me stay close. I'm not sure I'd be able to stay away if Olivia didn't want me around." The sound of something slamming shut comes from the guest bathroom at the same time the front door opens behind us, and we see Liam walk in.

Briefly, Drew and I exchange wide-eyed glances before jumping out of our chairs. Drew already has his Glock drawn from where it was hidden inside his waistband and aimed as we approach the bathroom.

Liam is hot on our heels, despite not knowing what we heard. To let him pass, I paused a few steps away, turning so that my back pressed against the hallway wall. I'm the only one without a gun, and on the off chance someone broke into the house, he should be closer to Drew.

Drew opens the door and they have it cleared in seconds—completely empty.

Liam glances back at me, one eyebrow raised, like, What the hell are we doing?

"What the fuck was that?" Drew demands, his eyes scanning the room for any signs of danger.

I shake my head, despite having a tiny idea of what it could be. There aren't any windows or other exits in the room, so whatever made that noise didn't leave. Which could mean one of two things: either we have some type of massive rodent problem, or there's something a little more supernatural happening.

My guess is the latter—this house belonged to Dan and Olivia before we moved in. They were married, had kids, and started a family here. It wouldn't be impossible to think he may still be hanging around here.

"You know what? Nope. You two can deal with it." Drew storms out of the bathroom toward his bedroom, avoiding the topic we both think is possible. The ghost of Dan is lingering around—pissed that his wife and kids don't live here anymore. When Drew and I first moved in, he was always accusing me of tampering with his stuff—hiding his keys, emptying his toothpaste, shutting the oven off while he was cooking something. I never copped to anything, but I also didn't mention that I thought it was Dan fucking with him. Based on his rocky start with Olivia, I always assumed this was Dan's way of getting back at him. Plus, I thought it was hysterical that a ghost could derail a Navy SEAL into thinking he was losing his mind.

Rather than look into it anymore, I chuckle to myself and walk back toward the kitchen and our most likely burned casserole. In the midst of everything going on, I'd forgotten that we had dinner in the oven. It doesn't matter if it's ruined at this point; we have at least a dozen more in the freezer, and it was worth sacrificing one to watch Walton's scheme go up in smoke as well.

Chapter Twenty

Isla

Every bump of the truck sends a new wave of pain through my nose and somewhere into the depths of my head. If it weren't for the pain medication the doctor prescribed, I'd have already passed out in the back of Hayes truck on the way to their house. The surgery yesterday went well, and I'm grateful they let me come home this evening—even if it's only a temporary home.

Three doctors had to sign off for me to leave, but after nearly a week in the hospital, I've finally been released. Dr. Chipper quickly signed off on Plastics this morning; Dr. Monroe with Neuro was next; and finally, the most stressful doctor of them all—Dr. Kemper, the psychiatrist who was brought in to assess the emotional toll of the domestic violence I experienced. She asked me question after question, trying to gauge my reactions and emotional state. Thankfully, she was satisfied with my responses and cleared me as soon as I scheduled an appointment with a therapist for ongoing support.

To be honest, it was probably for the best that they kept me for so long. My body went into some sort of shock following the entire ordeal. During the first three days, I let sleep consume me, only waking up when a nurse or doctor needed something. It was like my body was shutting down to protect itself from the trauma, and I can't say I blame it. Twenty-four hours of abuse—emotional and physical—and it deserved a little reprieve in the form of unconsciousness.

I vaguely remember the moments of lucidity, but I know one thing: Charlie never left my side. She's always been more of a friend than a boss, but in those moments, she was my lifeline. Doctors, nurses, police investigators, and even my parents—it felt like a million questions were being shouted at me from all different directions, and I was slipping back into The Darkness trying to remember it all. Charlie was always within earshot, though, never letting anyone steamroll me into saying something I didn't want to. She protected me, shielded me from the chaos, and made sure I had the space to heal at my own pace.

"The guys put all the bags you had packed into your room. They've been working for Olivia and me, too—covering the entire business." Charlie re-told me everything that happened to Olivia and the car accident she was in. Just hearing her name has me feeling immense guilt. Jeff went after her because he was pissed at me.

"How is she?" My voice breaks as I ask and I have to close my eyes once again to keep the tears at bay.

The leather of the front seat loudly creaks as Charlie moves around but doesn't say anything.

When I open my eyes, she's turned around in her seat and is staring at me. Annoyance is clearly clouding her features.

"Isla. Olivia is fine; she came to see you, but you were pretty out of it. She's healing and Drew is taking care of her. They're back together, happy, and moving forward. You need to stop blaming yourself for everything that Jeff did. His actions are not your responsibility."

Tears stream down my face, but I try to stay still. She has no idea how many times Jeff threatened to do something like this. So many times, I began to think it was just another empty threat. Only it wasn't. He was truly as evil as he threatened to be.

"Any time he was upset, he would go off on all the ways he could ruin every business in town. I told Olivia a few weeks ago that he was threatening to deny any permits or licenses she submitted to the city. I had no idea he would go further than that, until that night. He—" I pause, trying to steady my voice despite the shaking of my body.

Through a sob, I finally got out. "He told me he would start picking my friends off, one by one. Starting with Olivia."

A growl sounds from Hayes, who is driving, but Charlie only scoffs. "Yeah, fucking right. I hope you told him, 'We don't negotiate with terrorists!'"

Hayes chokes on a laugh. As I say, "Not exactly."

I watch as her green eyes grow wide enough that I can see little specks of gold in them. "What do you mean, not exactly?" she asks, her voice filled with concern and a touch of admiration.

I see through the rearview mode that Hayes is grinning from ear to ear, fighting off an even bigger laugh.

I take a deep breath before admitting, "I may have told him that he better pray that Drew didn't find him."

"That's not all you said." Hayes pointed out from the front seat. I gave him full access to our security system so that he could download the footage. We didn't have a camera in the closet, but there was one in the corner of the bedroom that was angled enough to see where we were standing. It also recorded the full audio.

Charlie's eyes bounce between us before she can't handle it anymore. "What did you say?!"

I groan and close my eyes. "Go ahead, Hayes! You probably remember it better than I do, anyway."

"She said, and I quote, 'Pray for Hayes. He's the most merciful of them all—a quick death. Meanwhile, I'll be praying it's Liam, and he skins you alive before disposing of you like the trash you are.'"

A loud gasp comes from Charlie before she lets out the loudest laugh I've ever heard. "Beautiful! Couldn't have said it better myself. What did he say after that?"

The only sound in the car is Hayes clenching his jaw, remembering exactly what happened next.

With a sigh, I open my eyes. "That was it. That's what set him off for the full-blown attack." Charlie's smile fades as she realizes the severity of the situation, her expression turning somber.

"I know you're not supposed to speak ill of the dead, but fuck that guy. Never deserved you."

Hayes nods his head dramatically in agreement, but instead of responding, I sit back and look out the window as we pull into town. The drive back to Three Sisters went quicker than normal. It looks mostly the same, except for how quiet the streets are. It's almost like the stores are closed, which is unusual for a Friday morning.

It isn't until I notice the number of vehicles lingering around the Sheriff Department and the road that leads to it that I realize what's going on. "Is all of that because of what happened?" I ask in disbelief. It hasn't been this crowded over here since Olivia's husband, Dan, was murdered. The entire town was practically shut down, grieving and avoiding the media circus that surrounded the Sheriff Department.

Charlie's entire body sags, but I can see from behind that

she's nodding. "Luke is handling it. The town is livid that Cyrus is turning this into some sort of political spectacle," she explains, her voice tinged with frustration. "Not one person from here believes the lies he's spewing."

With a gulp, I push down the feelings of guilt once again. I should've known Cyrus would react this way. Spinning narratives to fit his agenda is a specialty of his.

"What is he saying?"

Hayes and Charlie exchange a knowing look before Hayes speaks up. "He's claiming that the Sheriff's Department is corrupt. He's spinning it to say that if Everett is cleared, it's only because they're covering up evidence to protect their own."

I scoff, but remain silent.

"He's also saying that he thinks you and Everett were having an affair." My jaw feels like it's hit the floor. I can't believe Cyrus would stoop so low as to spread such a baseless accusation.

"You're kidding me."

Hayes shakes his head as Charlie turns around. "Isla, I promise you that no one in this town believes a word he's saying. Other than maybe his shady ass friends."

"What is Luke doing about it?" I ask, looking back out the window as we drive to their house.

"He's trying to keep the peace right now. Keep everyone updated without giving away too much information. It's gone viral, though. Every news station in the country has picked it up." I can't help but feel bad for Luke. He's been great as the sheriff since he took on the position. The town loves him, and outsiders fear him.

"Is there anything I can do to help?"

Once again, I see them make eye contact. Charlie immediately shakes her head, while Hayes arches an eyebrow at her.

"Spill. I don't need it sugarcoated."

Hayes turns his blinker on as we approach their driveway. "If everyone saw what happened before Everett got there, it would clear his name and yours." My stomach instantly rolls at the thought of the entire world seeing me go through that trauma. I don't know if I can relive that night again, but the alternative is that Everett continues to suffer.

The look Charlie sends Hayes is full of reprimand before she turns back to me again. "It'll clear itself up eventually, I. You don't have to put yourself out there like that."

Everett shouldn't be having his name smeared through the entire country because of me, though. He'd do whatever it took to clear my name, and I owe it to him to do the same. I just need to figure out how I can release the footage without jeopardizing the investigation.

Chapter Twenty-One

Isla

A loud knock, followed by someone clearing their throat, comes from the other side of the guest bedroom. It's been four days since I got home from the hospital, and I've mainly just laid around feeling sorry for myself. Everything hurts, but the pain is manageable enough that I feel human today. I even showered and put on fresh sweats today, an enormous accomplishment in my eyes.

I open the door, already expecting Liam. The giant, cold-hearted man has been lingering around, waiting on me—hand and foot. The first time he saw me, I swear tears sprang in his eyes before they quickly turned dark and vengeful. The only thing he said was, "I'm sorry it wasn't me who found him." *Me too, friend. Me too.*

"What's up, Liam?"

"Parents are at the gate. Do you want to see them?" I hadn't heard from them since the first day in the hospital, when I was still out of it. Not a text, phone call, or carrier pigeon in sight.

I drag in a long, slow breath and then puff my cheeks out as I let it go. "Sure."

He nods, sends a text, and then follows a step behind me as I walk toward the front entrance.

Charlie and Hayes house is a beautiful, two-story log home. Everything is open, light, and airy. They had it built around the same time Olivia had her new home built. I had only been working for them for a short time, but the busier they got with designing their homes, the more they entrusted me to help with CPM. Besides helping Bill and Gwen with the kids, it was the first time I felt like an asset rather than a burden.

I watch as the silver Range Rover makes its way toward the front of the house. The driveway is clear, but snow remains throughout the landscaping in big patches.

I sense the presence of someone stepping outside to stand next to me, but I resist the urge to turn and look. I had already had a feeling Liam would text Hayes. Out of the corner of my eye, I notice Liam take a step back so that it's Hayes flanking my side.

When my parents get out of the SUV, they look as posh as ever. My dad in his suit and tie, with silver streaks and confident aura. My mom, with her perfectly blown-out blonde hair, is wearing a fur coat and clutching her pearls nervously. Her heels click on the dry pavement as she walks a few steps behind my dad. She hasn't even made eye contact with me; she only stares at my dad's back. You'd think they were going to a funeral, not checking in on their only daughter.

I try to tip the corners of my mouth into a smile, but it feels more like a grimace.

Dad starts talking first. "Mr. Carrington. Thanks for taking care of our girl. You have no idea how much we appreciate it." He doesn't even look at me while reaching to shake Hayes' hand. Hayes doesn't move an inch, keeping his arms crossed over his chest.

Of course, my dad tries to play it off with a shrug and smarmy smile. "Hey, pumpkin. You ready to come home?"

A noise that sounds like a growl emanates from Liam, while Hayes' jaw is clenched so tightly that I swear I can hear his teeth grinding. This thirty-second standoff is charged with tension and unspoken animosity. I can feel the weight of it all, making me wish I could vanish into thin air. I've grown so accustomed to that feeling that my instincts urge me to do whatever I can to ease the hostility. It's that visceral reaction that has me squaring my shoulders and standing a little taller.

Instead of acknowledging them, I glance back at my mom, hoping to catch even a hint of concern for what happened to me. But when I see the deadness in her eyes, I realize it's a lost cause. Shaking my head, I turn to go inside, dismissing them the way they've always dismissed me.

"Isla. Don't you turn around on me." My dad snapped in the same tone I've heard for years. Not angry, but clearly trying to intimidate me with his commanding presence and firm voice, demanding my attention and compliance.

I stare at the YETI logo on Hayes chest while my dad continues to rant. "Do you know where we just were? The man you claimed to love? His funeral! It's time for you to set this all straight."

Hayes and Liam's chests nearly vibrate with each word my father says, but they remain silent. Waiting for me to take the lead. It's one of the greatest examples of genuine loyalty and protectiveness I've ever had.

My father, oblivious to their unspoken support, continues to demand answers from me, his voice growing louder with each passing moment. "Isla, do you hear me? Look at me!"

Whirling on my heels, a newfound fire ignites within me. "Look at you? Look at me! Do you *even* see me? Do you see what he did to me?" The bandage on my nose remains post-surgery, with bruises adorning my upper body and face. The emotional torment alone should speak volumes to him, yet he doesn't even blink. The more I gaze at my father, the clearer it becomes—he isn't simply indifferent to my state; he genuinely lacks any concern.

"You know what, dad? Fuck you. I never once claimed to love that abusive asshole. I hope he's rotting." I put every ounce of venom I have into my statement before turning away, knowing that I deserve better than his callousness and cruelty.

Neither of the guys look at me, they're too focused on what-ever vile things my dad is saying behind me. Bolstered by newfound confidence, I assert, "They're dead to me. Don't let them near me, again. Please." before striding between the two men and heading inside.

As I swing the door shut behind me, I see Liam is now shoulders-to-shoulder with Hayes, blocking my parents from entering or even seeing me. Despite Liam's height advantage over Hayes, together they stand like twin fortresses, an unyielding defense to ensure my safety. The siblings I never thought I'd have, ready to fight for me like family should.

When the guys finally come back in, they find me sitting at the kitchen counter, eating chocolate chip ice cream directly from the tub.

I point out the front window toward the driveway and say, "Thanks for having my back. I appreciate you both following my lead and letting me be the one to stand up for myself."

Hayes gives me a sympathetic smile, but Liam only glares at the ice cream container while I continue talking. "I spent most of my life making myself small to be who they wanted me to be. It wasn't until I started working for Charlie and Olivia that I began to find my voice. I was living in two worlds: being the perfect girlfriend and daughter and being Isla, the girl who wanted to drink beer and make crude jokes."

My spoon stabs at the hard ice cream as I try to convey the internal struggle I faced. "Before all of this, I had been holding on to a sliver of hope that they would understand why I was leaving him. I was trying to do everything right, down to breaking up in the right way." A humorless laugh bubbles out of me. "But damn," I say as I wave the spoon in my general direction. "If they could see me like this and still defend him, I know they never would have understood."

"I'm sorry, Isla. You deserved better than him and them." Hayes breaks the silence, his voice full of sincerity.

I nod my head as I scoop out a large bite of ice cream. "Yeah, even I can admit that."

He clears his throat before uncomfortably asking, "Do you, uh, want to talk about it?"

Shaking my head, I scoop out another bite of ice cream. "Nah, think I'll just eat my weight in ice cream and then take a nap."

Liam nods once and then I watch his large frame walk out the back door. He's a man of few words, hates attention, and looks like he's ready to snap a neck at any moment, but he's got a big heart hiding behind the scar tissue of his past.

The clatter of a drawer opening pulls my attention back to the kitchen. Hayes reaches in for a spoon while holding his own tub of ice cream. "*Mint* choc-chip. Can't beat it. Just don't tell Charlie I ate her ice cream."

"We both know the second I go take a nap, you'll be high-tailing it to the store to buy her a replacement."

With a grin, he sits next to me at the counter. "Yeah, but she'd be more pissed if I didn't make sure you were okay."

We both eat in companionable silence before I blurt out, "I need to see Everett before tomorrow afternoon."

Hayes spoon pauses, hovering in front of his open mouth, while his wide eyes look at me.

"There's a press conference scheduled for three. The governor is coming to support *Mayor* Walton and will be speaking." I almost refrain from rolling my eyes, but the second I say Cyrus' title, I can't prevent it.

Hayes lets out a slew of curse words before he stabs the spoon into the ice cream and wipes his mouth with the back of his hand.

"He's allowing me to speak before her, though. Share my side of what happened." I can see the war in his eyes, trying to decide whether this is a good idea or not.

"Isla..." He challenged in the softest voice I've ever heard him use, concern evident. "Are you sure you want to do that?"

"Everett's entire being is in question right now. The Waltons and my parents are on offense right now, spinning webs of lies and counting on me being too ashamed to share my story." I take another bite of ice cream, letting the petty work its way up. "Thing is, I am ashamed."

Hayes' mouth pops open in protest, but I talk over him. "I'm ashamed that I dated such a piece of shit. I'm ashamed that I let The Waltons, as well as my parents, walk all over me. I'm ashamed that I didn't let the people who love me help me. What I'm not ashamed of is finally standing up for myself and realizing my worth. It may have taken me longer than it should have, but I won't hide behind my insecurities anymore." My voice nearly snarled when I declared, "I won't let anyone make me feel small or unworthy ever again."

Pride fills his eyes, a smug look crossing his face. "Hell fuckin' yeah, Isla." He reaches out for a fist bump, and says, "You've got, *at least*, a half dozen highly trained operatives ready to go to war for you. Use us. We got you." He takes a large bite of ice cream and then mumbles something that sounds a lot like, "Some more than others."

"What's that supposed to mean?" I inquire, trying not to get my hopes up.

Hayes only smiles mischievously and shrugs, clearly enjoying the teasing. "So, how do you intend to see Everett? There's media that everywhere watching both houses."

"I have a plan," I say cryptically, not wanting to reveal too much just yet. "It may not work, but it's going to take another person to make it happen. You in?"

The laugh that escapes Hayes is full of confidence and excitement. "Damn straight."

Chapter Twenty-Two

Everett

"Hey!" I snapped into the phone at Hayes when he answered. "What the hell's going on, Carrington? Liam texted me *an hour ago*, that Isla's parents showed up and things didn't go well. But it's been fucking radio silence from you!" Hayes may have answered on the first ring, but that doesn't lessen the brewing anger I feel. I've been on edge since I heard that Mr. and Mrs. Shitchell showed up and tried to get Isla to go home with them.

He kept his voice steady when he replied, "Yeah, well, it was more important that I made sure Isla was okay before I sent you an update." He may have a point, but I was looking for a little more fight. Someone to verbally spar for a minute with. Should've known Hayes wouldn't bite, he's far too impervious to my outbursts.

"Shit. I know, sorry." Letting out a gust of air, I try to calm down. "I just can't believe they had the nerve to show up like that and demand she lie about what happened. *Manipulative assholes.*" My frustration bubbles beneath the surface, threatening to spill over despite my best efforts to keep it contained.

"Liam and I got firsthand experience with what she's had to deal with. Their interaction didn't even last five minutes, but it put things into perspective. None of us ever understood why she wouldn't dump that asshole and move on. Seeing her dad treat her like she wasn't the victim in all of this when she's still covered in bruises was both staggering and infuriating."

I saw in person the damage that Jeff had done, but hearing Hayes say "covered in bruises" hit me harder than I expected. My blood pressure feels like it spiked simply because of the words.

"It's killing me not to be able to see her, man. I don't know what to do, but I can't sit here while she's hurting. Luke and Detective Smith keep telling me to be patient and they're working as quickly as they can." It hasn't even been two weeks since I found Isla, but each day is grating on my nerves—especially considering she's less than a handful of miles away. If there weren't camera crews lingering around, I'd already have snuck over there a dozen times.

"I know, Ev. We're working on something, okay? Hang on for a little while longer and we'll figure it out. She's safe at our house, though. Healing and recovering. Her parents showing up might have actually helped her resolve. I think she's done with them."

"I hope so. Please let me know what I can do. Maybe have her call me later?" I'm not above begging just to hear her voice at this point.

We end the call, and I lightly toss my phone onto the loveseat in the living room. I quickly glance around the room, looking for something to take my mind off the situation but there isn't anything that sticks out. Cooper and Lincoln are on guard duty right now, but I haven't seen much of them. They're either running laps around the property or working out somewhere. Connie and Odessa stopped by for a bit, but they've been bouncing between the three houses. Isla's been quiet, only able to talk to me when she borrows Charlie or Hayes' phone. A few stray reporters will drive by, but since the big showdown at the CPM/EFSC building, it's been pretty quiet all around. Even this house is quiet. Too damn quiet. Every creak sets me on edge, like the house is warning me there's more to come. It's hard to avoid wondering if this feeling is why Olivia moved out so quickly after Dan died. It would've just been her and the kids, and when they went to bed, it'd be easy to feel the weight of the silence.

***

Two hours later, my phone dings with a text from Hayes.

> Close the shades on every window of the house.

Without hesitation, I started moving throughout the house to the windows. Each room becomes darker as I lower the blinds and then move the blackout curtains into place. I switched most of the lights off as well, only keeping on a few lamps.

My phone remains silent after that text, allowing my thoughts to start spiraling into worst-case scenarios. Ten minutes later, when I'm good and worked up, the security notification goes off as Hayes' truck pulls down the driveway.

Another text comes through from him, "Open the front door for me."

I do as he said, but step out onto the front porch as well. "What's wrong? "

With a shrug and smirk, he says, "Nothing. Charlie wanted me to drop this off."

My eyes nearly bug out of my head at his cavalierness. "What's with the cryptics then?!"

Hayes ignores my question and walks around the truck with the same stupid smirk. He opens the back door, pulling out an extra large storage container. The black box conceals everything inside, but the bright yellow lid has a huge red bow on top.

"Whatcha got in there? You hiding a dead body in that? Because I think I'm good on police investigations for a while."

Even from here, I can see the eye roll he gives me. "Early Christmas present. Open the goddamn door before I drop it." His jaw slightly flexes, but besides that, he looks completely at ease carrying it. At this point, I can't tell if the box weighs a hundred pounds or five.

"Okay? If it's your dick in a box, I don't want it." I open the door, moving out of his way so he can go in ahead of me.

He gently sets the box down and then turns around to look at me.

"Are those air holes," I guessed while pointing toward the fifteen or so holes in the top of the box. Gasping, I look back at him, "Did you get me a puppy?"

"Didn't want to take any risks. Linc scared off some assholes with a long-distance camera that were lingering down the road. Possibly, the media, but more than likely it's Walton doing some digging."

"Fuck." I feel like I'm living under a microscope. I thought it was bad going to the grocery store; now I can't even walk around my own home without being watched.

For a brief second, concern washes over him when he sees my demeanor change. He quickly shakes his head and starts walking past me again. "I'll be back in a few hours. Have fun."

162

My head rears back as I give him a quizzical look.

He only grins back, opens the door, and then hollers, "Merry Christmas!" Before slamming the door.

"Christmas is still nine days away!"

The sound of a pop startles me as I spin around to see the lid on the container fly up. "Holy shit!"

Small feminine hands shove the lid the rest of the way off as someone sits up.

"La," her name comes out more like a breath than a word.

She sits up gingerly, slowly stretching her back from being cramped in the box. The bruises have turned a greenish yellow color, and she still has the dressing over her nose, but she looks so much better than the last time I saw her.

With one step, I'm kneeling in front of her. I yank the bow off the lid of the box and stick it to her chest. "Best. Christmas. Present. Ever."

Her arms wrap around my neck and pull me in for a hug. "We might have gone overboard, but it was kinda fun hiding in there."

I put one hand under her knees and the other around her waist, so that I can gently lift her out of the box. "I'm so glad you're here. I've been a damn wreck since I left you in that ambulance. If it hadn't been Bill there, I don't know if even Luke could have stopped me."

The bow falls into her lap and she grabs it with one hand before looking up at me with those doe eyes and grins. "Bill is the best. I don't remember much of the ambulance, but he came to visit me in the hospital and has called a few times. Gwen has sent an exuberant number of casseroles."

Chuckling, I hold her to me for a few more seconds before setting her on her feet. "Think I've gotten a few of those casseroles as well. Everyone in town has dropped off some form of food at this point. I'd offer you some, but the guys have plowed through them all. Are you hungry, though? I was going to make pancakes." I don't give her a chance to respond before I latch on to her hand and pull her toward the stool at the kitchen counter. Having her this close has given me a surge of energy that I need to channel before I do something I'll regret. Like, kiss her before she's ready.

So instead of standing there and staring at her, I moved around the kitchen, collecting the ingredients for pancakes. I place everything on the counter closest to her, so I can still steal glances while I cook.

A silence hangs over us as I start measuring the ingredients. With each glance I steal, she has her gaze down, staring at the bow still in her hand.

"What's going on in that pretty head of yours?" I inquired, trying to break the tension.

She looks up, a sad smile playing on her lips as she replies, "Just thinking about how lucky I am to be here. I haven't had the chance to tell you in person, but thank you. For saving me. That night and all the times before. You gave me the courage to do what I needed to do." My heart skips a beat at her words—a reprieve from the racing thoughts in my mind.

"I'll be there any time you need me. For the big stuff, the small stuff, and everything in between. But Isla..." I let out a small exhale as I cracked an egg into the bowl. "You have to let me help you, even when you don't want to burden me. I care about you, and I want to be involved."

Her eyes softened as she nodded. "I promise, no more secrets or trying to handle everything on my own. I can admit I was in over my head and should've listened to your warning. I was holding on to some form of hope that they were decent people. Jeff, his parents, and even my parents. All of that's gone, though. What's that saying? 'When someone shows you who they are, believe them.' Feels pretty fitting here."

I started mixing the ingredients while she was talking, so I paused to look at her. Choosing my words delicately, I say, "I'm sorry that it took getting to this point for you to see their true colors."

"I'm sorry that you're being dragged through the mud because of them. It's not fair."

My breathing hitches, I know what I want to say regarding the Walton family, but it would probably be in poor taste to insult her ex's family after I just killed said ex. My wrist picks up the pace as I whisk, beating the batter until it's completely smooth, attempting to quell my inner turmoil. It doesn't work though, if anything it only gives the insensitive feelings time to compound.

Ungracefully, I drop the whisk and place my palms on either side of the mixing bowl. "I'm going to be brash right now, and I hope I don't offend you, but I want you to hear me when I say this so you understand the lengths I'd go to for you. I'm not sorry that I was involved. I'm not sorry that I was the one to find you, and I'm certainly not sorry that I pulled the trigger. In my opinion, Jeff deserved a much worse death than what he received. My only regret is not finding you sooner and making him suffer."

I watch her throat as it swallows, tears welling in her eyes before she quickly blinks them away. "If I'm being honest, same. I'm glad it happened the way it did and no one will be in trouble. However, I'd be lying if I said I hadn't wished him a painful death."

Feeling my shoulders relax instantly, I couldn't hold back any longer, moving around the corner to embrace her. "I heard a rumor that you wished it was Liam that found him instead of me," I chuckled as the words slipped out.

She laughs into my chest, so I thread my fingers through her hair and lightly pull back so I can see her face.

"Liam's a lot more scary than you are." My heart races with excitement as she blesses me with an equal smile part temptress and part mischievous.

"There's no arguing that, but I think I can be pretty intimidating when I want to be."

Her eyes sparkle with amusement as she leans in closer, her breath warm against my skin. "I wouldn't want to be on your bad side, that's for sure."

With a playful grin, I move so that our lips are nearly touching. "But lucky for you, you're always on my good side." The tension between us crackles like electricity, making it difficult to resist closing the distance between our lips. I want her in every single way, but I think a conversation needs to be had before I cross that line.

So rather than kiss her like I wanted to, I pulled away and moved back around to the other side of the counter. I need distance. *Maybe even a cold shower.*

When I glance back at her, she's staring at me with wide eyes, ever so slightly panting. Guess that answers my question about whether she's as affected by this as I am.

Instead of returning to the batter, I grip the countertop's edge and meet her gaze, mustering the courage to express my true emotions. "I understand things are complicated already, but I need to know where your head is at. Because I can't continue to pretend that I don't have feelings for you. I want you—to be with you, to date, to explore what could be between us." *Way to ease into it, Astor.*

Her smile slowly faded as she stared at me, absorbing my declaration. I'd give anything to read what was going on in her mind right now and to know what her hesitation was. Except I already know her hesitation, it's too soon after Jeff. I told myself I'd be patient and wait for her to tell me she's ready. Seeing her though, having her in my space, I lost all source of willpower.

Swallowing the rejection, I break our eye contact and grab the cooking spray. Out of the corner of my eye, I see her shake her head, attempting to clear her thoughts.

She takes a deep, ragged breath before steadying herself, squaring her shoulders, and lifting her chin confidently to meet my gaze. "I need.."

Chapter Twenty-Three

Isla

Everett confessing he has feelings for me sent butterflies to my stomach as well as nausea. I've wanted this—wanted him, wanted him to tell me he feels the same, wanted to have clarity. Now, the timing of it all makes me want to scream at him. If it were just him and me, I would be over the moon. But we have an actual investigation into our relationship, into my history of abuse, and into the details of what happened that night. Not to mention, the media is combing over both of our lives with a fine tooth comb. How could I not worry that all of that will bring us down before we even get a chance to start?

"I need you to understand that I have feelings for you and I want to be with you. You are everything I could ever want in a person and relationship." It's difficult to convey my reasoning when the only thing stopping me is the thing that I'm trying to overcome—caring what other people think about me.

He doesn't look at me when he says, "Sounds like there's a 'but' in there somewhere."

"Should we wait until things have settled down? I don't know if it's wise to start what could be this great love story with all this going on." Before I even finish my sentence, he lets out an offended huff, his energy shifting from nervous to irritated at my words.

"Well, baby, I've got bad news for you. No matter what, this is how the greatest love story started. It's messy and complicated, but this is it." He throws his hands out wide, gesturing to nothing in particular.

"I fell in love with you when you were stuck in a tough situation, striving to define your own path and identity. Because even then, from that first moment at the airport—watching you go out of your way to help others—I just knew. I knew you were it for me."

With a smirk, he continues, "This drop-dead gorgeous woman—wearing jeans that should be illegal—waltzing around the airport like it was her duty to help everyone else. I was fucking captivated, unable to tear my eyes away. And you know what? I have zero regrets about that."

"So if you want me to wait because you need time to grieve and process, I'll wait. But whether it's today or a year from now, I'm all in, Isla. All in."

"Can we go back to the falling in love with me part?" The words escape me, sounding more desperate than I intended.

He lets loose a laugh in disbelief while shaking his head, the corner of his mouth tipped upward. "I'm in love with you. Heart, body, mind, and soul. Haven't even kissed you, but I love you."

Without hesitation, I blurted out, "So do it."

"Do what?" He asks, picking up the batter and pouring perfect circles onto the electric griddle.

"Kiss me," I said, my heart pounding in my chest.

His hand freezes in place, hovering over the spot where he was about to pour the last pancake. He looks up at me, a mix of surprise and nervousness in his eyes. "What happened to waiting until everything settled down?"

"That was before you wooed me with all those pretty words and logical reasoning."

His expression stays neutral as he blinks at me. "I swear... I think you just broke me. The first thing that popped into my head was, 'So you're saying there's a chance? Yeah!'"

I can't help but let out an audible groan in response to his Dumb and Dumber reference. "Seriously? After all this time and training, that's the only line that comes to mind when a girl asks you to kiss her?"

"That's not the *only* thing, but it was, unfortunately, the first thing."

I roll my eyes playfully, unable to hide the smile tugging at my lips. "Fine, moment postponed. Finish making those pancakes; there's something else I need to talk to you about."

"Okay..." He glances quickly at me before grabbing the spatula and flipping the pancakes with a practiced hand. "What's on your mind?"

I take a deep breath, trying to calm my nerves, before mumbling out, "I spoke to Luke. He's agreed to let me speak at the press conference tomorrow."

"What?" His posture goes ramrod straight, his head whipping up to look at me.

"Cyrus is having Governor Greene speak on his behalf—the political agenda of police reform and brutality. Which, in this case, is a grotesque overuse of title and policies. However, if I don't share my side of the story, the world is going to believe whatever they say."

"Fucking hell, Isla." His tone doesn't hold an ounce of anger, but the despair is thick. "That's... Are you sure you want to do that?" Am I sure? Absolutely not. But sometimes doing the right thing isn't an easy thing.

"What else is there to do, Ev? Everyone thinks we had an affair!"

"No. Not everyone. The media? Sure, but they'll move on in a week when the next scandal hits. But, La, I promise you, no one from around here—no one that matters anyway—believes those lies." He waves the spatula at me while he's talking, emphasizing each point. "I have at least thirty texts and even more phone calls from people around here, reassuring me of that—and I've only lived here for seven months. Everyone knows how Jeff treated you; they know we were friends, and they know we never crossed a line. Because they know us. They know you."

I stare at the same spot on the counter in front of me, mulling over what he's saying. My phone looks mostly the same, though I've tried to avoid looking at it too much. Each time I do, I see an influx of messages from people in town offering their support, even a few busybodies encouraging me to start something with Everett.

But it's not even what the town thinks that worries me. It's the Waltons going after Everett. His good name, which he's worked so hard to establish as more than just an Astor, is at risk of being ruined. My father and Cyrus won't stop digging until they uncover everything about Everett and his past—his relationship with his parents, and the reasons behind their estrangement. They'll come after Odessa too, scrutinizing her career and speculating about her rise to fame. They'll stop at nothing... unless I stop them.

"You're right, the people around here have always treated me better than my family. It's taken a really long time to realize the way my parents treat me isn't normal. All they've done is think about themselves and the optics of their lives. If I don't stand up for myself soon, they'll do whatever they can to silence me. Currently, the only cards I hold are my truth and my voice.

I can share my story, the relationship I had with Jeff and what happened that night." They'll have no choice but to believe me, especially when Luke is able to share the body cam footage. It'll back up everything I say at the press conference.

"I know, but facing the same media that's been attacking you? They're vultures. One sniff of fear and they'll eat you alive." I nod in agreement; they'll definitely try to tear me apart if they sense any weakness. But I have the Sheriff on my side, and he's the one controlling the press conference.

"Luke has a plan for that. I need you to trust me on this."

With a small sigh, his eyes locked with mine, a bit of anxiety mixing with protectiveness. "I trust you. But I'm going to be in that room for you. Stand in the back; wear a disguise if I have to."

"You think Luke will let you? I guarantee he won't think that's very advisable for your case, or at least the surrounding perception."

"I've never been wise, baby. I've made every decision in life by trusting my gut. The wisdom comes after. Tomorrow will be no different. My gut's telling me to be there; consequences and perception be damned."

"Thank god. I'm so done caring about the optics of everything," I admitted for the first time out loud. "And on that note, I don't want to be concerned if people think it's too soon. I'm ready to prioritize my happiness and what I want."

"And you want to be with me?" he asked, his tongue quickly darting out to wet his lips.

Stealing the words from his mouth, I say exactly what he said to me. "Yeah. I'm in love with you. Heart, body, mind, and soul. Haven't even kissed you, but I love you." And there it was; he was already abandoning the pancakes before I finished my declaration to come to my side of the counter.

With a smile that reached his eyes, he gently cupped my

face and kissed me. The kiss was everything I had wanted and more—sweet, sensual, and brimming with promise for the future.

As we pulled away, the look on his face made everything we had endured to get here feel worth it.

"I'd have waited the rest of my life for that kiss, but I'm so damn glad I didn't have to." The love and relief in his eyes mirrored my own as we stood there, finally together after so much anticipation. In that moment, I knew we could face whatever challenges lay ahead. Having Everett Astor by my side felt like having a beacon of strength and unwavering support to guide me through the storm.

With him by my side as a friend, I felt strong.

With him by my side as a partner, I feel invincible.

Chapter Twenty-Four

Everett

Hayes pulled into my driveway at exactly 0700 with an uneasy look on his face. The irritated attitude he brought with him did nothing to quell the anxiety that brewed the second I woke up this morning. Despite sleeping better than I have in weeks, the second my eyelids opened, anxiety creeped its way through my veins like a slow-moving poison.

Isla left late last night, leaving me feeling the best I'd felt in weeks. Having her in front of me and being able to physically see that she's okay finally put my body at ease. The high I felt seeing her didn't even dissipate when I got the text from Hayes saying they were on their way. Thankfully, they had the foresight to bring Charlie's mid-size SUV this time so that they could park in the garage. No more smuggling bodies in storage containers.

Every road in a three block radius was congested with vehicles, New's vans, and curious onlookers trying to catch a glimpse of the action. Luke has every deputy working today, as well as every volunteer in town and even some off-duty officers from neighboring towns, to help manage the chaos. For a small town, they seem to know exactly what they're doing because Hayes can navigate the crowded streets without anyone even noticing us.

Captain Ellis is the one assigned to gate duty at the back entrance of the department. He's normally a serious-looking guy, but today he appears more intimidating than anything. His eyes narrow at Hayes but when he glances at me, they soften a touch before he gives me a quick nod and lets us through.

Hayes lets out a loud sigh and shakes his head. "Not that this pertains to the situation at all, but he was one of the guys that told Olivia about Dan. Don't think he's liked me since."

"Nothing to do with you, man. The only thing he has to associate you with is the day he had to tell the wife of the deputy he trained that her husband wasn't coming home."

He nods, but doesn't say anything in response as he drives through the lot to find a parking spot.

Through the corner of my eye, I watch as he puts the truck in park and shuts it off. My thumb begins rotating on my index finger, trying to calm my nerves.

I break the heavy silence first. "Do you know what Isla intends to do today? She wouldn't tell me, but I have a feeling I'm not going to like it."

"I do know and can confirm you're not going to like it."

My neck snaps toward him, waiting for him to tell me what he knows.

"You have to let her do it, though. As much as it's about you, it's not about you at all. There are some things she wants to clear up and address. She's finally ready to stand up for herself and take control of her life."

I understand why he's saying what he's saying, but it doesn't make it any easier. From the first day I met Isla, I wanted to protect her. Letting her share her story in front of the wolves goes against every fiber of my being. Especially because today is supposed to be a giant smear campaign against me and the Cascadia County Sheriff Department.

From the sounds of it, Cyrus has Governor Greene in his pocket. They aren't aligned politically, but apparently Mayor Walton has had a sudden change of heart since his son died. At this point, I don't even know what to do or where to go. I'm already regretting not following Odessa's advice and calling Eli.

Luke meets us at the back door, opening the locked door so that we can enter without a badge. He looks as perturbed as Hayes, his jaw locked tight as he leads us into his office without saying anything. There weren't many people in the building, but those that were sent me sympathetic looks as we passed through. *Like I'm walking toward my death sentence right now.*

As I pass Jill's desk, tears fill her eyes, but she tries to blink them away. Swallowing the lump in my throat, I offer her a half smile. She's called me at least once a day to check on me and remind me that the town still loves me, despite the lies Cyrus is spreading.

"Close the door behind ya," Luke says to Hayes as he pulls out his desk chair and sits.

The door clicks shut, and then Hayes plops down in the seat next to me, extending his legs. I don't take my eyes off Luke, though. Hiding behind the Sheriff mask he has on is a very tired-looking man.

Luke clears his throat, before shuffling some papers. "Sorry that you had to come down here so early. The roads are only about to get more crowded and security is about to get a hell of a lot tighter."

"Why's that?" Hayes asks, casually. When I glance at him, he's the picture of relaxed—hands folded on his lap, head tipped back, eyes closed.

Luke, for the first time in probably weeks, cracks a genuine smile. "About thirty minutes ago, I was informed that Governor

Greene's jet got sent to the private airport in Bend. Apparently, someone of higher precedence has landed at ours."

Hayes sits up so abruptly, it's as if he's been electrocuted. With his left eyebrow arched, he gazes at me, but I maintain a tight-lipped expression. Luke seems thrilled to have his moment, so I won't take it away from him.

"Deputy Astor over here forgot to mention that he has friends in high places. Friends willing to cancel international affairs so that they can fly Air Force Two to a small town to vouch for them." *Shit. I let my head fall backward and closed my eyes.*

With a light snicker, Hayes finally catches on. "Oh, fuck. V.P. Inkwell? I forgot you knew him! He was the one who helped us with the idiots in Brazil, right?" A few months ago, Delta received a call from some Army buddies that needed help with a government contract. The guys were kidnapped by a drug cartel and the United States government basically told them, "Sorry, we don't know ya." Hayes and Drew called everyone they knew from their days as SEALs but couldn't figure anything out. With one call to Vice President Elijah Inkwell, I had the information and backup they needed to rescue Delta's friends.

"I didn't want to involve him," I divulged, a tinge of annoyance creeping into my voice. This has Odessa written all over it. I love my sister to death, but occasionally, she needs to mind her own damn business.

Luke snorted at my response, "Buckle up, buttercup. Not only is he involved, he's on his way here. Secret Service will be here in fifteen minutes."

"Fuck." The curse comes out automatically like a groan.

He smirked in response before saying, "That's not all. It's going to be a packed room, but Isla requested you two be in the press conference for moral support. You'll stand in the back and be quiet." He points between the two of us, indicating that we have no choice in the matter. Then I watch the breath he lets out, his face softening slightly as he adds, "Isla is going to need you both to keep your emotions in check. Don't look at anything besides her if you have to."

I nodded, despite being uneasy about the entire situation. At this point, I don't know if I should be more concerned about Eli being disappointed in me, or about what Isla is going to say. The two of them seem to be keeping me out of the loop on purpose, so I know I need to go with it. Sitting back and letting other people fight your battles isn't exactly easy though.

Chapter Twenty-Five

Everett

The next few hours pass slowly, each minute stretching into what feels like an eternity. Eli's entire team had to vet everyone, set up their security measures, and coordinate with the sheriff's department on how they wanted things to be run. I had already met a handful of people on his team, so it didn't take long for me to get clearance. Despite that, I never left Luke's office. I sat in the same spot, waiting for my next orders, whether they would come from Luke or the Secret Service.

"Astor!" The familiar bark of Elijah Inkwell pulled me out of my thoughts as he walked through the open door.

With a grin, I push myself out of the chair and turn to see the man I think of as family more than a friend.

"You couldn't handle my decline to Christmas dinner so much that you had to fly out here and convince me?" My right hand automatically extends for a handshake, but he pulls me into a hug instead. He might be one of the most feared and professional vice presidents we've ever had, but he's always treated me like family.

He scoffs, but laughs while doing it. "That and Cassidy would have my hide if I didn't personally come out here and speak on your behalf. After all you've done for our family?" He shakes his head and I see his throat bob as he swallows. "This is the least I could do."

A few years ago, Eli and Cassidy's daughter, Harper, was kidnapped during a state visit. I had a gut feeling that I knew where they were keeping her. Thankfully, Eli trusted my judgment and we had her home in a few hours.

"I appreciate your being here. I wish it were under different circumstances, but it means a lot to have your support."

His eyes glisten with gratitude as he nods in acknowledgement. "You're family to us, always."

It doesn't feel like that long ago I was saying the same thing to Isla. Trying to convince her to take the help we were offering. Now I'm the one carrying the guilt of being a burden.

Without wasting any time, Luke gives the go ahead and escorts Eli into the conference room. He's allowing Hayes and me to slink into the back, as long as we can keep our heads down and mouths shut. It's a relief to have Luke in charge of the situation, knowing that he has our backs no matter what.

The conference room we normally use for SAR meetings has been set up for the press since the day the incident happened. A small podium is at the front of the room, and four rows of chairs are set up, each with eight occupied chairs. Thankfully, the room is big enough that the reporters can fit, as well as their camera crew, without everyone being squeezed in.

I try to keep my eyes trained on the front of the room, letting myself blend into the background of the wall as Luke gives his welcome speech. My brain is itching to seek the Mitchells and the Waltons, but I refuse to glance their way. They don't deserve a second of my attention after what they've done to us the last few weeks.

Mayor Greene sits off to the side of the podium, next to Eli. The sour look of a jealous woman who just lost the popularity contest is written all over her face. The only reason she is here is to push her own political agenda, transforming the tragedy that occurred into an opportunity for her to gain more power.

Eli, though, has nothing to gain from being here and backing me. If anything, it could hurt his campaign in the upcoming election. It doesn't stop him from sitting up there—next to a viper in a pantsuit—looking every bit as calm and collected as he always does, though.

Luke begins speaking, his facial expression impassive. "I appreciate you all being here, but I would like to remind you all of a few things—there will be no questions today, no outbursts, and no disrespectful behavior towards our guest speakers. There will be no second chances or warnings before your ass is thrown out." His tone leaves no room for misinterpretation, conveying a clear message of authority and control over the situation. Luke isn't just a big guy; he's also got a big presence that demands respect from everyone in the room. If I didn't know what a big softy he was, he'd be downright terrifying.

"Damn, that almost get you too?" I murmur to Hayes under my breath.

Without missing a beat, Hayes whispers, "Shakin' in my boots."

The laugh that wants to come out is so forceful that I have to cover my mouth with my clenched fist to stifle it.

"Alright, everyone. Vice President Inkwell would like to say a few words first." His right-hand gestures to Eli as he stands and buttons his suit jacket. They both shake hands, doing the standard exchange of pleasantries before Eli steps up to the podium. The room was already silent, but now it feels like the air itself is holding its breath, waiting for Eli's words to break the tension.

"Good morning, everyone. It's interesting to see some of you here that I normally see back home." He nods toward some of the reporters who are high up and well known in Washington. Surely, they had a tip that he'd be here today, but it's still mind-boggling to me that they'd fly all the way out here to cover it.

"I've shared this story a few times over the last several years — even giving an exclusive to one of the networks in the front row—so I'm in disbelief as to why the big media has allowed a defamatory narrative about Everett Astor's military achievements to be circulated when they know the truth of his heroic actions. Nevertheless, I'm happy to stand here before you and remind you to put an end to the false information being spread."

Eli takes a second to collect his thoughts before continuing, letting go of the scolding tone he had. With a deep breath, he began the story of how we met. "I had only been sworn into office for two months when my daughter, Harper Inkwell, served as an assistant to senior diplomat Westley Christianson in Kabul Province, Afghanistan. A suicide bomb ripped through a secure area, killing at least 75 people and wounding close to 500. The US embassy, although not as close to the explosion as our foreign counterparts, became the next target of the terrorist group responsible. Within seconds of the initial attack, the US Embassy was under siege and four staffers were kidnapped before we were able to secure the safety of the remaining personnel."

His hand rhythmically taps the outside of the podium, his eyes growing haunted. "Harper was one of the kidnapped staffers, and we immediately launched a rescue mission to bring them home safely. Chief Warrant Officer 2 Astor had eyes in the sky before I could even get to the command center to coordinate the operation. He'd been flying the city of Kabul for only six weeks, but his attention to detail, quick thinking, and skill as a pilot made him an invaluable asset to the operation that saved my daughter as well as the three other U.S. citizens."

Memories flood through my mind as he speaks. I may not have been there that long, but there's a unique mentality that only pilots understand. A focus that allows us to not just see what's happening below, but also remember the intricate details of the terrain and landmarks. There may be hundreds of different people walking through a city when we fly by, but a brick is out of place and we can tell.

"CW2 Astor flew for over six hours with his copilot, Chief Warrant Officer 2 Clause, only stopping to refuel. I was in contact with him sparsely through the entire ordeal, trying to gain intel from the other special forces units we had on the ground. I kept coming back to their team, though, trying to understand the logic behind their unique flight pattern. By chance, I had just tuned in when I heard him ask, 'Any of the victims seen wearing a gold, floral brooch covered in diamonds?'

Logan, known to us as Santa, joined us a few months after I did, always respecting my opinion and trusting my judgment. We'd been circling the same sparkling glint for hours, trying to determine what had caught my eye the first time we passed by. Every time we got close, something would distract us, pulling us away from the spot.

Finally, I started tracking each diversion, gradually narrowing my focus as I worked to pinpoint what had grabbed my attention. Just as the last bit of sunlight began to crest the horizon, I spotted the glint again and locked in on it. A sparkle peeked out from between loose rubble and a crumbling wall next to an abandoned mosque. Heat sensors hadn't picked up anything, and intelligence had already cleared the building, but my gut told me there was something there.

I flew low enough to capture an exact image and send it back to the command center.

"My wife and I had given our daughter a Cosmos brooch, adorned with diamonds, when she graduated from Duke a few years prior. To be honest, I never liked the thing. It was too expensive, too flashy, and barely the size of a silver dollar. Harper fell in love with it, though; from the second she saw it, she wore the gaudy thing everywhere." The breath he lets out is half a laugh and half emotion.

His head nods as he takes another deep breath and lets it out slowly. "There isn't a feeling in the world that can describe what it's like to feel your hope vanishing by the second. Knowing that your daughter is among three other hostages being held, God knows where, by a terrorist organization. Held by the same individuals who just killed and injured dozens of civilians. Having the most elite forces trying to track them down and not finding anything. To then have that hope reignited by hearing the words brooch covered in diamonds. I'll tell you, if I wasn't already a believer in miracles, I certainly am now. It was a glimmer of hope in the darkness that we desperately needed." He looks up at the reporters, knowing the impact of his words.

"CW2 Astor and CW2 Clause could have given up after the first hour—when they were taking fire, when their team couldn't find any leads, or when their superiors allowed the other rotary-aviator crews to give up the search. They didn't, though. Instead, CW2 Astor explained in detail to CW2 Clause why he was doing what he was doing, what they were looking for, and why trusting your gut is just as important as following protocol. Not once did he ever stray from his training, risk himself, CW2 Clause, or the mission. Yet, he honed in on one spark of light that hadn't been there in the days preceding this mission."

It felt as if I were tracking a lone cookie crumble that Hansel and Greta had left as a clue before they made it to the gingerbread house. Thankfully, Santa had my back the entire time, allowing me to focus on my secular mission while he covered our asses to make sure we weren't shot down. Our communication skills were always top-notch, allowing us to seamlessly coordinate our movements.

"If CW2 Astor hadn't trusted his gut, we wouldn't have known that a tunnel had been dug beneath the mosque that led to the outskirts of the city. My daughter, as well as the three others', were found thirty minutes after he found that brooch. A team of Navy SEALs used his intelligence to locate and rescue them, bringing them back safely and without any civilian casualties." Cooper had been on that mission, but I hadn't known him at the time. We didn't make the connection until one night when we were all having beers at the bar.

"Now, many of you may be wondering why I flew out here to give a speech I could've given in Washington. Well, neither my family nor I will ever allow someone to slander the mission that CW2 Astor and CW2 Clause accomplished. To be frank, I don't give a damn what political position you hold or which political position I'm going for— I will always defend and respect the hero who puts others before himself. The hero who fought for our country to make sure our families can sleep peacefully at night—and still does it. To me, that hero will always be CW2 Astor. He may be a "rookie" at the Cascadia County Sheriff Department, but he is a decorated veteran who continues to serve his community with bravery and dedication. To see his name and accomplishments slandered throughout the country over baseless assumptions and accusations is truly disgusting. The outright defamation spewed about him will be fought against fiercely." His eyes linger a second longer on Cyrus before they cross through the room again.

"Everett has proven himself time and time again, rising through the ranks to become one of the most respected pilots in our country. I only know the details that the public does regarding the night of December 5th, but I can say with certainty that he is a man of integrity and honor. I trust the other agency to handle the case without bias from either side and allow the truth to prevail. Thank you." With a single nod and hand wave, he leaves the room—Secret Service flanking his sides.

Luke approaches the podium once again. "Thank you for speaking, Vice President Inkwell. I'm going to take this opportunity to remind *everyone*, once again, that your presence is not necessary in this room. If I so much as hear a whisper, I will personally drag you out of this room." Luke's authoritative tone silenced the room once again. "Mayor Greene will speak after Isla Mitchell. Please remain quiet and respectful during their speeches. Thank you."

Shocked gasps rippled through the crowd as Luke's announcement about Isla caught them off guard. The reporters may have been privy to Eli coming to town, but I can guarantee they had no idea that Isla was going to share her side of the events.

With bated breath, I watch as Isla glides through the side door. She may still have bruises and a dressing covering her nose, but she carries herself with a quiet strength that demands attention. I can't help but admire everything about her. Tight jeans, a fitted blazer, and heels that click confidently as she walks. Her honey brown locks are curled and left loose, tucked behind her ears, reminding me of the first time I saw her. She's not wearing a stitch of makeup to cover up the evidence of her recent ordeal, and yet she's still the most beautiful woman in the room. As she approaches the podium, the entire room stares at her like she's about to reveal the secrets of the universe.

Chapter Twenty-Six

Isla

The podium at the front of the room is the only thing holding me up at this point. I spent two hours this morning trying to write a speech that would convey the gravity of the trauma I endured.

But now that I'm up here, staring at dozens of nameless faces, all my carefully chosen words seem to have evaporated from my mind. The weight of their expectant gazes feels suffocating, and I can feel my palms starting to sweat as I struggle to express the depth of my emotions.

It isn't until I catch sight of Everett standing at the back of the room that my breathing begins to level out. The reporters and camera crew fade into the background as I focus solely on him, drawing strength from his presence.

"My name is Isla Mitchell. You may not recognize me from the pictures that are being displayed across your screen, but my surgeon assures me that once everything has healed, I'll look just as I did."

A few awkward chuckles roll through the room as I take another breath to steady myself.

"To be honest, it's disappointing that I have to stand here at all, sharing a personal story about the abuse I endured—not even two weeks after it happened. However, I feel a responsibility to share my recollection of the events that occurred that night so that the rumors are shut down," I say pointedly.

Keeping my eyes trained on the crowd, but without looking specifically at anyone, I confided to a group of people that were just spewing garbage about me. "Thursday night, the night before Jeff attacked me, I came home later than Jeff had anticipated. He was expecting me to make dinner for him and his friends, and after they left, he was drunk and angry. After I had gone to bed, he cruelly woke me up to belittle me. I called his father, who promptly picked him up so that he could sober up at his house. The next day, I began packing my things. Jeff showed up that afternoon, still drunk, and when he saw me packing, attacked me. I was in and out of consciousness for hours, but eventually, was able to escape the house."

I inhale deeply, trying to push away the memories of pain and fear that linger. Despite everything, I know that sharing my story is a crucial step toward healing and moving forward.

"I'll admit, that was the first time he had been that aggressive toward me. Before that, he spent a lot of time belittling me and making idle threats against me and my friends. I stayed with him, not for love, but out of fear and guilt. Fear of the power he had—being Mayor Walton's son and working for his office. Guilt over being a disappointment to my family. It felt impossible to leave him without losing everything, and it wasn't until that night that I realized I'd rather lose it all, including my parents, than be with someone who treats me like that."

As I speak, my eyes instinctively find my dad first. He's sitting next to Cyrus like a loyal guard dog, an expression of impassive stubbornness etched on his face. Their wives sit on either side of them, both with stern eyes fixed straight ahead.

Neither of them has the courage to look at me as I share my story. My mother, who should be supporting me above all others, hasn't shed a single tear.

Without any hesitation, I lock my gaze on my mom, laying bare the pain and betrayal I've experienced. "My parents, as well as his, downplayed every argument, every fight, and every red flag that was waving right in front of their faces. They treated me like I was overreacting, like I was the problem. And I let them. I allowed myself to be treated as if my feelings didn't matter, as if my pain wasn't valid. I did everything I could to paint myself as the 'perfect daughter,' the 'perfect girlfriend,' and the 'perfect future daughter-in-law.'"

The only sign that my words are having an effect on my mom is the slight tremor in her hands. When I glance next to her, I see Cyrus whispering low into my dad's ear. *Keeping that leash on tight.*

"I was loyal to a fault, nearly to my own demise—almost to my own funeral. There will always be people who refuse to believe my truth; they'll say I deserved it or that I brought it upon myself. But I know the reality of what I endured, and I am stronger for having survived it."

I pause and glance at Everett, searching for strength in his gaze. "I'd like to warn you that the video about to be displayed is extremely graphic and may be triggering for some viewers. Viewer discretion is advised."

With a heavy breath, I nod to Luke to start the video behind me. I had asked to watch the entire thing beforehand, just to prepare myself for what would be shown. I thought it would be more difficult than it was, but seeing it again brings me a strange sense of peace. The sheer craziness of it all reaffirms that I wasn't the problem; I was simply a pawn in their game.

I know where it starts: the night before, when I had to call

Cyrus to pick up his son. I can see the events replay in the audience's eyes—the sick way he woke me up because I hadn't made dinner, the way he lunges at me when I stand up for myself, the tantrum he threw before his dad arrived to pick him up. Every face in the audience grows more solemn as they witness the raw footage of my abusive relationship.

After a brief pause, the second video begins to play—Jeff coming home to find me packing up my belongings, the threats he uses to keep me from leaving, all leading up to the physical attack. Each hit is followed by low gasps from the audience as they watch in horror.

Despite the chaos on the screen, I keep my focus on Everett at the back of the room. He hasn't broken eye contact with me; his expression filled with pride and love. He doesn't realize he's the one giving me the courage to stay up here and face this head-on.

When the second video ends, the silence in the room is deafening. My hands begin to shake uncontrollably, forcing me to clasp them together and set them on the podium.

Within a second, video number three begins—a montage of the outside security footage. I see myself, half-running, half-limping as I sprint barefoot through the snow. My desperate attempt to find a hiding spot beneath a tree along the road is all too clear. The timestamp shows twenty minutes later when Jeff starts searching for me, shotgun in hand. Moments later, the marked Cascadia County Sheriff Department vehicle approaches the driveway. I can hardly watch as the dark silhouette of me crawls on the ground, making a last-ditch effort to throw myself into the road, seeking safety. The footage captures the moment when Luke releases the audio of Everett shooting Jeff, as well as when backup arrives.

It's all laid bare, left for the entire world to see and form their opinions on.

When the clips finally end, I raise my chin, mustering every ounce of confidence I can find. "I literally crawled out of the woods to save my own life," I whisper, feeling a mix of relief and fear as the truth is finally revealed. The weight of the situation settles heavily on my shoulders; I realize there's no turning back now.

"Call it luck, divine intervention, or whatever you want, but I made it out alive because Deputy Astor found me on the side of the road. Everything that led to that moment was Jeff's fault. How Jeff conducted himself when he came into contact with a deputy after I was found is on Jeff. Period. I did not ask to be threatened. I did not ask to be physically assaulted. I sure as hell did not put a gun in his hands, nor did Deputy Astor."

Most of the reporters wear somber expressions as they listen to me speak, and it feels oddly satisfying to see their reactions. The rowdy crowd that once spoke over each other to ask Vice President Inkwell questions is long gone. A few women have tears streaming down their faces, while the men shift uncomfortably in their seats. There's something vindicating in knowing that my truth is resonating with them; it seems the video did exactly what it was meant to do—discredit the lies Cyrus spun about Jeff and me, about Everett, and about how the Cascadia County Sheriff Department trains its force.

"Vice President Inkwell just expressed his eternal gratitude to Everett for the courage he showed in saving his daughter in Afghanistan. I'd like to take a moment to express mine, especially since my parents will never do the same." The small dig toward my parents doesn't do much to quell my anger toward them, but I choose to leave it at that and be done with them.

"A lesser man might have bowed to the threats from the mayor's son. He could have handed me back over and left me to die. But Deputy Astor wasn't that man. He put himself, his career, and his reputation on the line to save me." I take a breath, letting the weight of my words sink in. "He's had a smear campaign waged against him across the country. His military accomplishments have been challenged, and his character, integrity, and devotion to helping others have been attacked. Yet, through it all, he has handled these challenging circumstances with remarkable tact and selflessness. His kindness, his friendship, and his unwavering commitment to doing what is right have never faltered."

Locking eyes with Everett once more, I try to convey just how truly thankful I am for him. "Deputy Astor, my friend, is a true hero in every sense of the word, and I will forever be grateful for him saving me that night."

With a single nod as my parting gesture, I leave the conference room and walk straight into Luke's office.

Chapter Twenty-Seven

Everett

The second Isla finished her speech, Hayes and I moved in sync to skirt around the cameras toward Luke's office. The next speaker is Governor Greene, and I don't care to listen to her fumble over her words after hearing Eli's speech and then Isla's. If she's smart, she'll keep her mouth shut and rattle off some bullshit about her faith in the investigation and how sorry she is for all involved.

With long strides, we catch up to her before she gets to the hall and follow behind her like bodyguards. Luke can kiss my ass if he has a problem with me staying with Isla. I'm not letting her out of my sight until she is safely back at Hayes and Charlie's house.

Her hurried steps finally come to a halt when she nearly slams into two men in suits blocking the door to Luke's office.

"Oh my god, I'm so sorry," she stumbles over her words, stepping back and crashing into me. My arms instinctively snake around her waist, pulling her closer.

"You're okay, La. It's just me," I murmur into her ear. She

instantly relaxes against me and then turns, wrapping her arms around my waist.

"You did so good up there." Understatement of the year, but it needed to be said. "Come on. I want to introduce you to someone." I gently slide my fingers down her arm until I reach her hand, lacing my fingers with hers.

She looks at me with such trust and admiration that I can't help but smile.

Hayes tips his chin toward an empty chair at the end of the hall, signaling that he's giving us some privacy.

I nod to the guys, and they step aside, allowing us into Luke's office. Eli is sitting behind Luke's desk, watching the TV on the wall. Five other men in suits stand around the room, their eyes flashing toward our intrusion, but none of them move.

"Eli, this is Isla—my reason." His eyes widen with unspoken understanding before a grin spreads across his face as he stands up.

Reluctantly, I let go of her hand and rest my palm on her back. "Isla, my friend Eli."

Isla splutters, her jaw dropping as she glances at me. "Oh my god. Eli? As in the friend you told me you normally spend your Christmases with? You didn't mention he's the Vice President of the United States!"

With a chuckle, Eli steps around the desk and pulls her into a hug. "Used to. He declined this year—something vague about having personal matters to attend to." His eyebrow arches in my direction as he pulls away.

"You already gave the lecture. I won't keep things as close to the vest anymore," I acquiesce.

"Fair enough. Isla, it's a pleasure to meet you; I only wish it were under better circumstances." He gives her a sympathetic look before continuing. "Next time, though, you'll get to meet my reason. Cassidy will be green with envy when I tell her I got to meet you before she did. This summer, come to our place in Virginia. It's right along the Potomac, with beautiful views and plenty of rooms."

Isla's jaw practically drops to the floor as she processes the invitation. "I would love to visit and meet your wife. Thank you for the offer," she replies, slightly stuttering but with genuine gratitude. The thought of spending time in such a beautiful location with my stunning girl and my second family brings a smile to my face.

"It's settled, then." He winks at her before turning to me and gripping my shoulder a little too hard. "Gwen will get in touch with the details. No more BS excuses, Everett. You're family to us."

Still grinning, I nod in agreement. "Promise. We'd love to be there."

"Great! Again, lovely to meet you, Isla. I'll see you both in a few months." With a final wave, he walks away, flanked by his Secret Service team.

Isla turns to me, curiosity lighting up her face. "What did you mean by 'my reason'?"

Instead of explaining right away, I lead her deeper into the office, settling into the same chair I occupied the night I found her. It feels like years ago that Luke escorted me back here, not less than two weeks.

Gently, I pull her down into my lap, holding her as close as I can. "A few months after the mission with Harper, Eli and Cassidy invited Santa and me to their home for Christmas. We were given plus ones; I brought Odessa, and Santa brought his wife, Sofia. Eli shares the story every year at Christmas about his own near-death experience during his time in the Navy. I'll save the details for him to tell you, but the moral is that the only reason he had the strength to keep going was because of

Cassidy—his wife, best friend, and biggest supporter. He knew he could never give up because she needed him as much as he needed her. She was his reason. For living, for fighting, for breathing."

As I speak, I notice her thumb begins to stroke the side of my face. It's a simple gesture, but I hadn't realized how much I craved that connection until she stopped. She keeps her hand resting on my cheek until I meet her eyes. "You were my reason that night. You'll always be my reason."

My hands tangle in her hair as I pull her down for a light kiss. We should be more cautious about what's happening in Luke's office, but in that moment, I couldn't care less if Detective Smith herself walked in.

She smiles as she pulls away. "I have something to ask you, but I don't want you to feel pressured to say yes. I can easily find somewhere else."

I shake my head, brushing my lips against hers again. "Yes."

"You don't even know what I wanted to ask!" She laughs, her eyes sparkling with amusement. "Can I stay with you? I'm sure Connie would want to stay with Charlie and Hayes, and with Charlie due in a matter of weeks, I don't want to—"

I hadn't realized my smile could grow wider, but hearing Isla ask for what she wants so openly feels like a dream come true.

"Of course you can move in with me," I say, pulling her in tighter. "I wouldn't have it any other way."

Her hands rest loosely on my shoulders. "Shouldn't you talk to your roommate before agreeing to this?"

"Nah, he's moving out anyway. I doubt he'll let Olivia be more than ten feet from him for a few years."

Before she can respond, a loud knock sounds at the door, and she practically jumps out of my lap.

Luke steps in, looking between the two of us like a parent

walking in on teenagers making out on the couch. "Am I interrupting something?" he asks with a smirk as he takes a seat in the empty chair behind his desk.

Isla blushes and stammers out a response while I chuckle at the situation. Luke shakes his head in amusement before switching back to boss mode.

He waves his hand dismissively. "Ignorance is bliss. But I do need to chat with you both."

Isla looks relieved at the change of topic, though curiosity flickers in her eyes as she waits for Luke to continue. He leans back in his chair, rolling his neck before letting out a sigh.

"I spoke to Detective Smith before I released the video. Since you both have given your statements and the footage aligns with your accounts, you are now free to communicate."

My shoulders sag with relief. "That doesn't mean the case is closed, though. It just means Detective Smith feels comfortable that allowing you to talk won't jeopardize it. I'd still advise you refrain from any public spectacles or discussing the case with anyone outside this room." Luke's tone is serious, but the relief in his eyes is evident. This hasn't just been a hard case for Isla and me; our friends, the department, and the town have all suffered in some way.

Isla squares her shoulders, narrowing her eyes at Luke. "I'm moving in with Everett. I don't have a home to go back to. Charlie is due with the baby soon, and they don't need to be taking care of me, too. Everett is graciously allowing me to stay with him."

I watch Luke's expression shift from concern to incredulity before he barks out a laugh. "'Graciously,' my ass, Isla. You two have been dancing around each other for months. The circumstances are shit, but I'm happy for both of you."

Isla's cheeks flush as she looks down, a small smile playing on her lips. "Thanks, Luke. It means a lot." Meanwhile, I sit, my eyes volleying between the two of them, trying to figure out what the hell is going on.

"So, we can go? Home together? No more hiding in storage containers?" I ask, looking at Luke.

He closes his eyes and pinches the bridge of his nose. "Ignorance is bliss," he chants lowly to himself a few times. "Keep it on the down-low, but I don't have any arguments. The case should be closed by mid-February. They usually want everything wrapped up in about ten weeks."

I let out a sigh of relief, feeling the tension finally start to dissipate.

I stand up, offering my hand. "Let's get out of here." She takes it willingly, waving goodbye to Luke as we walk out.

Hayes is already on his feet, taking long strides to position himself on the other side of Isla. I have no doubt Luke kicked everyone else out beforehand to avoid any ambush, but that doesn't mean Hayes or I won't be ready for anything.

"I take it you two got the green light?" Hayes asks, his eyes scanning in front of us.

"Yeah. And I'll be getting out of your hair soon. Ev said I can stay with him," she assures quietly.

Hayes stops mid-stride, grabbing her bicep to halt her. "You're joking."

We exchange glances before he shakes his head in disbelief. "Oh, shit. Charlie's gonna kill you. You know how hard it was to let Isla come here without her? She's going to freak."

I smirk, fully aware of Charlie's overprotective nature. "Well, it's a good thing she'll have you to take it out on."

Isla opens her mouth, then closes it again, looking at me with pleading eyes. "Give me one more night with her. Hayes is right—she'll need a little closure before I leave."

Hayes' lips twitch at the annoyed look on my face, clearly reveling in every minute of Isla taking his side over mine. I know it's good for her to spend some time with Charlie after everything that's happened, but that doesn't lessen my irritation. A sense of minor disappointment flares within me, but I force myself to shove it down. Isla's mine now; she's moving in, and one more night won't kill me. It'll also give me time to clear some space in the closet and empty out the drawers for her. Judging by the amount of stuff on her desk and in her gym locker, she's going to need the room.

With a groan, I nod. "Fine, but tomorrow you're mine. Charlie can deal."

A maniacal laugh escapes Hayes, his shoulders shaking. "I love it when Spicy Sunshine comes out and isn't directed at me. Just be careful—she's been on a real warpath lately, and I'm not protecting you."

"It'll be fine," Isla says reassuringly. "She just wants me to be happy. I can always shed a tear if I need to."

Hayes grumbles, "Damn, women and their crocodile tears."

I tug on the hand I still hold. "Let's go. You've got some appeasing to do, and I've got some rearranging to tackle."

Chapter Twenty-Eight

Everett

A low chuckle rolls out of me as I watch Hayes step out my front door. I just got back from helping Isla pack the few things she had unpacked at his house. Currently, he's hefting three of Drew's moving boxes out of the house, each stacked on top of each other. Only a few days ago, he was carrying a similar box into my house, but instead of personal items, it held Isla. Now, Drew's boxes are heading to Olivia's house and Isla's boxes will be moving in.

Hayes bends his head around the side of one box and shouts, "At what age can we just fucking hire movers?"

"I got the door, Tor!" Making my way to the back of his truck, I hit the button for the tailgate to lower.

"Doesn't even make sense, man." Hayes says as he shakes his head, but sets the boxes down as gently as he can. He grabs one from the stack and places it in the bed of his truck before sliding it toward the cab.

"Do they ever?" Drew grumbles grumpily. He's already halfway to his truck, not bothering to wait for an answer. "Let's get this over with. We've all got women that we should be taking care of instead of wasting time here." He throws the boxes haphazardly into the back, not caring that the contents could be damaged.

Hayes chuckles but mutters "testy" before following suit and tossing the boxes into the back of his truck.

"Hey, asshole. How's Olivia feeling?" I shouted toward him while following him back into the house.

With a heavy sigh, he pauses in the living room. His gaze swivels around the living room, but it doesn't feel like he's looking for anything. "She's doing better," he says cautiously.

Hayes and I remain stark still, waiting for him to elaborate on how Olivia is truly doing. Drew knows how to internalize his feelings with the best of us, but occasionally, when things get too overwhelming, he lets a crack show in his tough exterior.

"I think hearing Luke say 'officer-involved shooting' brought up more trauma than she thinks it did. Losing Dan will always be a wound that never fully heals for her. Any time I leave the house, she's worried I won't come back. The kids are going stir-crazy already—she won't let them out of her sight except to go to school. I don't know if it's because she's holding on to so much guilt or the pregnancy, but anytime she thinks about Isla, she just sobs." He keeps ranting, pacing the length of the living room but my attention is still stuck on that last little piece of information he dropped. Hayes must have caught it as well, because his jaw is practically on the floor.

Drew doesn't notice our shock and continues on, oblivious to our reactions. "Jeff almost murdering her doesn't help much either. Isla was right; he's lucky I didn't fucking find him first. I would've done more than just skin him alive. I hate that—"

Hayes arm snakes out and smacks in the back of the head as he walks by him. "Hey, idiot. That's how you're going to tell us you're becoming a dad?"

Drew turns, eyes as wide as Hayes just were. "Do not fucking tell Olivia."

"We won't, but what the hell? When did she find out? When did you find out?"

His hand rubs the back of his neck before he smiles—the first goofy smile I've seen on him in a long time. "She found out at the hospital that night. Told me the next morning. We're planning on telling the kids Christmas morning and y'all at dinner."

Hayes pulls him into a hug first. "Damn, way to lock her down after the shit you pulled."

"Oh, fuck off. It wasn't like that. But I'd be lying if I said I wasn't excited and terrified at the same time."

"Time for a Melanie sandwich!" I declare, before wrapping my arms around Drew and Hayes.

Drew squirms but Hayes only wraps his arms tighter, locking Drew between us. It takes less than three seconds before Hayes is yelping and jumping back.

"You fucking pinched me?" He roars back, holding the underside of his bicep, causing us both to cackle like hyenas. The eye roll he gives before storming to grab more boxes would rival Odessa any day.

With a pat on Drew's shoulder, I offer my sincerest "happy for you, man."

As Drew and Hayes pull out of the driveway, Lincoln's Tacoma and Charlie's Aviator pass them. It takes all of me not to run down the driveway when Charlie stops to talk to Hayes. Isla is so damn close that my patience is wearing thin. Instead, I pop the tailgate of the truck and then pause.

My eyebrows hit my hairline when I see three medium-sized boxes in the back. "Do you have more in the cab?"

Linc's already hopped out of the truck and started shaking his head. "Nope—this is it. She didn't want anything else from the house, and this was what she had packed before it happened."

The passenger door closes with a soft thud, but I don't look up to see Liam get out. I'm too focused on the lack of boxes, considering we had both of the guys truck beds full when they left and Drew had only lived here for a few months.

The dull ache in my heart is back. Looking at these boxes, you'd think she was a minimalist and not the pack-rat that I know her to be at the office. Knickknacks line her desk, as well as photos of her with all of us. The kitchen has at least four mugs that she rotates through seasonally, as well as enough baking supplies to open a small bakery. Even her little cubby at the gym is full of workout gear, lotions, and random supplements. I've even seen the state of her Audi, and while it's clean, she has things tucked in every compartment.

"Starting fresh or didn't feel comfortable there?" I wonder aloud.

Lincoln, surprisingly, has an answer. "I wish I could say both, but that house was void of any Isla touches. When I installed the cameras for her, it felt like I was on a showing for a new house. Same thing when we picked up her stuff—pristine, white, replaceable."

My head cocks to the side, brow furrowing when I ask, "Replaceable?"

His shoulders sag while Liam's jaw audibly snaps shut, clenching. "Isla gave us permission to review all the footage we had stored. Once a month or so, he'd go on a bender and come home piss-drunk. Start throwing shit—photo frames, vases, candles, you name it. But the next day, everything would be back in its place, as if nothing had happened. It was like she had a duplicate set of everything, ready to replace whatever he destroyed."

I shake my head in disbelief, even though I shouldn't be

surprised. At work, she's always one step ahead, ready for any crisis. Once she's off the clock, though, she's normal, fun, and carefree. Or at least, I thought she was. Now, I'm starting to realize that this side of Isla was reserved strictly for us.

The sound of a car turning off snaps me out of my thoughts and I turn to see her closing the passenger door. Charlie groans as she slides off her seat, her hand going under her belly for support.

"How ya doin', mama?" I ask as she waddles toward the front bumper.

Her eyes narrow on me, like I'm the root of all her problems. "Got a bone to pick with you, Astor."

My hands instinctively raise and I sidestep closer to Isla. "Don't hide behind your girl. I'm mad at her too!" She stabs her key in Isla's direction and then plants a hand on her hip.

"Is this one of those, 'I should already know why so you're not going to tell me moments?'"

Isla giggles from next to me and I sidle up closer to her, wrapping my arm around her waist.

"As a matter of fact, you should know! Moving her in with you? She's my best friend! I finally had her safe in my house. Where I could watch her every move and keep track of every sneeze."

Isla whispers under her breath something about being suffocated and I have to stifle a laugh. Charlie is earnest in her hormonal outburst over her best friend, but Isla seems to take it all in stride with her usual humor and wit.

"Char, I promise you that I will keep her equally, if not more, safe. I also promise to text you any time she sneezes." That earns me an elbow to my ribcage, but I can tell by the twinkle in Isla's eye that she appreciates my attempt at lightening the mood.

Charlie, thankfully, backs off. "Okay because you know,

Doctor Chipper gave really strict instructions on how she should sneeze and care for her nose after everything. I'll send you all the documents I have and all the webpages I saved."

With a small chuckle, I nodded. "I'll read them all."

"You better," she replied, tears welling in her eyes. "Don't think this means I'm not happy for you both. I love you both, and I've been hoping you two would figure your shit out and be together. It just... it feels chaotic and sudden, and I was really scared. I'm sorry; I'm a blubbering mess. But I'm happy for you."

"Hey, it's okay," I said softly, stepping closer to her and pulling her into a hug. "I know you're just looking out for our girl. I get it. We both know what a mess I was last week."

Isla chimed in behind me, her voice teasing yet scolding. "Now you're gonna make me cry!"

Lincoln chuckled, shaking his head. "Bunch-a saps around here."

A snort escaped Liam. "Says the guy who broke a knuckle last week." I had heard whispers that Lincoln had punched something in reaction to the security video, but the details were hazy—everyone was still reeling from the events of the last few days.

Gingerly, Lincoln rubbed his thumb over his knuckles, scoffing at the memory. "Don't act like you didn't become a monk for 24 hours after *you* saw it."

Liam grabbed a box from the truck, a smirk spreading across his face. "Had to stick to the schtick."

Lincoln rolled his eyes and gestured to Charlie. "Come on, it's freezing, and Hayes will skin me alive if you're out here too long." He winked at Isla before holding out his hand to help Charlie up the stairs.

As I watched them move, my heart swelled with gratitude. With each step inside, it felt more real—Isla and I were taking this leap together, and I knew that despite the chaos, we would find our way through it. Just then, Isla placed her hand on my chest, pausing us before we followed the others.

"Wait. Can we have a second alone?" Nerves skirt their way all the way down to my toes as I nod my head. When everyone is in, she looks up at me, her anxiety warring on her.

"Are you sure you want me to move in? Everyone in town is going to have an opinion. I don't want you to feel pressured because of the situation.

I take a deep breath, placing my hand over hers on my chest. "La, baby. I want you here with me. The town already has an opinion about us, some good and some bad. At this point, it's only about what makes us happy. If you're not ready, I'll be bummed, but I can wait."

Her eyes soften, and a smile plays at the corners of her lips as she leans in for a quick kiss. "I'm ready."

I've been wanting to hear her say that since the first day I met her. Those two little words could have a million different meanings, but in this case, they mean my dreams are coming true.

I finally have Isla, and there's no way I'm going to lose her.

Chapter Twenty-Nine

Isla

Tap, tap, tap.

The lightest knock came from the front door, and I swiveled so fast in the chair that I almost fell off. I've barely had a sip of the delicious coffee that Everett made for me, and the sun is just starting to brighten the sky outside—yet someone is already knocking on our door. Everett's in the shower, but knowing how paranoid he is, I'm sure he's already checked the alert to make sure whoever is here is safe. It's sweet how protective he's been the last few days, ensuring I want for nothing and know how loved I am—a stark contrast to my last living situation.

My bare feet softly pat against the wood floors as I wonder which member of the "Bod Squad" has come by to see if Everett can play. Olivia jokingly coined the nickname for the EFSC guys when they first arrived in Three Sisters, and it's been stuck in my head ever since.

Fully expecting a large, buff dude, I'm taken aback to find the short brunette who coined the nickname in the first place. Instantly, I sense that something is off. Her hair is thrown together in a messy bun, her pale face devoid of makeup, and she's still in her flannel pajamas, the pants tucked into a pair of worn-out boots. Meanwhile, the sun rises in the background, casting pink hues over the natural desert landscaping in the front yard. The wild look in her light-brown eyes sends my heart racing. She looks both guilty and sad—not exactly the best combination to greet me with after the last few weeks.

My mouth drops open, but all that escapes is a visible breath in the chilly air. Thankfully, she speaks first, wringing her hands nervously. "Can I come in?"

I step aside and open the door wider, stumbling over my words. "Of course! What happened? What's wrong?"

She glances down, toeing off her boots as I close the door behind her. I can't help but stare at her, waiting for the blow that's about to come. It's been one thing after another, and I'm not sure how many hits I can take before I stop bouncing back.

Without responding, she starts walking toward the kitchen.

I follow behind her, swallowing my unease, waiting for her to say something.

Her gaze flitters around the house as she moves; she seems comfortable, even though I know it can't be easy to be back here. As she reaches the kitchen, her hand glides over the wooden dining table. For a moment, it pauses, and then she turns to look at me.

Her eyes sparkle with unshed tears before she says, "Nothing new has happened, but I need to tell you something. It's been eating away at me for weeks, and I don't know if there will ever be a good time to tell you."

My head begins to nod unsteadily. "Coffee? This sounds like it's going to be a long conversation," I suggest, trying to lighten the heavy atmosphere. She nods gratefully, and I quickly grab a mug from the cabinet and pull out the fresh pot.

"WAIT, no!" Olivia suddenly shouts, her urgency slicing through the air.

A loud shriek escapes me as I slam the pot back into the machine as if it's on fire. My heart pounds in my chest as I whip around to face her.

The bathroom door flies open, hitting the wall.

"What happened?!" Everett demands, concern etched on his face. My gaze flicks to him and lingers on the sight of him wrapped in just a towel, water still clinging to his skin and dripping from his hair.

"Shit! Sorry! I didn't mean to yell," Olivia says, throwing her head back and groaning in frustration. "I'm messing this all up. I've already had a stupid cup of coffee today."

The tension in my body hasn't dissipated, but Everett's shoulders sag, and a grin spreads across his face when he looks at her—the grin he gets when he knows something he shouldn't.

"We have that raspberry leaf tea that Charlie drinks all the time. It's in the drawer by the oven," he says, gesturing with his head.

Without pause, I react to his retreating shape. "Charlie only drinks that because she's pregnant."

Looking back at Olivia, I see that she has her head in her hands now, a small laugh shaking her shoulders.

"You're pregnant?!" It's my turn to nearly shout at her.

"I'm so bad at keeping secrets. Don't tell Andrew! Unless he already blabbed, in which case he's—" she points toward Everett—"not as intuitive as we think he is."

"Is that why you're here?" I ask, a mix of confusion and excitement bubbling in my voice. Olivia is one of the best moms I know, and her kids are among my absolute favorites in the world.

"No, it's not that," she replies, her tone heavy as the solemn mood sweeps over her again. She lets out a sigh that seems to carry the weight of the world.

"Then what is it?!" I press, my voice rising a little more dramatically than I normally would.

"The Waltons didn't pay off your medical debt," she replies, her voice remains steady but is clearly laced with concern.

"Wait, what?" I exclaim, incredulity flooding my tone.

Her face remains composed, but her eyes betray the worry she's been hiding. "While you were in the hospital, someone made an offhand remark about you thinking your parents felt like they owed the Waltons."

I raise an eyebrow, skepticism creeping in. "They do. I couldn't complain about a hangnail without my mom saying I needed to be thankful for the life I have because of Cyrus."

She frowns, crossing her arms tightly. "Well, he isn't God, and he sure as hell didn't pay a dime toward your medical expenses."

"You're shittin' me, right?" The words tumble out of my mouth before I can think better of it. A slow grin spreads across Olivia's face, and a loud cackle echoes from the hallway as Everett catches me slipping. He rounds the corner, fully dressed now. A simple white t-shirt tucked into his dark jeans shouldn't look that good on anyone, but Everett looks down-right lick-able.

"Not my fault! Sweet Home Alabama is a classic. We watched it the day she moved in, right after Drew dropped the baby bomb and Hayes and I gave him a 'Melanie sandwich.'"

Olivia's eyes narrow on him, but she shakes her head, waving her hand dismissively. "I'll dive into that later."

Everett plants a gentle kiss on my cheek, takes the coffee pot I'm still holding, and sets it back in the machine. "I'll make the tea. You should sit, La."

I steal a quick glance at his expression, noting the mix of concern and confidence on his face. He must already know what this conversation is about, and it sends another flutter of nerves through me.

I awkwardly laugh, my body buzzing from the casual chaos.

Olivia continues as I take the seat next to hers. "So, I don't know how much you remember about the year you moved to town, but I did some digging and called Elise."

Elise Anderson is a family friend of Olivia's, someone she's known forever. Her husband, Cal, was a teacher for years before becoming the district superintendent a few years ago. She has been giving swim lessons to all the local children for many years, volunteers at every event, and is well-liked throughout the community—exactly why my mother despises her and wouldn't let me swim.

"Apparently, from the beginning, Lovey and Elise were concerned. There was something about the way your dad immediately started following Cyrus that was off-putting. She said it was like Cyrus sunk his claws into him, and your dad wouldn't blink without asking for permission first."

A light scoff escapes me. Sounds like not much has changed in the last twenty or so years, then.

Everett sets the steaming tea mug in front of Olivia, and she gives him a gracious nod, her lips curling into a soft smile.

"Thanks, Everett," she says, wrapping her hands around the warm cup.

With his coffee in hand, he sits in the chair on the other side of me, scooting it as close as he can. His jeans-clad thigh presses against my bare legs. The roughness surprisingly offers the slightest bit of comfort in the midst of our tense conversation.

Olivia leans in, her expression serious. "Lovey couldn't figure out what he was holding over his head to make him act like that, but she was determined. She always thought Cyrus was a snake in the grass, and she was genuinely afraid for you and your mom."

I blink, stunned. "She really cared that much?"

"Absolutely. Elise said she called all over the state, trying to track down where you received your care. But because of HIPAA laws, it was harder than she thought." Olivia runs a hand through her hair, frustration flickering across her face. "Finally, she spoke to someone who knew of a charity that had set up a public donation fund meant to benefit an Isla Mitchell."

I lean in, curiosity piqued. "What did she find out?"

Olivia's brow furrows slightly. "There were a few thousand dollars already applied to your fund, mostly from teachers and families from your previous school who wanted to help. The rest of the 'goal' amount had yet to be paid."

Surprise washes over me, and I shake my head slowly, leaning back. "I had no idea..." I don't remember much about my school before my parents pulled me out, but I never would have expected such generosity from people I barely knew.

Everett shifts in his seat, sliding his arm around me and gently running his fingers through my mostly tangled hair. I realize with a slight pang of embarrassment that I haven't even had the chance to brush it this morning. At least Olivia is in a similar state, looking like she just rolled out of bed. Everett, of course, looks effortlessly like a model.

It takes me half a second to refocus on the conversation, but Everett keeps us on track. "So, the charity was directly linked to the hospital or something?"

"Yep. Lovey wrote a check for the remaining amount, hoping to get your parents out of debt."

"And my parents just assumed, like I did, that it was the Waltons?"

"I don't know. I think that might be part of it? But Andrew had Linc look into your parents' relationship with Cyrus." She takes a deep breath, her eyes serious. "Did you know your dad was the prime suspect in a potential homicide case before he went to law school?"

Shock ripples through my core. "What?!"

"Who died?" Everett asks, his curiosity piqued.

"Marcus's coworker, Tony." I frown, trying to grasp the details. I don't remember much about that time; I would have only been around three or four. All I knew was that my parents found out during my dad's senior year of college that my mom was pregnant. She was only a freshman, so she dropped out. My dad had to defer going to law school to support my mom and me. I can't even recall where he was working or what type of job he had back then.

A low curse escapes Everett's lips, but he doesn't say anything else.

"I hope it's okay, but I asked the guys to look into it," she continues. "The only thing we know is that there was an accident at work and a few months later, your dad suddenly had enough money to go to law school. Linc and Luke are both digging into it to see what connection Cyrus has—if he has one, that is."

All I can do is nod at this point. The last remnants of loyalty I had toward them evaporated during the press conference. Whatever they find won't change anything, but maybe it'll explain why Cyrus has always had such a hold over my father. Perhaps it'll give me some closure, even if it doesn't change the past.

Everett gently pulls me into a hug, ensuring that my face is turned away to prevent him from bumping my nose. "We've got you," he reassures softly, his voice steady against the swirl of my thoughts.

"Whatever you need," Olivia offers, her hand reaching out to squeeze my arm.

I nod, tears filling my eyes at their acceptance of me. Shitty family and all, they've never judged me for my past and my parents.

"So, now that the cat's out of the bag... How do you feel about gloomy forever teenage vampires?"

Olivia stands up quickly. "On that note, I'm out of here. Andrew's probably freaking out that I bolted like I did this morning."

"You have no idea!" Everett exaggerates. "He's already called twice to make sure you're still here. Man's got it bad." He chuckles next to me.

"Well, that's what the big blabbermouth gets," Olivia smirks.

I leap out of my chair, rushing to cut her off before she reaches the living room. "Wait! You're having another baby! Who else knows? What did Drew say?!"

The scrunch of her face tells me she knows she's been caught. "Charlie. Well, she guessed, and I didn't confirm or deny it. No one really knows the details. Or should I say, no one should know." She gives Everett a pointed gaze, and he throws his hands up in surrender. "We're telling the kids on Christmas morning so they can feel included. Then, as a family, we will make the big announcement to fill in all the details."

The excitement in her eyes speaks volumes. It's hard to believe it was only a few weeks ago that Everett and I were concerned they might not find their way back to each other. Now it's as if the entire Heather ordeal never happened, and they're starting a new chapter together as a family.

Then again, who am I to judge? I mean, in just three weeks, I went from zero to hero—once stuck in a dismal, sexless rut to now happily enjoying a bangfest worthy of a rom-com montage.

With one last hug, I agree that mum's the word, and she heads toward the entryway to put her boots back on. Everett grabs his jacket, insisting on walking her out to her car. He's clearly still a little on edge after everything that's happened recently.

As he walks Olivia out, I collapse onto the couch and look around. It's not lost on me that I've only just moved in, yet this house already feels like home. In just two days, he managed to find the heaviest, fluffiest blanket, which now waits for me on the couch. He took the time to frame photos of every big moment we've shared over the last year and place them around the house. And then there's the warm vanilla sugar candle sitting on the coffee table—one that Ev bought before I even moved in. He swears he saw it and just knew it would be my favorite. Apparently, his freaky sixth sense extends to candles, too.

Within a minute, he's back in the house, hanging his jacket on the wall hook. When he turns around and catches me staring, he gives me an almost bashful grin. "What?"

I pat the seat next to me, smiling back. "I just can't believe this is my life. You, looking all hot after caring enough to walk my friend to her car. It's nice."

As he sits down next to me, he begins to explain, "That would be a Grandpa Astor thing." His cold hands grab my legs and drape them over him. "Walking guests out, opening doors, and all that. He was a gentleman to the core."

"You really miss him, huh?" I ask softly.

"I do. He was a good one."

I smile at him, wanting to lighten the mood. "You're a good one too, ya know."

He leans in closer, his eyes sparkling with mischief. "Oh,

I'm good at plenty of things—walking friends to their cars, being charming, and making you..." He watches my cheeks flush, his grin widening. "...flush."

My heart races, a blend of nerves and delight, and I can't help but laugh softly. He's always been a flirt, but I'm still not used to his brazen advances now that he's dropped all filters. "You're going to give me a complex with all these compliments."

I close my eyes and let out a content sigh, sinking deeper into the cushions. A girl could get used to this level of comfort and bliss.

Everett continues to click through the guide before he casually asks, "So, you really had no idea your dad might be a murderer?" His tone sounds casual, but I can see the twitch in his lip that he's fighting off a smile.

A full-on laugh escapes me at his candor. "I feel so removed from the life I had that, after the initial shock, I don't even feel fazed. My dad's a professional at evading the truth, answering just enough of a question to satisfy without actually revealing anything. And my mom, well, she's always been an expert at turning a blind eye to anything that might disrupt her perfect image."

"I know a thing or two about that. Our parents certainly know how to put on a facade, don't they?"

That they do, Ev. That they do.

Chapter Thirty

Everett

"I told you we'd be late," Isla groans while fidgeting with the hem of her ugly Christmas sweater dress while we make the short drive to Olivia and Drews. It's mostly black, fitted, and has a tiny Christmas tree print. The words 'Merry Christmas' adorn the top with tassels resembling Christmas trees below them. It's truly appalling; however, one look at her curves and I couldn't leave the house without getting under it.

With a lopsided grin, I reach out and cover her hand with mine. "Worth every minute of grief we get."

Her cheeks flushed slightly before she laced our fingers together. "Says the guy who has no shame," she retorted, a hint of a smile playing on her lips. Her bandage and splint were removed yesterday, and her bruising has faded so much that she easily covered them with makeup. She looks like my Isla again, with a newfound confidence that fills my heart.

"Psh, nothing to be ashamed of," I replied, squeezing her hand gently. "Charlie and Hayes have tortured us with PDA for years. Olivia and Drew were sneaking off to the bedroom every chance they got. It's our turn to be so madly in love that we're late to some parties."

She laughed, her eyes sparkling with adoration. "You're right. I used to envy Charlie and Hayes for the relationship they have and how connected they are on every level." She leans in to kiss me softly on the cheek. "It's quite surreal that it's barely been a week since we have been living together, but I already feel that way about you."

I gently squeezed her hand as a sign of agreement. "We were half way there before anything romantic ever happened. The sex just brought it to an entirely new level," I added with a wink.

She returned the smile, a blush creeping into her cheeks. We'd spent the last few days diving deeper into what we both felt before she broke up with Jeff. On paper, it could look like an emotional affair. Despite never crossing a line, we were both yearning for a deeper connection.

Life isn't black and white; this gray area makes it easy to justify why we grew so close. Jeff was an asshole, and her parents weren't supportive. I couldn't care less about the consequences—I just wanted her. Would I have backed off if she were happy with him? Sure, I'm not a complete jerk. But from the first time she mentioned him, I knew she wasn't happy. She was my love at first sight, and I would've waited as long as it took for her to realize that.

The driveway is already full of cars, confirming we aren't just a little late—we're the last ones to arrive.

Without knocking, I throw open Olivia's door. It looks like Mrs. Clause threw up in here. The halls are decked, there are three trees all sparkling with lights and ornaments, and the smell of freshly baked cookies fills the air.

Ben is the first one we see, a blur running through the entryway toward the other side of the house, a laser gun in hand. He slides on his socks while trying to stop when he sees us, nearly falling but recovering at the last second.

"You're here!" He shrieks, running back toward us and wrapping his little arms around Isla first and then me. Before we can respond, he turns and sprints back to wherever he was originally going.

The entire house buzzes with people and noise, but the kitchen and living room are the main hubs of activity. Charlie and Olivia are busy preparing dinner, cackling as they chop ingredients. At the adjacent counter, our friend Ethan, a former NFL player who now owns the Ponderosa Pine Tavern, is mixing drinks. Delta, Liam, and Odessa sit opposite him, eagerly downing whatever he concocts.

Levi hovers over the appetizers laid out on the kitchen island, practically inhaling them. Meanwhile, Drew, Lincoln, and Ben team up against Hayes, Cooper, and Ethan's son Jake, who are running around the house, chasing each other with laser guns.

Connie and Ellie are busy trying to build a misshapen gingerbread house while Zeke, Ellie, and Ben's grandfather oversee their efforts. Everyone is decked out in some form of ugly Christmas sweater, as Olivia requested. It's pure chaos—but the best kind.

"Dad!" I shout toward the grown-ups, who haven't noticed our arrival. "I walked all day and night to find you!" Each Christmas, I choose a movie to quote throughout the day, and this year it's Elf. I even wore a sweater featuring Will Ferrell.

The room erupts with a mix of faux groans and genuine excitement at our arrival.

Isla leans in closer to me, whispering, "Really, really late, apparently."

I can't help but laugh as I pull her the rest of the way into the party. No one bats an eye at us being together—or showing up late.

The house has been buzzing with Christmas cheer since we arrived a few hours ago. At dinner, Olivia and Drew announced their pregnancy, and the dining room nearly shook with excitement and congratulations. They haven't been together long, but when you know, you know—and those two definitely know.

Being out in the open with Isla feels incredible, especially knowing everyone here supports us. Even Charlie seems less upset with me about "taking her best friend away." It's as if we've all collectively decided to let go of the weight from the past few weeks and embrace a day filled with nothing but happiness.

After dinner, Ethan and Jake left to spend time with his family, while most of the guys from the EFSC team headed to a bar in town that claimed to be open. Meanwhile, Zeke, Levi, Hayes, and Drew kicked off a gingerbread house competition, which I cleverly sidestepped by volunteering to be the judge. The women gathered around the kitchen island, gossiping animatedly. Hearing Isla laugh as she chats with them feels like a balm for the stress of the last few weeks. Every moment of anxiety was worth it if I get to hear her laugh like that every day.

Across the room, Ellie and Ben are playing with a mountain of gifts received from their new extended family of friends and loved ones. They embody the essence of "kids on Christmas morning"—full of joy and excitement. I can't imagine how hard it must be for them to navigate life after losing a parent so young, but they're fortunate to have so many people who care about them. Odessa and I grew up with two parents, but we never experienced this level of love in a household. If it weren't for Hayes and Drew sticking up for me in the sixth grade when I was the new kid without any friends, I wouldn't have known what a normal family looked like. The Carrington and the Reynold family spent every holiday together, welcoming Odessa and me into their fold. Our parents barely noticed we were gone, too wrapped up in their own lives to care.

The contrast between the challenges of the last month and the happiness of today is more emotionally draining than I expected. The extreme lows and high highs have always taken a toll on my social battery, and today is no exception. That's why, while everyone else is occupied, I slip into the formal living room near the entryway, sipping a beer and watching the glow of the fireplace.

Odessa must have either sensed my absence or sensed my unease because she was seeking me out within two minutes. Barreling into the room, worry darkening her features, as if whatever weird intuition gene we share was lighting up like the Christmas tree.

Her Christmas sweater jingles loudly as she plops down next to me on the loveseat. I can't help but tease her: "This is a kid-friendly party. What exactly compelled you to wear a sweater that says, 'I have some bells for you to jingle?'"

Odessa cackles, swaying slightly from the champagne. "I couldn't resist," she replies, pointing to her sweater. "It was either this or 'I'm so good, Santa came twice.'"

I grimace, shivering in disgust at the thought of her hooking up with Logan. She chuckles at my reaction. "I know, I couldn't go there. But I did send it to Sofia," she adds mischievously, waggling her eyebrows.

"God. Way to inflate his already enormous ego," I reply, shaking my head. Logan and I have stayed tight since our days stationed together, but he chose to remain in, dedicated to retiring in another decade or so.

She takes a sip of her champagne, flipping her sleek hair over her shoulder. "What's got you sitting over there looking like a bah-humbug?"

I scoff, but my thumbs start swirling counter-clockwise on my index finger. "Not a bah-humbug, more like reflecting," I admit, feeling a bit sheepish. "Seeing everyone here—one giant mismatched family—laughing and having a good time makes me realize how lucky we are."

She nods understandingly, taking another sip of her champagne before blurting, "I'm buying a house. Subdivision off Main Street."

My thumbs freeze, and I slowly crane my neck to look at her, surprise and happiness spreading across my face. "You're joking." I can't help but exclaim, genuinely thrilled for her. "Moving here full-time? What about modeling?"

She quickly looks away, avoiding eye contact with her nose slightly stuck in the air—her classic defiant pose. Coolly, as if she's been rehearsing, she replies, "I have a few contracts to finish up, but I'm ready to be around family."

I bump my shoulder into hers and say, "Congrats, little sis. Can't believe you bought a house before me, but I'm proud of you."

She laughs and nudges me back, then tilts her head toward Isla. "I have a feeling you'll be next. Or will the wedding come first? Maybe a baby?"

"Someday," I say vaguely. Isla and I need time to simply be together, to enjoy each other and focus on us. All of that will come eventually—I already have future plans brewing—but nothing needs to happen today.

Just then, Olivia and Drew's front door swings open, and a cold gust of air sweeps through the room. Dess instinctively sits up straighter, crossing her ankles against the chill—or maybe it's because of who walks through the door.

Luke breezes in, looking as gruff as ever—his slightly disheveled hair, cowboy boots, and wranglers complimenting the scowl etched on his face. His step falters when he sees us, but he quickly recovers, plastering a fake smile on his lips.

I stand up to shake his hand, greeting my boss as I normally would, but there's an unusual tension in the air. Luke's eyes flicker to Dess for less than a second before he excuses himself, making his way to the kitchen without another word. She rolls her eyes but says nothing, choosing to focus on her glass instead.

"Did I miss something?" I ask, planting my hands on my hips.

Her eyes flick to mine before she finishes her drink. "You're asking the wrong person."

I tilt my head, arching an eyebrow, waiting for her to expand. "Why the long face, Buddy?"

"It seems I'm not an elf," she says with a sigh. Before I can respond to her Elf reference, she stands up, twirling her empty glass, and walks toward the liquor cabinet.

I watch her pour herself another drink before she goes to sit with the kids, pretending nothing is wrong. For a busybody who is always in everyone else's business, she certainly keeps her own feelings well hidden.

When Luke notices it's only me in here, he comes back carrying two beers. "So, I heard some news from the grapevine. Mayor Walton is thinking about resigning from office next week," Luke says, handing me a beer.

I raised an eyebrow in surprise, wondering what could have prompted that decision. "Why's that? The investigation?"

His mouth twitched slightly. "Yes. But not yours. It appears him and Mr. Mitchell have been involved in some shady dealings that date back pretty far."

"Hmm," I say trying to play it cool. "Any idea what happened?"

He lifts one shoulder in a half-shrug. "Not sure. It's above my pay grade." Considering he's at the top of the food chain in the sheriff's department, I doubt that, but I understand his need for discretion.

"Should we be concerned?"

Luke frowns, his forehead creasing as his thick eyebrows draw together. "I think when it comes to the Walton's, you should always be concerned. However, in this case, I think he's going to be preoccupied trying to save his own ass for a while."

Not the answer I was hoping for, but the one I was expecting. I've seen how Cyrus operates, and I know just how sneaky and manipulative he can be. I wouldn't put it past him to weasel his way out of anything or try to drag everyone he could down with him—including Isla's dad.

At least if he's distracted with his problems, it might give us some breathing room to recover. Detective Smith said she needs at least another seven weeks to get through all the evidence, write up her report, and present her findings. Until then, it'll be a lot of Isla and I lying low and staying under the radar. My favorite place to be, as long as she's next to me.

Chapter Thirty-One

Everett

Pulling into the driveway behind Odessa, my eyes bulge as I openly gawk at her new house. We have only briefly talked about it since Christmas, but she's kept the details pretty tight-lipped. Not once, in the last forty-five days, did she mention how nice it was or how amazing the location was.

I threw open my door, sliding out of my 4Runner to get a better look. It's a beautiful stone-blue colored home, with white trim and natural stone accents. The timber framed front entry and matching gable brackets are stained darkly and provide the perfect contrast. It oozes all that Three Sisters charm while still being modern. It screams—I have money, but I'm still down to earth. The fact that it's only a few blocks from Main Street and in a picturesque neighborhood, is the cherry on top.

Odessa doesn't notice me yet, too engrossed with whatever is in the back seat of her other expensive new purchase—a white Rolls-Royce Cullinan. She asked me to meet her while she finished signing the paperwork and got the keys to her new house this morning. Then she invited me over to be the first one, besides her, to see the place in person.

"Alright, alright, alright!" I compliment the house when she finally gets out. "This place is almost as incredible as that car."

She doesn't pay me any attention, only slams her driver door and opens the back passenger one. A large black dog sits patiently, tongue hanging out of its mouth, staring at me.

Blinking rapidly, I try to process the unbelievable sight of a black and tan mutt drooling all over the luxury seats of Odessa's nearly half-million dollar car. A quick burst of laughter burst from my throat when the initial shock wore off. Through breaths, I ask, "*You* got a dog?"

Nonchalantly, she says, "Found him a few days ago when I was hiking." She pats her leg and the dog jumps out, looking like a giant big-headed Labrador. "The vet thinks he's a Labrottie mix."

I place the back of my hand out, letting him get a sniff. His tail wags but he doesn't leave her side. "What's his name?"

With a sigh, she looks at him lovingly and then begrudgingly says, "Dog."

I can't help the cackle that comes out of me, it's loud and obnoxious. "You named your dog, Dog?"

"It's the only thing he would come too!" She stomps her foot like a petulant toddler, but I see her trying to hide a grin. She clearly loves this dog already, which is surprising considering not once have we ever owned a dog or has she mentioned wanting one.

"I like it. He seems like a good boy—already protective," I remarked, noticing he hasn't left her side. It's a relief knowing that she'll have another being watching out for her, especially one that has teeth that will rip a throat out. When she's back in the city, or traveling, she has bodyguards. Being here, though, she hasn't needed them.

Her attention moved to the house, staring at it like she wasn't sure what to think. Probing, I ask, "So, what made you pick this one? The craftsmanship or location to Ponderosa Pine?"

She chuckles at that, but shakes her head to both. "The availability and the fact it's turn-key."

I trail behind her and dog as she unlocks the door. Over her shoulder, she explained, "It's not huge by any means, but I like that it has a little yard in the front and there's a pool outback with some cute landscaping." I can see by the small smile on her face that she likes it more than she's leading on, though. Odessa's always been at war within herself, fighting between a desire for luxury and a desire for simplicity. This house seems to strike a perfect balance between the two, making it the ideal choice for her. The car, however, is all flash.

"Olivia has a landscaping crew that's awesome," I mention. "I'm sure they could add you in since it would only be the front that needs to be mowed."

Surprisingly, she shakes her head, looking at the yard with pride. "Nah, I want to learn to do it myself."

"You?" I ask, faking a gasp. Odessa may be turning a new leaf and settling down, but she's never been known for doing manual labor. Then again, she wasn't known for being an animal lover, either.

"Yep, me," she replies, her smile turning into a scowl. "I can take care of my own home, inside and out."

My eyes instinctively narrow on her; she normally takes my jabs and gives them right back. "Did someone say you couldn't?"

Odessa's scowl softens a touch, but she still avoids looking at me. "Nope. Just wanted to prove that I can handle it all."

I nod, despite my gut telling me she's hiding something. "Hmm. I have no doubt you can, but that doesn't mean you have to." All the women in my life are fiercely independent and even more guarded. Generally, it's easier to get the guys to reveal their feelings than the girls in my circle. But Odessa, with her insane determination and refusal to show vulnerability, is on a whole other level.

Without another word, she unlocks the front door and continues the tour, completely overlooking my unspoken concerns. As the tour goes on, I gradually let go of my suspicions and focus on absorbing the information she shares about the property. The bedrooms are enormous, each with its own walk-in closet and en-suite bathroom. The kitchen isn't just a place to cook; it's a work of art, featuring top-of-the-line appliances and marble countertops. Everything here is high-end, from the hardwood floors to the custom lighting fixtures.

She stops in the kitchen, running her fingertips over the marbled island. With a shrug of her shoulder, she looks out the French doors toward the pool. "So, that's it. Pretty vanilla."

"Vanilla, huh?" I reply, unable to hide my amusement at her understatement. It's clear that Odessa's definition of impressive is on a whole other level.

With a heavy sigh, she admits, "Maybe vanilla is the wrong word. It is beautiful and in a great location."

"But?" I probe, waiting to see what she thinks is missing.

"I don't know. It feels so cookie-cutter. There are five other houses on this block that have the same layout, the same interior, and the same everything. For now, it's great. Someday, I want something with more character."

I nod in understanding, realizing that Odessa's taste is more eclectic than what the current house offers. "I get it. You know, Olivia subdivided her property when she bought it. You could always buy one of the lots and build. Preferably next to the one that I just purchased for Isla and me."

She nearly gives herself whiplash, snapping her neck toward me. "You're joking! Does Isla know?"

"Not yet. Olivia and Drew are going to keep it a secret until

I propose. I want to do it on the property." I can't prevent the grin that overcomes me when I think of proposing to Isla.

She looks at me with wide, excited eyes. "Proposing! When?"

"Easy tiger. It'll be a minute before I do, but I have no doubt it'll happen."

Groaning and rolling her eyes, she playfully punches my arm. "Just don't fuck it up before you get a ring on her finger. She's already a sister to me and I don't want to have to kick your ass if you break her heart."

I chuckle at her protective nature. "Not a chance in hell. She's it for me, ya know?"

"I know. We've all known," she drawls out, reminding me of how obvious my feelings for her have been to everyone around us. "You're it for her too. You can tell just by the way she looks at you."

"Thanks," I say, shifting my tone to convey sincerity. "I don't say it enough, but I really appreciate you being my sister —always having my back and especially for being here through this whole scandal. It means more than you know that you showed up for me—for both of us."

She clears her throat, her eyes darting away from me. However, she nods, prompting me to continue. "I do have to ask, though. Are you sure you want to live here? Giving up modeling to settle in a tiny town in the middle of Oregon? You're not moving because of everything that happened, right?"

For a brief moment, I notice her nostrils flare as her lips twist to the side. Then, in the blink of an eye, she forces a smile. "I know it's a big change," she admits, "but no. I want to watch all my nieces and nephews grow up. You and Hayes got a head start with Ellie and Ben, but I'll become the favorite soon enough."

My loud guffaw doesn't faze her as she continues, "You don't stand a chance with the new ones."

"How dare you?" I demand, channeling my inner sixteen-year-old fighting climate control.

Normally, Odessa is the only one to nail every quote, but she stares at me, blinking. "I...fuck. Why don't I know that one?"

"Because you don't care about the environment," I chastise at her.

Odessa's eyes widen in mock horror. "I care about the environment! I recycle—sometimes."

"Using the same coffee cup twice before tossing it in the trash doesn't count, Dess." That one earns me a proper dead arm as she strikes me so hard that I yelp in pain.

"Ow! Okay, okay, I take it back," I say, rubbing my arm. "You're a regular eco-warrior." *Flying around on your private jet.*

Odessa smirks triumphantly, not knowing that my inner monologue won that battle.

"Back to those new ones, you heard from Charlie at all? She's due like any minute, right?"

The genuine grin she gives now only confirms there was something amiss earlier. "I talked to her on my way here. Her due date is next week, the 12th, but she's hoping the baby comes on Valentine's Day. She's been at the office, trying to get everything done before her maternity leave."

"Isla mentioned that. She was excited about her first day back today, but she's bummed the three of them won't work together until next fall." Between Isla taking a month to recover, Charlie's four-month maternity leave, and then Olivia taking her maternity leave right after, the office will be pretty quiet for a while.

Odessa moves around the kitchen, opening and closing

empty cupboards. "I know. It's crazy that Olivia is pregnant too, but also so exciting! Our little five-some family has more than doubled. I couldn't believe how many people showed up for Christmas." She's not wrong; Olivia has more pseudo-family than we have biological family. The best part is that they've welcomed us with open arms, making us feel like we truly belong. It does remind me, though.

"Speaking of Christmas, what was the deal with you and Luke?" The tension between them never left, which is odd considering I hadn't realized they had even really met.

The nostril flare is back, coupled with a tilt of her chin upward. She quickly turns around, busying herself by opening the oven to look inside. "Not sure what you mean," she says over her shoulder. "He can barely stand to look at me, let alone talk to me." The oven door slams shut, rattling violently as she closes it with more force than necessary.

"You know what happened with him, right?" I try to ask gently. It's not my story to tell, but after the Drew debacle, I feel compelled to make sure there aren't any misunderstandings.

She huffs through her nose, slamming another cupboard. "I do. Doesn't mean I deserve to be treated like I'm invisible." Her voice wavers, betraying the hurt beneath her tough exterior. "I get it; I look like her. Not my fault." Luke's girlfriend, Maddy, was in a car accident on the same day that Dan was killed. She survived but suffers from anterograde amnesia. I hadn't met her, but I have seen a few pictures, and she does resemble Odessa—down to the blonde hair, blue eyes, and model height.

"Sorry, Dess. I wouldn't take it personally; there's a complicated history there."

The look she sends me is half confusion and half intrigue. "What—" she starts to ask before shaking her head and changing the subject. "Has he said when the investigation will be over?"

"Uh, yeah," I say, rubbing the back of my neck. Luke called while I was on my way to meet her for the keys, and I hadn't wanted to overshadow her good news with mine, so I kept it to myself.

Both of her perfectly kept eyebrows rise, waiting expectantly for me to continue. "He said that Detective Smith reported to the review board yesterday afternoon. They're all in agreement that my actions were objectively reasonable," I finally reply, trying to sound casual about it.

Her eyes light up with relief and excitement, a smile spreading across her face. "That's great! I'm so happy for you," she exclaims, pulling me into a hug. "Does that mean you're cleared to go back to work?"

I nod. "Tomorrow, actually," I say, feeling a wave of gratitude wash over me that it's finally over. I can't wait to return to normalcy and put this whole ordeal behind me. I'll be on light duty for a few weeks, but at least I get to be reinstated and back in my uniform. Odessa's expression shifts in an instant to irritation.

"I'm going to kill you! Why the hell are you just now telling me? We should be celebrating! I'm calling Mom, and we are going to the office. Right now!"

With a chuckle, I nod and watch as she quickly hurries to check on Dog and lock up the house, muttering to herself about "men not knowing a good thing if it hit them in the face." I don't say anything, though—she's not wrong.

This truly is news worth celebrating. If I hadn't been so stunned, I would've called Isla immediately to share it. But I don't think I've fully processed the information yet. Still, I can sense the hopeful energy beginning to brew, and I know that this is just the start of a brighter chapter ahead.

Chapter Thirty-Two

Isla

Grinning, I strolled into the office holding two new photos for my desk, one of Everett in his flight suit by his helicopter and the other of the two of us at Christmas. It's my first official day back at work, and I'm practically giddy. I've been back a handful of times to check in with the girls, but they wouldn't let me lift a finger during my nine-week leave. As much as I grumbled about wanting to be back, it was incredible to spend that time at home. I went to therapy twice a week, laid around with Everett for days on end, and started to feel whole again. Everett still hasn't heard from Detective Smith or Luke, so he was able to be there the entire time with me. You'd think we would have gotten sick of each other, but somehow there wasn't any time.

Equipment clatters from the gym, but I bypassed the guys working out and rushed to get up the stairs. Charlie starts maternity leave next week, so I want to capitalize on the next two days of having the three of us together. I'm not sure if that'll happen again until the fall of this year, considering Olivia will start her maternity leave as soon as Charlie is back.

Charlie's standing over her desk, holding her bump, and organizing papers. She doesn't even glance up as I walk through the door.

"Hey, mama. How are you feeling today?" I asked with a little too much enthusiasm.

Her response is more of a grunt than actual words, but I get the gist—not good. "Well, you look beautiful. That dress is so cute!" She has on a black mini knit wrap dress, her bump accentuated perfectly.

This time, she gazes up at me with apprehension and declares, "I look like Shamu, Isla." I try not to laugh at her self-deprecating humor, but I can't help it.

"You may feel like a whale, but I promise you that you don't look like it," I say, trying to reassure her.

With a huff, she nods before grumbling out, "You have no idea." She goes back to looking at her paperwork, scanning each document before setting it in the tray it belongs in.

My desk is off to the side, already full of framed photos. I make room, pushing some backward and cramming them together so that Everett can be front and center. The man is the definition of sex appeal, as he casually leans on the helicopter with one leg crossed over his ankle. The ruffled blonde hair, sunglasses, and massive grin all add to his charm. I can't help but smile every time I look at the photo, grateful for the reminder of the wonderful man I get to call mine.

When I glance up, Olivia is heading toward me from the kitchen common area, her eyes lighting up. "Isla! We missed you so much," she exclaims, enveloping me in a warm hug. The new baby hormones must be hitting her hard because tears fill her eyes.

"I missed you too! Where do you want me to start?" I ask, still smiling like it's my first day. Olivia's mouth pops open, but the guttural noise behind me is the only thing I hear.

As I spin on my heels, I spot Charlie hunched over in front of her desk—her knees bent, one hand clutching her belly and the other pressed against her back, her face contorted in pain. Olivia and I share a fleeting glance and nod simultaneously, silently agreeing that this is serious.

"Get Hayes!" I order, yanking my phone out of my pocket in case I need to call 911. Thank God Hayes works in this building. Olivia is already moving, shouting for Hayes as she goes.

With two large steps, I'm standing next to Charlie. "Contractions?"

She grits her teeth, shaking her head. "No—back pain. I must have slept wrong because it's been hurting off and on all day."

"Okay, let's sit down. Can you make it there while we wait for Hayes?" I gesture with my head toward the rec room, which is essentially just one giant playroom situated between our office and the guys' office. There are couches, chairs, and even Ben's oversized, enormous beanbag chair, which is more like a bed.

With a single nod, she starts moving out the door and into the other room. The closest thing to her is Ben's beanbag chair, and she half collapses and half sits on it. Her green eyes go wide and her jaw drops as she sucks in a breath.

"Oh my God. Did I just pee?" Sure enough, a small, dark spot is forming on the gray chair beneath her.

Before I can react, Hayes is barreling into the room like a bull in a china shop, his eyes wide with concern. "What happened?" he demands, kneeling beside her. "Are you okay, Sunshine?"

Tears fill her eyes, and she shakes her head. "I think I just peed myself," she whispers, mortified. Her body goes stiff, and she groans in pain again.

Hayes, momentarily stunned by the situation, hasn't so much as blinked since he entered the room.

A light chuckle comes from behind me. "It's not pee, Number Three." *Number Three?*

I glance over my shoulder and see Levi whispering to Olivia. It dawns on me that "Number Three" refers to how he's been calling Charlie his third favorite girl since before I met them. Olivia nods, her expression growing serious, before turning around and jogging back down the stairs.

I keep an eye on Levi as he stands still near the doorframe. I've known him for a few years now, and I've never seen him this serious. His eyes flick between his watch and Charlie, clearly tracking the time between what must be contractions. When the next one hits, he smirks and grabs the jug of hand sanitizer. He applies it to his hands and forearms while still watching her. Once the contraction is over, he steps deeper into the room, his expression shifting to one of suave charm. "Charlie-girl, if you wanted me there for the delivery, you could've just invited me into the hospital room."

Charlie looks like she wants to shoot laser beams out of her eyes to eviscerate him. Her teeth are still clenched together when she says, "I will kill you."

Levi, being Levi, continues to grin, but I see the worry etched in his tight features. He takes a step closer in my direction. Under his breath, he says to me, "Olivia is calling dispatch. Grab some hand sanitizer and then pass it to Hayes."

"You can kill me later, but right now, I want to check you out." Levi kneels on the opposite side of Charlie, reaching for her wrist. He smirks again before joking, "Not like that. Your husband is here."

Hayes rolls his eyes and huffs, but he doesn't say anything. Taking the opportunity, I grabbed the same jug of hand sanitizer Levi just used and covered my hands and forearms the way I saw him do it.

I side-step so that I'm mostly behind Hayes, and gently touch his arm with the jug. He looks at it, and then looks back at me, confusion and annoyance flashing in his eyes.

I quietly explain, "Levi's orders."

Hayes begrudgingly cups his hands together and shoves them out, allowing me to continue with the necessary precautions.

We both look up as Olivia flies back up the stairs, carrying a huge duffel bag. She sets it next to Levi and comes to stand by me. With her phone back up to her ear, she watches Levi, waiting for more instructions. If anyone had told me we'd all be waiting on Levi's orders like this, I wouldn't have believed it. He's the jokester, the flirt, and the one who never takes anything seriously. But here we are, following his lead unquestionably, as if he's suddenly become the most competent one among us. Then again, when it comes to delivering a baby, he is absolutely the most competent. Olivia may be next, but only because she's had two herself. Charlie and Hayes look as lost as I do right now.

When Levi's done with his count, he stares up at Charlie. "Alright, Char. I need to be direct with you; you are currently in active labor, and that precious boy may not wait much longer to make his grand entrance into the world. If you're comfortable, I'd like to check your cervix to see how dilated you are. I need to know if we are delivering here or if we can make it to the hospital."

Hayes looks downright petrified, ghost-white, as his jaw comes unhinged. The only thing that snaps him out of his shock is when Charlie lets out another groan, the contraction hitting her hard. Levi doesn't wait for her to respond; he moves the duffel bag to the left of him and unzips the largest pocket.

When the contraction lets up a fracture, she mumbles, "Where's Bill or C—?

"Charlie Carrington, you insult me! I can assure you, I'm more qualified to be delivering your baby than those fools." He remarks while pulling supplies out of the bag and laying them on a large disposable under pad.

She nearly growls at him, "Levi, just because you've seen more vaginas than a gynecologist doesn't mean you know what you're doing."

For one brief moment, he stills, his hand hovering over the bag holding some type of scissors. Her words clearly striking a nerve before he quickly shakes his head and continues preparing for the delivery, ignoring her comment. As he finishes setting up the rest of the equipment, he solemnly explains, "When Olivia found out she was pregnant with Ben, Dan and I spent one Saturday a month, for nine months, learning everything there was to know about emergency deliveries. Same with Ellie. I am confident that if this baby is coming right now, I have more than enough training to keep you both safe. Please. Let me help you. Both of you." The crack in his voice reveals precisely how serious he's taking all of this.

Charlie nods, tears streaming down her face. Levi puts on the gloves and begins to explain everything he is about to do before he does it. It doesn't even seem like he's started the exam when he calmly states, "Everything looks great. Just keep breathing through the contractions and try not to push yet." His head turns so that he's fully addressing Olivia. Lightly, he says, "Liv, let them know the baby is crowning."

When he turns back around, he pats Hayes on the shoulder. "You ready to catch your baby, Dad?" Stunned doesn't begin to describe Hayes' face, but he nods and moves to be kneeling next to Levi.

"Alright, Charlie. Next contraction and I want you to push.

He's right there, ready. I'd say, knowing how strong you are, three pushes. Think you can do it?"

The next contraction hits, and he begins coaching her like he's a Lamaze professional.

"Isla!" He barks at me when she's in her brief recovery moment. "Grab the gown, left pocket. Help her out of the dress so she can do skin to skin." I move quickly, grabbing the hospital gown and helping Charlie get her dress off. I use the gown as more of a blanket, covering her top.

"Dad, next push, and he's here. You'll place him on mom's chest for now, and we'll get him covered. When we're ready, I'll help you cut the umbilical cord."

Three heads ascend the stairs, all wearing the Cascadia County medic uniform. Bill's the first one in the room, halting once he gets in. He watches Levi for a moment before glancing at me and giving me a reassuring nod. The other two medics stand back as well, allowing Levi to finish what he started.

Charlie's contraction hits, and with the final push, his little shoulders are out. Hayes' hands were already poised, and before I could blink, he was holding his newborn son. He looks terrified and in awe at the same time, staring at his baby while he gently places him on Charlie's chest. She immediately holds on to him, weeping at the overwhelming rush of emotions.

Levi barks more orders, but this time they're at the medics on duty. They all fall in line and start working on Charlie and checking on baby Carrington. It's a blur of movement as Levi continues to give Charlie the care she needs before she's ready to be transported to the hospital.

After a quick argument about how to safely get Charlie down the stairs and a lot of complaining from Charlie, they had the three of them loaded into the back of the ambulance within ten minutes of her giving birth. Levi didn't stop directing them until the doors were closed and they were driving away.

Olivia, Levi, and I stood there watching the ambulance drive away, still in shock by what happened. Drew and Delta must have come out at some point without my realizing it because they were suddenly behind us.

Olivia turned around first, wrapping her arms around Drew. "You're officially an uncle," she says grinning.

With a light chuckle, Drew replied, "I guess I am. Who would've thought she'd give birth in the office?" He releases Olivia before turning to Levi and extending his hand. "Owe you a hell of a lot more than a simple thank you, but it's a start. Thanks, man."

We all watch with bated breath, trying to see how Levi will respond. He's been giving Drew the cold shoulder since the week before Olivia's car accident, and a chilled shoulder since they first met.

Levi takes the extended hand, giving Drew a firm shake and a small nod. "No need to thank me," he says gruffly. "Charlie's as much of a sister to me as Olivia." With a heavy sigh, he turns around and trudges back up the stairs.

Delta and I exchange an anxious glance before following Levi's retreating form.

When we get up there, Levi's already scrubbing his hands in the kitchen sink. He must stand there for a full three minutes, lost in his thoughts, before Olivia breaks him out of it.

"Hey, Vi. Ready to elaborate on the fact that you may be the most prepared off-duty medic in the world?" Levi huffs but doesn't respond, which only spurs Olivia on. "The enormous labor and delivery duffel bag? You just keep that thing in your truck at all times."

He shuts the water off, grabbing a dish towel to dry his hands. When he turns, he lifts his shoulders in a nonchalant shrug.

Delta and I both shift uncomfortably, sensing the building

tension in the room. Olivia may be the only one around, besides his dad, who truly calls him out. Whatever nerve she's hitting appears to be the same one Charlie hit earlier. Levi's jaw tightens as he avoids making eye contact, a sure sign that Olivia's words are getting to him.

"What's wrong with you? That was the best-case scenario; you were practically a midwife."

"Fuck sake, Olivia," he roars. "Drop it." He throws the wadded up dish towel onto the counter like it's a gauntlet, his frustration palpable in the air.

Drew steps in front of Olivia, as if he's trying to protect her from Levi's anger. "Hey, what's your fucking problem?!"

Levi's eyes bug out of his head, as if he can't believe anyone is even questioning him on this. "Do you know how many things could've gone wrong? Do you understand how lucky she was? If the cord had been around his neck, if he had been breached, if..." He throws his hands in the air in exasperation before pointing his finger at Drew. "You don't fucking get it! Even during normal, routine childbirth, mothers bleed out or babies die from perinatal asphyxia. I was playing out a hundred different worst-case scenarios each step of the way, and even with all the extra training, sometimes it's not enough." Any outsider looking in can see there's some PTSD playing out right before us. Levi's been a first responder for over a decade. He was the first on scene for his brother's murder and then, a few weeks ago, first for Olivia's car accident. Somehow, I don't think this is about either of those, though.

"No, man. You're right," Drew agrees, but shakes his head. "Sometimes it isn't enough. There's a lot of factors playing into every circumstance, call it luck, fate, or divine intervention, but the people involved can't control everything. You can prepare for it. You can educate yourself and train relentlessly on how to handle those worst-case scenarios. You can do everything by the book, but even that won't be enough." He looks at Olivia with a sad smile. "No matter how much training you have or how perfect your hands are, you'll never be God. But you may be the last face that person sees—the one who brings comfort and hope in their final moments. Doesn't mean you don't train and try your hardest to save them; it only means you forgive yourself when you can't."

Levi's eyes turn downcast, not willing to accept what Drew is telling him. He buries his hands in his blonde hair, pulling at the ends. I should be taking pity on him, but instead I want to shake him, all of my feelings bubbling to the surface.

"God. Boo-freaking-hoo, Levi." It feels like the air is sucked out of the room, everyone's face turning to me with a mix of shock and disbelief. But I stand my ground, knowing that tough love is sometimes the only way to break through someone's denial and self-pity. Levi needs to face reality if he's ever going to move forward. "Less than, like, ten weeks ago, I thought I was going to die. Fully believed I was a dead woman. *I was that patient.* Would I have wanted Everett to feel at all responsible for not finding me in time? No. Would I have thought it was Bill's fault if I coded on the way to the hospital? Abso-fuckin-lutely not. The only person to blame that night was Jeff."

I realize my voice sounds more like a shriek at this point, so I back off and take a lighter tone. "If something had happened to Charlie or the baby, not one of us would have blamed you. She mentioned she was having back pain, none of us questioned her further. Would that have been our fault? No, because we only know what we know. We don't know what's going on her in body, the severity of her contractions, or the pain level. We went by her word."

By the time I finished my impassioned speech, Levi looked wilted. Out of the corner of my eye, I see Delta retreating toward the balcony as silently as he could. *Pussy.*

Olivia moves around Drew to be closer to Levi, her mouth opening and closing like she's trying to find the right words. "Isla's right, a little dramatic," she says and then winks at me. "But she is right. You only know what you know, Levi. That's it. You can't focus so hard on the things that could have gone wrong that you don't celebrate the things that went right. The fact that you've taken so much time to learn about emergency deliveries is beyond what anyone would ever expect or what most people would do. So yes, maybe things could have gone a hundred different bad ways, but right now, you are the only one in this building that has the training to recognize those things."

"Now. I have that training now. But having it now doesn't mean I can forget about the past." With his head ducked, he walked out of the room and then jogged down the stairs. His med bag forgotten in the rec room, with the supplies he used still strewn out on the floor.

Olivia, Drew, and I exchange uneasy glances. I flinch when I hear the front door slam shut behind him.

"What was that?" Olivia asked, still reeling from Levi's outburst.

"Too harsh?" I ask, my tone dripping with sass.

Drew snorts while trying not to cackle. "Boo-freaking-hoo, Levi!" he repeats, trying to mock my tone. Olivia's hand reaches out, slapping him on the chest, which only makes him laugh harder.

"I'm sorry, it's not funny," he says while wiping his eyes. "But Everett seems to be infecting Isla. That's totally something he would say."

I can't prevent the smile that tugs at the corners of my mouth, despite the seriousness of the situation. It feels good to be associated with Everett's wit and humor, even if it's in the midst of chaos. He's helped bring out a fiery side of me that I spent so long trying to repress. I know that an apology to Levi is in my future. I shouldn't have kicked him while he was down, but that doesn't mean my stance has changed. If there's anything I've learned, it's that the longer you hold on to anger and resentment, the heavier it becomes to carry.

"Speaking of Everett," Olivia says, looking toward the stairs. I glance over to see Everett, Odessa, and Connie walking in with massive grins and three bottles of champagne. Their smiles all fall at the same time when they notice the supplies strewn around them.

My eyes widen, and I whisper, "Did anyone call them?"

They both shake their heads, then suddenly break into laughter. This is the chaos our group has come to know and love, and honestly, I wouldn't change a thing. Moments like these remind me why we're in this together, fully embracing the unpredictable ride of life.

Chapter Thirty-Three

Everett

"Woah!" Odessa loudly gasps, as we walk up the stairs at the office. I nearly run into her when she stops short, taking in the chaos in front of us. It looks like someone left a kindergartener unattended during first aid training. A medical bag lies open, its contents scattered across the floor.

My heart nearly stops until I hear manic laughter behind me. Drew, Isla, and Olivia stand in the kitchen, doubled over in fits of laughter at our shocked faces.

"What the hell is going on?!" I demand, striding toward them. I'm barely aware of Connie's phone ringing; my focus is on Isla, whose cheeks are streaked with tears from laughing so hard.

Drew is the first to respond. "Baby Carrington made his appearance early."

"Here?" I gasp in disbelief.

"Yep," he replies, popping the "p" like it's the most exciting news ever. "Thankful Levi was here and delivered him."

I hear Odessa shriek from another room, her excitement building along with Connie's voice.

"Holy shit! He was okay? Healthy and all that?" I ask incredulously, realizing Connie must be on the phone with Hayes and Charlie. I glance back over at them. Odessa is grinning widely, while Connie wipes tears from her eyes, a mix of happiness and relief.

Isla wraps her arm around my waist, resting her head against my chest. "He was perfect. Came really quickly, but Levi was a pro." My hand threads through her hair, pulling her closer to me.

"That's amazing, but also, holy shit! An office baby? How does that even happen?!"

Olivia slaps her hand on the counter, excitement lighting up her face. "It was seriously the fastest birth I've ever seen, and I've had two!"

Isla nods, then pulls her head away to look at me. "Her water broke, we called 911, and then Levi pretty much delivered the baby. The other medics arrived just as he was coming out, but Levi didn't even need them. Did you know he's had all sorts of extra training for emergency deliveries?"

I find my shoulders shrugging involuntarily as my head shakes in surprise. Not that he isn't capable or extremely hardworking—he is—it's just that he's an odd one to understand. One minute he's the life of the party, and the next, he's lost in his own world. I think he struggles with wanting to be the same guy he was before he lost his brother, while knowing he can never be that person again.

I hear the excited cheers coming down the short hallway as Olivia chimes in, "Wait, so what's with the champagne?"

"Celebrating!" Odessa declares, lifting the bottle she's carrying like a prized trophy.

"What are we celebrating?"

"Apparently a few things," I mutter through a smile.

All eyes look to me, waiting for me to elaborate. "Well, of course, Baby C coming into the world."

Drew snorts, making a mocking sound. "You didn't even know that."

"Odessa closed on her house today. She's now officially a Three Sisters resident!"

Cheers erupt around the room as everyone hugs Odessa. She laughs, trying to downplay it as if it's no big deal, but we all know that her settling down here is a significant step for her.

"Alright, that's enough about me," Odessa says, narrowing her eyes at me. "Everett..." She gives me a pointed look, making sure I don't downplay my news. She lectured me in the car all the way to pick up Connie for not being more excited and made me promise to wait to tell her until we got here.

"And..." I say, keeping my face impassive and my voice even. "You can't touch this."

Olivia and Isla both stare at me, clearly confused. Connie and Drew, on the other hand, immediately get it. A slow grin spreads across Drew's face as he starts to chuckle. Connie gasps, covering her mouth with her hand.

I might be more of a movie quote guy, but when the moment calls for it, I can't resist breaking into song—and that's exactly what I do, channeling a little MC Hammer.

"My, my, my, my!" I belt out, dancing around the kitchen like the guys and I used to do in middle school—even though we'd never admit it.

"Music hits me so hard

Makes me say, 'Oh, my Lord'

Thank you for blessing me

With a mind to rhyme and two hyped feet."

It feels good when you know you're down,

A super dope homeboy from the Oaktown.

And I'm known as such.

And this is a beat, uh, you can't touch.

I told you, homeboy,

You can't touch this!"

"I don't..." Olivia starts to say, clearly lost in my musical moment, while Isla looks shocked and asks, "You're cleared?"

"Cleared?! Luke called and you're just now telling us!" Olivia shouts, and when I nod, I can see tears fill her eyes. *Pregnant women. Yikes.*

"That's what I said!" Odessa replies, still exasperated with me.

But it's not until I catch a glimpse of Isla's face that my mood shifts entirely. Her jaw is slack, her breathing ragged, and her eyes seem unfocused as she stares blankly at the wall behind me. A wave of worry hits my gut like a freight train. The last thirty seconds replay in my mind as I try to figure out why she isn't celebrating.

She continues to look as if the wind has been knocked out of her, and it hits me—casually rapping a song to announce my news may have been a bit insensitive.

I reach out to touch her arm, asking softly, "Isla—"

Before I can even finish my apology, she launches herself into my arms. The relief is instant as my arms wrap around her, easily supporting her weight.

"It's done!" she exclaims, her voice brightening. "No more worrying about some crazy 'Hail Mary' they're going to send our way. That's it! You're off the hook!"

Her excitement radiates, and I can't help but smile, feeling the weight lift as we share this moment together.

There's still a lot we don't know about her parents and the Waltons, but at least this is one thing we don't have to worry about anymore. We get to be us without the cloud of an investigation hanging over our heads. I can return to work, and Isla doesn't have to worry about me anymore.

We get to move on with our lives, and in that moment, I realize I may be the luckiest guy alive to have her by my side.

Chapter Thirty-Four

Isla

One of my favorite things about spring in Central Oregon is that I finally feel justified getting iced coffee again. The mornings may still be chilly, but the warm afternoons are all the incentive I need to stop by my favorite drive-thru coffee hut, Maisie's, on my way home.

Maisie was a few grades above me back in school, best friends with Ethan and Olivia. Something changed when Ethan left; now, she won't even be in the same room with him. It's been a topic of many wine-filled conversations with Charlie and Olivia over the years. Olivia swears she doesn't know what happened, but she admits feeling torn between them. Regardless, we still visit Maisie a few times a week—her coffee is simply the best, and her desserts? To die for.

When I drive up to the window, her bright smile greets me from behind the window. She opens it, smiling even wider somehow. "Hey, pretty girl! I haven't seen you in so long. How ya doing, love?"

"Better," I admit with a smile. Maisie texted me daily to check in when she found out I was in the hospital. She was also one of the first people I told that I was dating Everett. For one millisecond, her eyes went wide and then she grinned like it was the best thing she ever heard. Since then, I haven't been worried about what anyone else around here thinks.

"How are you? You must be swamped right now with everyone on spring break."

Like I manifested it, she yawned and then tried to shake her head to clear the sleepiness. "I'm exhausted but surviving," she giggles. "It's definitely been a busy week. Whatcha havin' today?"

"Feel like surprising me? Something iced, highly caffeinated, and extra sweet would be perfect," I replied with a smile.

She nodded. "Love it. I have the perfect thing in mind," she said before turning and starting her creation. Over the espresso machine, she shouted, "How's Charlie feeling? August is so freakin' cute!"

"Right? He's the perfect little one-month-old. Charlie seems to be adjusting well. It's Hayes who is becoming a control freak," I chuckled, shaking my head at the thought of Hayes' overprotective nature. "But they're all three doing great," I added.

Maisie grabs a pink straw and puts it into the concoction she made. I nearly drooled at the caramel drizzle and whipped cream on top. "Here you go, one caramel macchiato with extra love," she said with a grin. I took a sip and closed my eyes in temporary bliss.

The screech of tires yanked me from my coffee-induced nirvana. Recognition hit me as I saw the black Corvette—Cyrus behind the wheel, his eyes blazing with rage.

Two could play at this game. I refused to look away as he passed, determined to show him he had no control over me anymore. Over the past few months, I've learned plenty about him and my dad—things that, had I known sooner, would have changed my adult life entirely.

It didn't take long for Lincoln to connect the dots between my dad and Tony, the Operations Manager at the logging company where my dad worked as a timber broker.

The biggest piece of information he uncovered came from Tony's wife. She revealed that he had been looking into the company's wrongdoings and was considering becoming a whistleblower. From the start, Tony was wary of my dad and planned to file a lawsuit that would implicate both my dad and the owner, Gary. Tragically, before he could go public with his evidence, Tony was killed in an "accident" on a logging site.

The police ruled it an accident, unable to prove any foul play. However, their suspicions were raised when someone from the rigging crew claimed to have seen my dad at the logging site on the morning of the incident. My dad maintained he was just searching for a serial number on a piece of equipment, but the rigger sensed something was off. After all, my dad had never stepped foot on a logging site before, and on the very day he did, Tony, who was filling in as the yarder operator, found himself suddenly trapped when the equipment tipped over. Despite the firefighters' best efforts, Tony died on the way to the hospital.

Given everything that has unfolded, we can only assume Gary learned about the lawsuit and the whistleblower situation and then informed his old high school buddy, Cyrus. With Cyrus's shady reputation, it's plausible he advised Gary that it would be cheaper to eliminate Tony rather than face a court battle. Unfortunately, all evidence against them remains purely circumstantial.

The only "smoking gun" is the money my dad received a few months later. Both Gary and my dad insist it was a no-interest loan because Gary believed in him, yet my dad has never repaid a cent and continues to act as Gary's lawyer— for free.

Fortunately for us, Lincoln has made it his personal mission to uncover the truth, creatively obtaining and giving information to the FBI's ongoing investigation.

As I watched his shiny car drive away, the tension slowly began to melt from my body. Something about seeing him still set my nerves on edge. I want to believe he wouldn't dare come after me, but after everything Jeff did, I know better than to underestimate the vile family he belonged to.

Whenever that anxiety tightens my chest, I remind myself of the support surrounding me—both emotional and physical. I have family and friends who have shown me their love and proved they would go to battle for me.

I reached into my bag to grab my wallet, but as I pulled out the cash, Maisie shook her head. "Nope, let's call it a 'Glad you survived that evil family and found your prince charming, gift.'"

The corner of my mouth turned up and I couldn't help but laugh. "Fine, but that means you'll let me buy you a real drink soon. Even if it means getting out of," I swirl my finger in the air, gesturing toward our town, "here to do it."

She beams at my suggestion, nodding eagerly. "Deal," she agrees, "but only if you promise to tell me all the juicy details about your fairytale romance." *Easy—Everett's my favorite thing to talk about.*

Once I'm home, I set up my laptop and grab the documents I'll need to work on while enjoying my coffee. The encounter with Cyrus is still unsettling, but I try to push it out of my mind. He has no control over my life anymore and I know that I'm safer now than I have ever been.

An hour into compiling a spreadsheet of renter information, I heard a very distinct *pop* sound from my bedroom. It's
not loud enough to be alarming, but it definitely catches my
attention.

My hands freeze on the keyboard while my ears strain to
hear any other sounds.

I don't hear anything, but I refuse to take me eyes off the
hallway as my hands fumble on the kitchen table for my phone.
When my fingers lock on to it, I unlock it and try to make
thoughts connect.

Everett is at the air field today, working on "Bell." It's his
first day back that he's been able to go check on his beloved
helicopter. He practically skipped out of the house this
morning and the thought of ruining that over my overactive
imagination gives me pause. Hayes would be option two—he
lives right down the road and is probably home with Charlie
and baby August, but that's precisely why I choose not to
call him.

Taking a deep breath, I try to remind myself that it was
most likely just the wind or a loose floorboard. But as I hear
another creak, I can't help but feel a chill run down my spine.
Drew!

I find his name in my contacts in half a second, hitting the
call button and praying he answers and is at Olivia's.

He answers before the first ring finishes, confusion mixed
with alarm when he says, "Isla?" We're friends and all, but he's
not exactly someone I call every day, or ever. Normally, I'd call
Olivia and have her ask him whatever was needed.

"Hey," I say, my breath a little shaky. "Are you home? I'm
so sorry to—"

He interrupts my apology with a sense of urgency in his
voice: "Isla, never apologize for calling me. What's wrong? Are
you okay?" I briefly explain the situation with the popping

noise and creak, hoping he can provide some reassurance or advice. The sound of a truck engine starting sounds through my phone speaker as I realize he's already on his way to the house.

"I'll be there in three minutes," he guarantees. "Just stay on the phone and wait for me. Did you call Everett or Hayes, yet?"

I shake my head, even though he can't see it. Stammering, I answered, "No, Everett is at CC today and I didn't want to bug Hayes since they're not really sleeping."

He makes some sort of grunt before saying, "I'm glad you called me, but don't ever think either of them wouldn't want you to interrupt their day. We've had too much shit happen not to take every creepy noise seriously." *Ain't that the truth?*

"Thanks," I say, feeling a bit reassured. I appreciate that he's not downplaying my concerns and is always willing to help out, even if it means interrupting his day.

All I can hear for a minute is the sound of his blinker and the rev of his engine before my phone pings, indicating that someone has arrived in the driveway. I fly out the front door, unable to sit at that table any longer now that the cavalry is finally here.

His truck practically skids to a stop, dust still kicking up as he jumps out of it. By the time he's rounding the front of the truck, he already has his pistol out.

"Do you want to wait in the truck while I check it out?" he asks while keeping his eyes trained on the front door.

I shake my head, not eager to be alone right now. "I'll stick with you. It was probably nothing anyway."

The tick of his jaw confirms he doesn't love that plan, but he doesn't argue. Instead, he says, "Stay behind me. Keep your phone in your hand in case you need to call anyone." *Meaning 911, great.*

I follow him back into the house, keeping a few feet between us. He clears each room methodically, like he's done this a hundred times before. I can't help but feel a sense of relief as we make our way through the house, knowing he's there to protect me if anything were to happen.

When we get to the partially open bedroom door, he looks back and mouths, "Wait."

I give a single nod, and he pushes the door the rest of the way open. In less than a minute, he shouts, "All clear."

With a heavy sigh, I walk into the bedroom. At first glance, everything looks the same. Our bed is made, pillows still fluffed, but something catches my eye—Everetts security safe is unlocked and partially open.

Drew must notice my concerned expression because he immediately walks over to inspect it. After a few moments, he bends down and picks up a weathered looking envelope. Around it is a ribbon, tied in a neat bow.

He holds it up between two fingers, one eyebrow raised. When I shake my head, he flips it over and says, "It's addressed *'To the future Mr. Odessa Astor.'*"

As I stepped closer for a better look, I noticed a diamond band attached to the ribbon. When he flipped it over, we both saw that "Grandma Astor" had signed the back.

"That's weird, right?" I ask, shifting my weight from foot to foot.

Drew nods and flicks the door of the security box open with his index finger. Inside sits another identical envelope, but I can't see what it says because it's tucked beneath two of Everett's handguns. A wad of cash secured with a clip rests behind the guns.

He clears his throat before asking, "Notice anything missing?"

I peered at the contents before shrugging. "Honestly, no idea. Everett was using that one," I say, pointing toward the smaller of the two handguns. "When he had to turn in his service one. It was sitting on the dresser for a while, but Ellie and Ben came over the other day, so he must have put it in there."

Drew's head bobs up and down as he continues to scrutinize the open lock box. "I'll call him and double check, but these battery operated locks aren't foolproof. It could've been a glitch for no reason, or Everett may not have closed it all the way when he put the SIG in there."

His brow furrows once again, and his chin tilting to the side. "What?" I ask, noticing his puzzled expression. "Is something wrong?"

Drew shakes his head, a thoughtful look crossing his face. "This one is top of the line." He points toward the green light on the lock box. "It shouldn't have malfunctioned like that."

When he sees my terrified face, he quickly adds, "But don't worry, I don't think anyone was in here. Weird shit happens in this house all the time. The number of times I lost my keys only to find them in the most unexpected places is ridiculous." Drew chuckles, trying to lighten the mood but it doesn't work.

"Andrew Reynolds, are you seriously implying there's a ghost in this house?"

His mouth twitched as he fought off a smirk. "Only saying I'm glad it's not just me that Dan likes to fuck with."

My jaw went slack as I processed his nonchalant response. The thought of Dan being a mischievous ghost in the house is both terrifying and strangely comforting at the same time.

"Daniel Turner! Don't you dare mess with me!" I shout while stomping my foot.

Drew laughs, amusement dancing in his eyes. "Doesn't work. I tried. Then again, I'm dating his wi—" Before he can finish his taunt, a loud *beep* sounds from the safe, and the green light turns red. We both scream in unison, and the letter

Drew is holding flies out of his hand as we scramble out of the room.

As we catch our breath in the hallway, Drew whispers, "I think I pissed off Dan."

"No shit, Sherlock," I reply, rolling my eyes and walking into the kitchen. "Olivia home? I'm not staying here alone." I say while grabbing my purse, keys, and laptop.

Drew watches over me, his eyes flitting around the room, like he expects Dan to pop out somewhere. When I have everything gathered, he grabs my bag for me and follows me out the door, still looking over his shoulder nervously. *Even big, bad Navy SEALs are terrified of ghosts.*

"You okay to drive or do you want a ride?" he asks, shouldering the bag and walking toward his truck.

"Ride. Let's go talk to Olivia and then we can call Everett." Somehow, telling Olivia that we think her dead husband is haunting us sounds easier than trying to explain it over the phone to Everett. Plus, I really don't want to ruin his day. He deserves one good day, uninterrupted by the disarray of our daily lives.

Chapter Thirty-Five

Everett

Clocking back into work has never felt so good. I've been on cloud nine walking through the department since I was reinstated last month, but today I get to spend the day at the Cascadia County airfield, lovingly referred to by most simply as CC. We haven't had any flight time or call-outs yet, but the weather is unseasonably warm. Which means hikers, bikers, and wilderness enthusiasts are flocking to the outdoors. Luke took a two-week leave to spend some time enjoying the weather as well. Levi's father, Zeke, who was also Luke's predecessor, and Captain Ellis are standing in for him during his small absence. It's been fun around the department; pranks and jokes have been flying left and right. It's giving major cats away and the mice get to play. I may have instigated a handful myself, but really, Zeke is the mastermind behind most of them. It's been nice to see everyone letting loose and having a good time after everything we had to deal with in December. Spring has sprung, and we're all relishing the good weather and better moods.

The CC airfield is less than a mile from the department,

and the sheriff's department has a hanger, with a shiny new helicopter in it. I wasn't sure I'd ever spend a dime of my trust fund, but when Luke mentioned he was having a hard time finding the funds, I couldn't resist a hefty donation. Within two days, I had picked out, upgraded, and ordered the Bell 407GXi. When they informed me it was ready, I paid extra to have it delivered to the Sheriff's Department as an anonymous donation. The price tag may have been over twenty million, but damn, if it wasn't worth it. Donating the money toward the department felt like the right thing to do anyway—even if it is a little self-serving. Plus, my grandpa Astor would've loved it.

Bell sits pretty in the hangar, with not a fleck of dust to be seen, thanks to the meticulous care of the maintenance crew. I'd barely spent fifty hours of actual flight time with her before everything happened, so simply seeing her sparkle in the sun peeking through the door has me excited. All dark green, with tan accents and the word "SHERIFF" in large letters on the side, she's a sight to behold.

Despite what the contractors do to keep up with maintenance, there's still a lot I can do to make sure everything is running smoothly before Luke is back and I can return to my normal duties. Today's a day to get my hands dirty, checking all the systems and ensuring she's in top condition for when duty calls.

I get lost in the motions, looking over every inch from the rotor blades to the engine. Everything is top-of-the line, from the Rolls-Royce M250 turboshaft engine to the Garmin G1000H® NXi integrated flight deck for enhanced pilot awareness. Which means not only is she powerful, she's also smart.

My work cell phone rings from the pocket of my maintenance coveralls, breaking my concentration. I quickly wipe what I can of the grease on my hands before fishing it out to see Zeke's name flashing on the screen.

Lightheartedly, I answer his call, 'Go for Everett, Big Dog.'

"You still at CC?" Zeke asks, then adds quickly, "I've got Peter and Claire heading your way. Luke needs you near Crooked Canyon Falls for a medevac." His tone shifts to all business. If he's sending one of the doctors who volunteer with SAR along with a medic, it must be a critical situation.

"Hold up," I say. "Does that mean I'm off my 'low-key' shift?" Despite the question, I'm already mentally preparing for the urgency of a medical transfer mission.

A long pause comes from Zeke's end of the call, but I can hear a commotion happening behind him. He mutters something low that I can't catch, then snaps back, "How long do you need until you can be in the air?" If his voice didn't sound so strained, I'd ask again about being cleared. *Or maybe not. 'Never look a gift horse in the mouth' and all that.*

Instead, I quickly calculate the time needed to gather my gear, do my pre-flight checks. Confidently, I respond, "Fifteen minutes."

There's a quick huff before he barked, "make it ten."

Rather than respond, I sprint toward the hangar to change into my flight suit. Whatever's happening has Zeke in a tizzy, and I'm not about to make that worse.

Thankfully, I've been at the airfield all afternoon, and the Bell is ready to go. I have my routine down to a science; everything is always prepared and waiting for moments like this.

I'm nearly finished with my checklist when I catch movement out of the corner of my eye. Doctor Peter Lewis and our paramedic, Claire David, jog across the field just as I complete my checks. Peter's a smaller guy, balding with bifocals, and he looks like he's spent more time with his nose in a book than on a trail, though I know he's an avid hiker. Claire, on the other hand, has an athletic build and long, dark hair that's always braided—she looks like she was made to hike up a mountain. *Or kick someones ass.*

I nod at them before handing over the gear they'll need. Claire takes it and climbs into the cabin, ignoring my existence like she always does. I've been around her long enough to know she isn't one for small talk or people in general.

"What do we have?" I questioned Peter, preparing myself to communicate with air traffic control for takeoff with whatever details they have.

Peter's eyes flick toward mine briefly before he goes back to getting his gear on. "Scout River Trailhead. Individual presenting with a polytraumatic condition resulting from envenomations. St. Charles Bend has vials waiting." *"Envenomations?" Meaning rattlesnake bite? Or multiple bites?*

"Copy that," I respond without much more thought. Medical terms have never been my strong suit, and although it may seem too early in the spring for rattlers to be out, I know better than to underestimate nature's timing.

Without another word, he climbs into the cabin, secures his helmet, and gets ready for takeoff.

It's not my first time flying with Peter, but there's an uncomfortable tension in the air, as if he's intentionally avoiding looking at me. That could mean there's more going on than I realize or that he's on Team Cyrus. Most of the town has rallied behind Isla and me, but there are still a few who remain loyal to the Waltons.

Rather than dwell on it, I turn my attention back to my preflight checklist, making sure all systems are ready to go. The familiar hum of the engine starting up pushes aside any lingering doubts, allowing me to focus entirely on the flight ahead.

Once I confirm the area is clear, I roll the throttle to idle and check the voltage before hitting the starter. It may have been a few months since I've been in the seat, but it feels just like riding a bike—albeit a very high-tech, high-stakes bike.

Radioing in to air traffic control, "MEDEVAC Three Nine Four, Delta Tango," I begin my communication with our flight plan and intentions. Every time I give the tail number, I'm reminded of why I chose it to begin with—life can change in an instant simply because you let your guard down. It's a small way of honoring Dan, with his badge number and initials, while also reminding myself of the importance of staying focused and vigilant.

The acceleration, the gentle lift-off from the ground, and the rush of wind against the cockpit windows all come together in a symphony of motion and emotion, igniting a familiar adrenaline spike that pumps through my veins. Thankfully, I've done this enough that the rhythmic hum of the engine and steady communication with air traffic control keep me grounded as we ascend into the sky.

It's a seven-minute flight to Scout River Trailhead, followed by another ten minutes to the hospital in Bend. I'm not sure why AirLink isn't handling this case, but I'm not questioning it —simply seizing the opportunity to be in the air.

The view is stunning today, with sunshine and temperatures in the seventies. It's the perfect day for an early spring hike or some rock climbing along the cliff by the trail.

I'm not an expert on the area, but I've gone on a couple hikes with the crew, trekking past the falls toward the caves. Olivia led us along the river for nearly five miles, navigating through brush and rocky terrain. It wasn't an exceptionally difficult hike, but it required some agility and endurance—especially once we passed the falls and approached the caves. That didn't stop Ellie and Ben from running circles around us, though.

As I follow the river north, I maintain altitude above the rimrock-lined canyon, trying not to focus on the rugged terrain below. Given the natural landscape and the slope of the canyon, I anticipated that landing would be challenging. The only advantage I have right now is Bell's top-of-the-line systems, which enable safe landings in tough terrain. The Vertical Situation Display (VSD) provides terrain details aligned with our flight plan, altitude limits, and wind conditions. It's basically set up to give me a nearly foolproof way to navigate challenging areas like hillside plateaus.

From a distance, I can see the canyon beginning to widen, transforming from steep, solid rock faces into a broader slope. A plateau large enough to land on matches the exact coordinates I was given, as if the person who sent them knew the ideal place for my landing.

As soon as I spot the people waiting for us, I recognize Luke. He's kneeling on the ground, his broad shoulders hunched over another person, his massive frame shielding them from the dust that's already starting to stir. Even from four hundred feet, I can feel the tension radiating off him in waves. The rigidity of his shoulders, the dark energy swirling with the dust. *What the hell is going on? Who—?*

Questions swirl in my mind, but I push them aside and refocus on my job. Speculating about what I'll discover soon is only a distraction that doesn't serve any purpose. Being a pilot doesn't mean getting to be a nosey bastard. *Even if I want to be.*

As I carefully descend toward the sloped hill, I align the helicopter with the incline to minimize any sideways movement. The gentle swaying of the aircraft as it adjusts to the slope adds complexity to the landing procedure, but it's nothing I'm not used to. Delicately, I manage the collective and cyclic controls, coordinating their movements to counteract gravity and ensure a steady descent.

Once the skids make contact with the ground, we settle onto the uneven surface. The tension in my shoulders begins to ease as I feel the helicopter shift from hovering to resting securely.

With a final adjustment of the controls to keep the helicopter running, I nod to Peter and Claire. They jump out of the cabin door the moment they can, jogging toward Luke, who is still protectively covering the patient just off to the side of where we landed. They're only about 75 feet away, but they're now slightly out of my line of sight.

I take a quick glance at the screens, confirming that our flight path to the hospital has updated, that the system is running properly, and that everything is as it should be.

Through their headsets, they relay updates on the patient's condition and ask Luke about any changes. Part of me wants to check in on them, but that's not my role. It's more important that I keep my focus on getting us back in the air and that means staying in my seat and waiting. Whatever happens with the patient is beyond my control; the only thing I can ensure is that I get them to the hospital safely.

While they load the patient, I scan the surroundings in front of me, looking for anything I may have missed on the way in—dead trees, utility wires, or some idiot civilian who might get a little too close to the scene. When I don't spot anything out of the ordinary, I recheck the gauges and prepare for liftoff. It's only a matter of time before I get the all-clear to go.

Out of the corner of my right eye, through the high-vis crew window, I glimpse a long, ash-blonde ponytail cascading down toward the ground—the same unique shade as mine. I nearly give myself whiplash straining to catch another look, but it's not blonde hair I see anymore.

It's black and tan.

A true nightmare materializing before me as I spot Dog sitting beside the open door, waiting to get in.

The realization that Odessa is the 'critical individual presenting with a polytraumatic condition resulting from envenomations' hits me like a freight train. *What the hell does that even mean? Odessa's dying? From a rattlesnake bite?*

Fuck.

I should have asked more questions.

Epilogue

Isla

Two and a half years later—

"It's like boho chic. Is that even a thing? Deep V-neck, long-ish dress with crochet inserts," I say to Olivia, trying to explain the dress I chose for Charlie's baby shower. Baby Carrington number two isn't due for another two months, but they're having the party a bit early. They decided to wait to find out the gender this time around, so Charlie asked everyone to wear neutral colors. I ended up going with white, and even though it could be seen as a touch bridal, I feel absolutely radiant in it.

"Send me a picture, Isla! I have an overly fancy option and then a more casual summer dress. What shoes are you wearing? No heels, right?" This is typical Olivia conversation. She can close a deal in minutes or talk any tenant into renewing their lease, but god forbid she picks out an outfit.

"No heels. I was thinking of the short Ariat booties you got me for my birthday." Olivia has always had an impressive collection of boots, and once I mentioned how much I loved the pair she was wearing, she insisted on gifting me my own.

I quickly snap a photo of myself in the dress to send to her. The angel sleeves are mid-calf length, and they make me feel both comfortable and stylish, perfect for this in-between season where summer is over, but fall hasn't officially begun yet. I can't help but twirl a bit, enjoying the way the fabric flows around me and the sense of confidence it brings.

"Perfect! You look amazing! I think everything is set up; the decorations and food are already here. Is Everett still dropping you off?"

Everett left about an hour ago to run a few errands in town but promised to be back in time to give me a ride. The guys are going to hang out at the Carrington's while the girls celebrate at the Reynolds/Turners' residence. Olivia and Andrew celebrated their one-year wedding anniversary last spring, and Olivia legally changed her name to Olivia Turner Reynolds. She found a way to perfectly honor the past while embracing the future—holding on to their memories while creating new ones for a blended family.

"Yeah, are you sure you don't need any help? I can come earlier."

Olivia and Ellie planned almost the entire party, barely letting me do anything. At almost nine years old, Ellie was excited to take charge, wanting to do most of the planning, which left Olivia just "guiding" and "paying" for it. It's adorable how much Ellie wanted to contribute to Charlie, especially now that she's legally her "Aunt Char."

Olivia is quick to deny any help needed, insisting they're all good before hanging up the phone.

· · ·

An hour later, I'm slipping on my boots when I hear the unmistakable sound of rotary blades slicing through the air. It's not an everyday occurrence, but Everett has been known to get called in to work on his days off. I have a feeling this is his way of telling me he can't be my chauffeur.

Popping open the door, I hurry outside to at least wave at the shiny green and tan helicopter flying past. But when I step out, it's already beginning its descent, stirring up dirt in the field across from our property.

"What is he doing?" I can't help but ask aloud. He often flies by the house, but he's never landed around here.

I start my walk down the driveway toward him as he shuts everything down. It's hard to tell from here, but he's definitely not wearing his usual flight suit.

By the time he gets out, I'm close enough to appreciate how divine he looks in his champagne-colored suit, the tailored fabric hugging his shoulders perfectly. The contrast of the light suit against his sun-kissed skin makes him look even more striking, and the white linen shirt he has left open reveals just enough of his toned chest to make my breath hitch. He looks so much like a true Astor—old money and effortless swagger. Drool-worthy.

"What are you doing, Everett Astor?" I shout, despite the road still separating us.

"Giving you a ride!" he shouts, the mischievous grin I love in full force.

He jogs the rest of the way, ignoring the fact that dust is surely covering his shiny brown loafers.

Reaching me, he pulls me in, kissing me breathless. We're both left panting at the end of the driveway before he says, "I thought we could go in style." He throws in a wink that should be illegal. "Luke cleared it, but I can always take it back and drive you there."

"Hmmm..." I pretend to ponder, as if it isn't obvious I'll choose the twenty-million-dollar helicopter over my very sensibly priced Jeep Grand Cherokee, which I'm still making payments on.

He steps back, raking his eyes over me, ignoring my fake indecision. "You are the most beautiful woman I've ever seen."

I laugh, feeling the thrill of his attention. "You clean up pretty well yourself there."

Without hesitation, he grabs my hand, pulling me toward the helicopter. "Ready for the second-best ride of your life?" he asks, his voice smooth and sending a thrill down my spine.

"Ha. Ha." I respond sarcastically as he helps me into the helicopter. The interior is just as sleek as he is, with leather seats and state-of-the-art controls. I've flown with him before, but every time, I'm just as impressed as I was the first time.

Once I'm settled in, he hands me a headset and gives me a quick kiss on the cheek.

I buckle myself in, watching as he moves around, ensuring everything is set up on his end. The way he commands the aircraft is mesmerizing; there's a confidence in his movements that makes me admire him even more.

As the rotor blades begin to spin, adrenaline rushes through me. There's nothing quite like feeling that surge of energy course through you as the helicopter lifts off the ground. It's terrifying and exhilarating all at once, yet Everett seems completely at ease.

"Alright, alright, alright," he calls over the noise as we ascend into the blue sky, and I feel my stomach flutter with exhilaration.

Everett adjusts the controls smoothly, glancing over at me with a grin that matches my own. "Mind being a little late? I want to show you a few things."

My lips part in shock as my mind begins connecting dots

that may or may not exist. He raises one eyebrow as if he's daring me to voice my hypothesis. Instead, I do my best to compose my features and stay grounded in the moment. *Which would be a lot easier if we weren't hovering several thousand feet in the air.*

He begins to point out various places, the landscape unfolding beneath us—hayfields, rivers, and canyons. "Scout River Trail—great for hiking, but not if you have ophidiophobia," he jokes, that playful smirk returning to his face. I can't help but roll my eyes as he continues to point things out. "Smith Rock—great for rock climbing, picnicking, and getting caught making out in your car like teenagers."

Groaning, I bury my face in my hands. "I think we scarred Ellie for life." It was our first summer as an official couple, and we all decided to kick things off with a sunrise hike. Unfortunately, only Everett and I managed to arrive on time, and let's just say we got a little carried away. There's nothing quite like the sound of a six-year-old banging on your window to remind you that you're definitely not alone—and maybe that you should tone down the enthusiasm a bit!

"Ah, good times," he says wistfully. "Not that her mom and Drew haven't been caught doing the same thing before."

He gestures toward an open space, the runway clear from where we are. The ground below is a patchwork of tan soil speckled with tiny brown and green juniper trees, roads weaving between them. "And over there is the Redmond airport, where I fell head over heels in love at first sight," he continues, his voice taking on a softer tone—the day he walked into my life and changed everything.

"Back this way is the little town where I hope to spend the rest of my life, starting my own family right next to the people who welcomed me into theirs," Everett says, warmth and hope lacing his words.

I smile at him, my heart swelling at the thought. "That sounds perfect."

He glances over at me, his expression turning serious. "I have something for you." He hesitates before adding, "It takes the surprise out of what's about to happen, but my grandparents insisted that the woman I want to marry read it first before I propose."

With that, he pulls out a simple envelope and hands it to me, the weight of it feeling significant in my palm. I recognize it immediately—though it's different from the one I saw a few years ago in Everett's safe. Instead of saying "To the future Mr. Odessa Astor," it now reads "To the future Mrs. Everett Astor," and it's missing the ribbon.

My breath catches, and the pounding of my heart is so loud that it puts the rotary blades to shame. I look up at him, searching his eyes. "Everett, is this...?"

He doesn't answer my question but instead says, "We're almost there." As I begin to recognize where we are, I note Charlie and Hayes's house and their large pond. Beyond that, I can just make out Olivia and Drew's house.

"Isla," he says urgently, "Need you to read that *right now*, baby." There's a hint of nervousness playing in his pressing tone.

The pounding of my heart was so loud that I couldn't hear anything as I slid my shaky finger underneath the Astor seal. I'm faintly aware of his preparation for landing, but I focus all my attention on the letter in my hand. The weight of the paper feels significant, like I'm getting a small glimpse of what it means to be an Astor.

"To Whom My Grandson Falls in Love With,
As I write this letter, I feel a deep sense

of joy knowing that my grandson, Everett, has found someone so special to share his life with. It is with great pleasure that I pass down my engagement ring to you, with the hope that it brings you the same love and happiness it has represented for me.

My grandson is an extraordinary young man. His intelligence and intuition have always amazed me, but it's his zest for life that truly sets him apart. He approaches each day with passion and enthusiasm, bringing joy to everyone around him. The fact that he is giving you this letter means you must be as special as he is. I have no doubt that you will complement each other perfectly and create a beautiful life together, filled with love and happiness.

While it pains me to acknowledge that my daughter and her husband were not the best parents, I firmly believe that Everett will break that cycle. He possesses a kind heart and fierce determination, and I know in my heart that he will be an incredible father. Together, you will create a warm and loving family—one where your children will thrive.

The ring I am giving you is from my mother-in-law—a Van Cleef & Arpels—and while it may appear simple at first glance, its significance runs deep. It embodies the enduring love and commitment of generations, a reminder that love is not measured by the size of a diamond, but by the strength of the bond it represents.

As you wear this ring, may it serve as a symbol of the love and trust I have in you and my grandson. I wish you both a lifetime filled with laughter, adventure, and boundless love.

Please take care of my sweet boy; he wears his heart on his sleeve and feels emotions deeper than most.

With all my love,
Grandma Astor

Blinking through tears, I look over at him and am surprised to see he's already pulled off his headset and shut everything down. I was so wrapped up in the letter that I hadn't even registered us landing or where we really are.

"Give me one minute, and I'll help you out." He winks at me before climbing out and walking around the helicopter.

This gives me a moment to glance around and try to make sense of where we are. He's positioned us on a concrete pad that offers a view of the mountains and the natural landscape, but nothing behind us. The last I can recall is seeing Olivia's property and the land she subdivided, but we could really be anywhere in Three Sisters.

The nerves that were once fluttering in my stomach have now turned into a full-blown storm. Taking a deep breath through my nose, I try to grasp reality while shakily letting it out. I've been thinking about this moment for so long that it's hard to believe it's finally here. We went from friends to dating to living together so quickly that I appreciated the slow buildup to this proposal. Now, the thought of waiting another second for him to ask feels like a lifetime.

I watch through the window of the door as he takes a steadying breath. When he opens it, a slow smile crosses that perfect face. His hand reaches out, gently taking mine as he helps me out. I nearly fall into him, and he catches me, pulling me flush against him.

Murmuring into my hair, he says, "I love you so damn much." When he steps back, he wears the widest grin I've ever seen, with not an ounce of nerves left. I swear the rest of the world blurs around him as I focus on the way his eyes shine with love and adoration—at me! It still feels like I'm living a dream that I get to be the girl he loves.

Then, he drops to one knee and slowly pulls a white bow made from silk ribbon from his pocket, revealing the ring tucked inside the delicate knot.

"Isla, I've watched more movies in my life than I can count, and the plot of most of them centers around love at first sight. Somehow, I always knew there would be a woman to knock me off my feet from the moment I saw her." He takes a shaky breath before letting it out and continuing, "I have been truly, utterly obsessed with you for the last three years, nine months, ten days, and— roughly—three hours. By now, I'm sure you know that I would kill for you and die for you without thinking twice about it. But what I need you to understand—the most important thing—is that I will live for you. Every day, my choices, my actions, and my thoughts are all for you. You are my reason for living. My purpose. My everything. Will you marry me?"

Tears flow freely as I manage to mumble a yes before throwing myself at him. He catches me and laughs, kissing me like no one's watching. It's only when the sound of cheers behind us breaks through my moment that I realize we aren't alone. Pulling away from the kiss, I turn to see a mass of people beneath a large white tent—bright colored outfits, smiling faces, and decorations suited for an engagement party.

"What is happening?" I ask, still bewildered by the whirlwind of events. It's as if my brain can't catch up to the outpouring of love.

My gaze quickly scans the crowd, which is shouting what sounds like nonsense but is definitely a chorus of excitement. I take note of the friends I've known for most of my life, who have treated me with nothing but understanding throughout everything. Then my gaze lands on those closest to us at the front of the crowd—our unique family that has formed bonds stronger than I ever knew were possible. I've become "Aunt La" to the kids, like a daughter to Connie, and I've gained more than a handful of people I think of as siblings. My heart swells with gratitude for how lucky I am to have him in my life—*all of them*, really.

He gently tips my chin up toward him, his fingers warm against my skin, ensuring I'm looking directly into his eyes. "Charlie's baby shower was just a cover for our surprise engagement party," he grins before releasing me once again. "I wanted to make sure all our friends and family were here to witness this moment." *Oh my God—oh my God—Oh. My. God.*

My hands tremble as I watch him methodically untie the bow. "The moment you said yes marked the beginning of our fairytale happily ever after. Right here, on the lot I bought from Olivia not even two weeks after we moved in together." He holds the ring up between us, scanning my face. "So, whether we build a castle or a tiny house, have a dozen kids or none, as long as it's you and me together—against the world—I'll be the happiest man alive."

His free hand latches onto my right hand, pulling it toward him. My throat feels too thick with emotion to even respond as he places a beautiful emerald-cut ring, accented by two baguette diamonds, on my finger. It's stunning—simple, classy, and a true honor to wear a ring from a woman I'll never meet, yet who played a part in raising Everett into the incredible man he is.

This time, it's me who kisses him—making sure to pour as much love and appreciation into the gesture as possible. I pull back slightly, looking into his eyes, my heart racing.

"I love you! This is..." I begin, my voice buzzing with elation. "It's beyond what I could have expected. It's perfect."

The day I met him at the airport changed everything for me. I can still picture that moment clearly: the chaotic blur of travelers, the rush of announcements echoing through the terminal, and even the rough fur of the brown teddy bear dropped by a little boy. In that crowded space, my heart skipped a beat when I saw him for the first time. He stood there, already looking at me like I was the answer to his prayers —as if he hadn't simply found his ride from the airport, but as if he had found *me*.

Never in my wildest dreams had I expected to find someone who understood me so deeply and cared for me so completely. From our very first conversation, it felt like he saw beyond the surface, recognizing the quirks and fears I had always kept hidden. He quickly became a friend, a wish, a lifeline.

From there our love story became filled with blurred lines and unexpected twists—avalanches and hurricanes that tested us at every turn. Yet, through it all, we've emerged on the other side to experience the most beautiful sunrises. We have a fated love that not even the weight of a million other opinions could tear apart.

Already ready for more Cascadia County? Read on for a sneak peek of Book 4 in The Cascadia County Series—Behind the Yarrow.

Behind the Yarrow
Prologue

Drew

Present Day—

"So, I think it'd be best if you told Liv about what happened at the house." I joke toward Isla as we pull out of her driveway. She had called me less than fifteen minutes ago, rattled by a noise she heard in her bedroom while Everett was at work.

Isla shoots me a side-eye, the corner of her mouth quirking up. "Lovely! Can't wait to tell your baby mama that her other baby daddy is haunting her old house."

Just then, my phone buzzes with an incoming call.

"Think her ears are burning?" I ask, raising an eyebrow as I reach for the button to connect Olivia's call. "We were just talkin' about ya, Boots! Isla's with me; we'll be there in a few minutes."

She sniffles and says, "Okay," then adds "Can you hurry?" My body goes tense, instinctively alert at the tone of her voice.

"What happened?" I demand, a little too forcefully as I put more pressure on the gas.

"I—" she falters, and I can picture her biting her lip, trying to hold herself together. "I don't know," she admits. "Pops called; Levi's on his way to hang out with the kids. Something happened to Odessa—she's being transported to Bend." Her words land like lead weights, quiet and devastating. Odessa's as much of a sister as my actual sister Charlie is to me.

"Isla's with me. We'll be there in a minute," I say, forcing calmness into my voice while the needle on the speedometer climbs higher.

In the background, I catch snippets of Olivia speaking softly to the kids, her voice only slightly trembling as she explains our sudden departure.

I hit the turn into our driveway a little too fast, feeling the truck's back end slide. "Sorry," I mumble to Isla, casting her a quick glance. She waves a hand dismissively, leaning forward with anticipation; I can see the same worry etched on her face as mine.

Before I even put the truck in park, Isla flings her door open and bolts toward Olivia, who's standing with her purse in one hand and her phone in the other. I quickly trail behind, catching the tail end of Olivia leaving a message for Charlie.

Levi pulls in behind us, jumping out of his truck and joining the frantic scene in front of the house.

"What's going on, Vi?!" Olivia's voice sharpens as she spots Levi approaching.

He raises his hands defensively, shaking his head, just as confused as the rest of us. "I don't know much. Pops called about five minutes ago and told me to haul ass here."

The distinct sound of rotary blades cuts through the otherwise quiet air, pulling our attention skyward. The familiar green and tan of the Cascadia County Sheriff Department heli-copter flies south toward the hospital in Bend.

Olivia gasps, "Is that—?"

Isla's the only one who moves, instinctively gliding toward the distant helicopter. Everett's the only pilot on the force; it has to be him flying it. *Coincidence? Or is he the one flying his sister to the hospital?*

Levi seems to share my anxiety; he kicks at nothing on the ground in frustration, shouting, "Fuck!" His fingers rattle through his short hair before his hands drop. He closes his eyes briefly, trying to steady himself. If anyone understands the weight of dealing with siblings in crisis, it's him.

Instinctively, my hand reaches out to squeeze his shoulder. He shakes his head, and I see the pain in his eyes. "You good?" I ask, even though we both know he isn't.

He nods, looking back at the distant dot of the helicopter. "I got the kids. Text me updates."

"Come on, time to go." I lace my fingers through Olivia's and start to pull her along.

Glancing behind me, I notice Isla hasn't moved from where she stands, her body visibly shaking.

"Isla!" I shout, not out of anger, but to snap her out of it. The sound startles her and I instantly feel bad. "Sorry. Levi's got the kids; we need to go."

As I pull out of the driveway, Olivia's phone rings with a call from Charlie. She answers, her voice shaking slightly as she begins to explain the situation. We all hear the shocked gasps from Charlie echo through the truck.

"Hey," I hear Hayes take the phone from her. "What's going on?" His tone drops, serious and probing. It doesn't take long for Olivia to explain the situation again to Hayes but in the background, Charlie's muffled sobs cut through—heartbreaking. I glance at Olivia and Isla, who mirror the same distress, their faces reflecting a mix of worry and despair.

Reaching out, I place my hand on Liv's lap, trying to instill some confidence. "It'll be okay. She'll be okay."

When she nods, I take the phone from her hands. "Hey, mom there?"

He exhales deeply, a sound heavy with concern. "Yeah, think she's taking a nap. I'll find her, we'll meet you there."

As Hayes leaves to get Connie, I pass the phone back to Liv. The tension rises when Charlie's voice bursts through again, frantic. "I don't understand! How does no one know what's happening?!"

We hear drawers slamming in frustration. "Fuck," she groans, irritation mingling with panic. "I forgot to repack the diaper bag when we got home. I can't find anything!"

It hits me then—she's planning to bring August with them.

"Wait, Charlie, are you sure you want to bring a baby to the hospital?" I ask, urgency threading my voice.

"What?!" Charlie gasps, disbelief clear in her tone.

"Charlie, he's tiny! There are germs, infections, fucking bright lights, and shit."

Charlie hesitates, my point sinking in.

Olivia jumps in. "Levi's at my house! He's great with babies."

Hayes must have returned because he agrees, determination rising in his voice. "Drew's right, Sunshine. Let me call him."

Charlie hesitates for only a moment before yielding. "Fine. We'll see you there," she says, her voice heavy with sorrow. Then, raising her voice, she demands, "Drive safe," before hanging up the phone.

I'm almost to the turnoff for the highway when lights and sirens blare in front of us. Three marked Cascadia County

Sheriff cruisers and one unmarked vehicle fly toward Bend. My arms go rigid, but I pull out immediately behind them, following as they break every speed limit. Our own little police escort into the unknown.

The drive gives me time to shift into mission mode. It's been a long time since I was in the field, but the adrenaline surging through my veins feels familiar—like a rush that sharpens my focus, allowing me to see everything through a wide-angled lens.

Olivia has been taking calls and answering texts, working to piece together who knows what. It helps that she knows everyone at the Sheriff Department and throughout Three Sisters. Meanwhile, Isla sits silently in the back seat, gripping her phone tightly and staring at it, waiting for any word from Everett.

By now, he's likely landed at the heliport and gotten Odessa into the emergency department. The real question is what he'll do next. He can't leave the helicopter there for long, in case Airlink needs to land as well. Which means he'll park it at the private airfield just a few miles away, but someone will need to fetch him and bring him back to the hospital. I mentally start mapping out a route to drop the girls off before heading to get him. I wouldn't put it past him to run to the hospital if nobody arrives quickly enough.

Three of the cruisers head directly to the hospital, but one speeds on, not slowing down.

Glancing at Olivia, I ask, "Do you know who was in that one?"

My gut tells me whoever is driving that cruiser is picking up Everett wherever he's touched down, but I don't want to be wrong and leave Everett stranded out there.

"Will."

"Can you call him for me? Speaker, please." I ask gently, my voice barely above a whisper.

She nods, her fingers trembling as she holds the phone out toward me. We wait in silence, the ringing tones filling the air.

He answers on the first ring as I pull into the hospital parking lot.

"Olivia—"

"She's here too. You picking up Everett?"

"Affirmative."

"Thanks. See you soon." Olivia ends the call just as I throw the truck into the first available parking space. We rush into the Emergency Department, the usual thirty-minute drive condensed into twenty adrenaline-fueled minutes.

A few deputies I recognize from around town stand at the front desk as we storm in. Olivia approaches them, and they motion for us to follow as the medical assistant leads us through two sets of locked doors and down a dimly lit hallway.

We enter a separate waiting room, sealed off from the rest of the department. "You can wait here until we have more information," she says before retreating back the way we came.

"Luke!" Olivia suddenly shouts as I follow her inside. She rushes to him, kneeling in front of his chair and taking his hand in hers. Sweat and dirt cover his entire body, but his vacant stare is focused on a single tile in front of him, lost in his own world.

"Are you okay?" Olivia asks, her voice trembling with concern. "What happened? Were you with Odessa?"

Luke doesn't flinch at her barrage of questions; he doesn't even look at her. His gaze remains fixed on a single tile he's been staring at since we entered the waiting room.

He's clearly in shock, but at least he doesn't seem to have any visible injuries. Mentally, though, he looks like he's been through the wringer. Guilt? Is he blaming himself for Odessa's injuries? My gut tells me that's not it, but something is definitely weighing on him.

I catch the eye of Corbin, one of the deputies I've hung out with at Ponderosa Pine Tavern before, and gesture toward the hallway.

He follows me and steps to the side so that we have privacy.

"Any idea what's going on?"

He runs a finger along his jaw, considering his words. "We don't know much. Turner called us individually and asked us to come, to be here for whatever Luke may need. Said Odessa was being transported by Astor to the hospital, and we needed to be here. LT Will went to pick him up from Powell Butte Road."

"Anything else," I plead, desperate for more information.

"Sorry, man. Nothing. He's keeping everything under wraps."

"That's about what we know too. Thanks."

We walk back into the private waiting room, where Olivia sits on one side of Luke and Isla on the other. Olivia gently rubs circles on his back, a soothing gesture that once would have sent me spiraling. If this situation weren't so intense, I might chuckle at my former worry about something more between them. I know better now than to think Luke is attracted to Olivia. Especially now, looking at the devastation etched across his features, as if he's just had his heart ripped out and stomped on. But I still can't figure out why? Last I heard he couldn't even be in the same room as Odessa.

I lean against the doorframe for a few minutes, analyzing the situation, when a commotion behind me catches my attention.

Everett barrels down the hallway, nearly sprinting past our room. How he got past the keycard doors, I have no idea.

"Astor!" I call out, reaching for his arm and spinning him

around before he can pass. Fury ignites in his eyes, and he pulls back his fist, ready to throw a punch.

It takes just a moment for him to snap out of it and relax, but my patience is wearing thin.

"What the hell's going on, man?" I ask, urgency creeping into my voice.

"Odessa was fucking bit by a goddamn rattlesnake!" he shouts, frustration spilling over.

"A rattlesnake?" I challenged, as loud gasps rippled through the waiting room behind me. "It's March!"

"I know!" he shot back, a tense standoff hanging in the air between us. After a moment, he inhaled sharply and stammered, "I think. Shit! I don't know. Doctor Lewis was speaking in tongues. I dropped her off with Luke; he'll know."

I gesture toward Luke, and Everett's eyes widen as he steps into the room. "Luke! What the hell's going on?" *Just said that.* "Where's Odessa? Is she okay?"

Luke remains motionless, as if he hasn't even heard him. Isla's shoulders sag, shaking her head in disbelief. Tears stream down Olivia's face, and when she looks at me, I try to offer a sympathetic smile, though it's hard to maintain.

Everett glances between the three of them before turning his questioning gaze back to me.

"He hasn't moved since we got here—ten minutes ago—not even an inch."

His mouth opens and closes, but nothing comes out. The situation has us all off-kilter.

"Okay, so what do we do? Just wait?"

I nod. "The doctor will be out any minute to give us an update."

Frustrated, he huffs and takes a seat next to Isla, the tension radiating off him like heat from a fire. Sensing his distress, she gently places a hand on his arm, offering quiet comfort amid the chaos.

Corbin and the other two deputies greet Everett quietly from where they're standing off to the side. He asks them the same questions I did, everyone trying to piece together what's going on but still not having enough information.

"We saw you fly by the house," Isla offers during a quiet moment. "Drew had picked me up, and we had just gotten back to their house when you went by."

His head shifts, confused. "Why was Drew picking you up?"

Isla's gaze nervously bounces between me and Olivia, unknowingly sending mixed signals about our relationship. Fortunately, Everett knows me better than that.

Finally, she says, "I heard a noise and called him."

"Why didn't you call me?" A chuckle escapes me at the hint of jealousy in his tone, knowing I'd probably feel the same.

"You were working!" she replies, exasperated.

"Okay, fine. What was the noise?" He turns to me, his eyes searching for answers, so I glance at Olivia to see if she's listening. *And of course she is.*

Clearing my throat, I say, "Your safe popped open."

"No way," he admonishes the idea right away. "It's one of the best. Even if the batteries died, it wouldn't open by itself."

I shrug, trying to avoid that rabbit hole while we're in the hospital.

"Was anything missing?" he asks, his brow furrowing with concern.

"Not sure—Your Korth and SIG were in there. As well as two envelopes and a little cash."

Isla adds, "Well, one envelope had fallen out."

"What? Back up. What do you mean one had fallen out?"

Isla sighs and then explains everything in detail, starting from the beginning.

Everett's only response is a dismissive "humph."

"What?"

"Math ain't mathin'," he shrugs casually. "Someone had to have opened the safe, which means someone was either in our house or—" I can see the moment he connects the dots with the rest of us. His eyes go comically wide, and he draws in a sharp breath, raising his shoulders. "You don't think—?"

I glance at Olivia, who looks between us, clearly anxious. "Think what?" she prompts gently.

Thankfully, Isla steps in. "It was probably just a fluke, but the only other, not really reasonable thought is... uh, well, ha, a ghost?"

Olivia's head reels back in confusion. "You're joking—" Then she quickly adds, "You're not joking?!"

We all sit in an awkward silence as she glances between us like we're crazy. "I lived in that house for almost a decade and there was nothing ever that weir—OH MY GOD! You think it's DAN!" Her shriek has us all cringing with guilt. It really is crazy to think Dan would be haunting us. *Right?*

Low voices suddenly drift in from the hallway, and I take full advantage of the opportunity to step out and avoid that conversation. I greet Charlie, Hayes, and Connie, filling them in on what little we know and buying myself some time before walking back in.

By the time we all go back in there, the conversation is steered back to Odessa.

For another twenty minutes, questions are rapid fired through out the room, everyone—except Luke—trying to piece it all together.

"Rattlesnake bite?"

Every person has a different hypothesis, a different question, but I haven't said much or even really paid much attention to who's talking.

I only stare at the still, unmoving man before us. I have seen this man during crisis' and not once has he ever shown any sign of weakness or vulnerability. A rattlesnake bite for what should be acquaintance at most? He's the Sheriff of a small town he grew up in—this should be nothing to him. Yet, here he is—poke him and he'd topple over, statuesque, Luke.

"No!" Luke's rough voice suddenly booms through the chaos, and the room falls silent.

"No, what?!" Everett demands, the tension in the room escalating.

"We're—it's—" Luke stumbles over his words, his chest heaving as he struggles to gather his thoughts. "Complicated."

"When the hell did that happen?"

He leans forward, taking a moment to catch his breath, his forearms resting heavily on his thighs. His eyes dart around the room, searching for the right words. "At the beginning of January, we..."

Available 04-05-2025

Also by TJ Deal

The Cascadia County Series

Behind the Cascades

Behind the Juniper

Behind the Larch

Behind the Yarrow

Behind the Pine

Behind the Wildflowers

About the Author

TJ Deal is a Pacific Northwest-based aspiring author who often daydreams about writing stories in the incredible places she travels to around the world. Thanks to her husband's unwavering support and her lifelong obsession with reading, she has decided to follow her passion for writing. Her days are mostly spent drinking coffee, relishing in the daily grind of motherhood, and capitalizing on every free moment to work on her latest novel.